PRA

"The Gears are the preeminent historical novelists of our times, offering fascinating and brilliantly researched insights into war, suffering, tribal life, and the beliefs that inspire people to act above and beyond what they thought possible. No one reads a Gear novel without being transformed in beautiful ways. The Gears, separately and together, rank among the most significant novelists of modern times, and their work will endure for generations."

RICHARD S. WHEELER

SWITCHING GEARS

ALSO BY W. MICHAEL GEAR AND KATHLEEN O'NEAL GEAR

Big Horn Legacy

Dark Inheritance

The Foundation

Fracture Event

Long Ride Home

The Mourning War

Raising Abel

Rebel Hearts Anthology

Sand in the Wind

Thin Moon and Cold Mist

Black Falcon Nation Series

Flight of the Hawk Series

The Moundville Duology

Saga of a Mountain Sage Series

The Wyoming Chronicles

The Anasazi Mysteries

The Peacemaker's Tales

SWITCHING GEARS

AN ANTHOLOGY OF WESTERN SHORT FICTION

W. MICHAEL GEAR
KATHLEEN O'NEAL GEAR

WOLFPACK
PUBLISHING
— EST 2013 —

Switching Gears: An Anthology of Western Short Fiction
Paperback Edition
Copyright © 2024 W. Michael Gear and
Kathleen O'Neal Gear

Wolfpack Publishing
1707 E. Diana Street
Tampa, Florida 33609

wolfpackpublishing.com

Paperback ISBN 978-1-63977-513-2
eBook ISBN 978-1-63977-512-5
LCCN 2024945107

Cover photo credit: KS Jones

To all the
O'Neal, Alsup, Buckner, and Garren
ancestors who have
inspired us with their stories of
murder and mayhem

CONTENTS

INTRODUCTION

Ask about our identity as writers and we will tell you we are novelists. Oh, and yes, we have hundreds of nonfiction articles on bison behavior, genetics, history and the like, not to mention the articles on the craft of writing and anthropology. But our true forte lies in the novel. Eighty-six of them to date. With eighteen million copies of our novels in print worldwide, we've been translated into at least thirty languages. We received the Western Writers of America's Wister Award and were inducted into the Western Writers Hall of Fame because of the novels.

We never had time to write short fiction. Our book contracts and looming deadlines precluded it. Though for a time in the early 2000s, we did consider hosting an anthology. The indefatigable Martin H. Greenberg met with us in New York to pitch the idea of an anthology of prehistory short fiction. We'd write the first couple of stories, and he'd solicit the rest from established authors. Then we raced home to beat another of those relentless deadlines and never got around to it.

There is something safe about a novel. Start with the opening scene and setting, understand the conflict to be resolved, and turn the characters loose. If you know what they want and the extremes they'll go to to get it, just follow their lead. They'll work it out as they take you to the end. To be honest, short fiction intimidated us. Not that we ever wasted words on a novel—each scene and chapter had to advance the story—but short fiction is different. Compact. Hard hitting. Like slamming the bolt home on a hunting rifle.

Then Wolfpack Publishing approached Kathleen and made a pitch about submitting a short story for their upcoming *Rebel Hearts* anthology. It was to be a first for Wolfpack. She worked on "No Quarter" for over a month, handing drafts to Michael to read. Writing well is always about learning the craft, figuring out the rules, using language to its best impact.

Her short story won the Western Writers of America's Spur Award for the best short fiction of the year in 2023. Then came the news that it was a finalist for the Western Fictioneers' "Peacemaker Award." And finally, it received a Medallion from the Will Rogers Medallion Awards.

As her summer of awards was unfolding, Michael was asked for his submission to the subsequent Wolfpack anthology, *Ridin' With the Pack*, composed of some of Wolfpack's finest male authors. Given Kathleen's success with "No Quarter" she'd set the bar pretty darn high.

As Michael wrote, it was as if God was staring over his shoulder, reminding him with each sentence: *Kathleen won a Spur, what if you don't even place?*

No pressure, huh?

And then Michael's "Bad Choices" won the 2024 Spur Award for short fiction, and he, too, won a Will Rogers Medallion Award. Maybe the key to good writing comes from putting a gun to the side of your head and repeating, "Do better, or else."

Better yet, we had fun; writing short stories is a challenge! Not only were we learning a new craft, but for the first time in four decades, the schedule was clear. We could indulge ourselves. With each story in *Switching Gears*, we've experimented with different voices and styles. Scratched the creative itch.

Hopefully, you'll find a new favorite in the following collection. And even visit some old friends and new worlds.

SWITCHING GEARS

THE ONLY WAY TO WIN

A 'SAGA OF THE MOUNTAIN SAGE' STORY

W. MICHAEL GEAR

Michael has created some extraordinarily rich and complex characters over the years, but two of my favorites are Travis Hartman and Baptiste de Bourgmont. I've always wondered how they met. We get hints here and there in The Mountain Sage series, *but never the complete story...until now. Travis the salty seaman, and Baptiste the runaway slave, are both being pursued by ruthless men who want to see them swinging from ropes. An unlikely duo brought together out of necessity, but the reader knows right away that this is a friendship that will last a lifetime. (KOG)*

Baptiste de Bourgmont and Travis Hartman were first introduced in my fur trade era novels The Morning River *and* Coyote Summer, *While* The Morning River *was campaigned for the 1996 Pulitzer Prize, the books have developed a dedicated following. Hey, I get it. I love those characters, too, and they've called to me over the years. I had always considered doing a series based on Baptiste but could never find a publisher for it. It would have started with Baptiste's first meeting with Travis Hartman, which would have gone something like this. (WMG)*

Louisiana—1811

A swamp is a noisy place after sunset. The bloodhounds could be heard over the chirring night insects and the croaking of the frogs. Baptiste shivered, the chill running down his torn and bleeding back. Up to his waist in black water, he sloshed forward, his feet sinking into the sticky mud with each floundering step. Lost in the night, he had only the sound of the hounds to orient himself.

That, and the smell of death. Something about the stink rising off the water, filling his nose with the odor of decay and ruin. Like onions when they rotted into brown slime.

In the bald cypress overhead, an owl hooted. The death bird. Its eerie call carried over the clicking of the insects. All the world was black: a cloud-dark night with midnight-shadowed trees, hanging vines, and ebony water swirling around his waist. Baptiste fought his way through the shallows. Moss and water lilies tried to tangle around his legs.

Fatigue had begun to burn through the muscles in his calves, thighs, and back. Breath came hard, desperate, as his body began to flag. Didn't matter. Wasn't nothing but to go on. Run the race right to the end. All a man could do.

Behind it all lay the memory of Lizza and their two children. The expressions on their faces as the overseer slashed away at Baptiste's back with that blacksnake whip. Wasn't no pain of the body to compare to that hopeless look behind their eyes. And nothing he could do but cry out as the tears ran down his face.

He swallowed hard, thirst pulling at his throat.

Couldn't drink the water. Not this deep in the swamp. He'd seen the effects. Been on work crews where desperate slaves tried to slake their thirst on the black water. Seen them hours later with the scours, bent double and shooting streams of liquid brown even as the overseer beat them with a whip handle. Nothing the poor fools could do but cry out, clamp their guts tight, and shit some more.

Baptist tripped over a sunken log slimy with mud and moss. He floundered, went down. Should have dropped the double-bitted axe he carried. Couldn't. Just... couldn't.

Water gurgled in his ears, ran cool and stinging into the shredded skin on his back. The instinct was to gasp, to let the water take him. Nope. Couldn't do that, neither. 'Scaped slave gonna let hisself drown like that? 'Specially after what he done to Master?

Baptiste half-swam his way across the slippery log, got his feet under him, and pushed up. His head broke water, and blinking, he scrubbed his face with his free hand. The axe, normally not so heavy, was trying to drag him down like an anchor.

"Gotta keep...goin'. One foot...ahead o' 'tother," he promised between panting breaths.

Something splashed off to his left. Fish? Gator? Didn't matter. If the swamp didn't kill him, that posse of hunters back there would. If a gator got him? That was fair. Gator'd get a meal out of him, and them bastard slavers would never find his body. Ole Baptiste, he just vanished into the swamp. Maybe he still there? His ghost, it be wavering in the mist. Just yonder, at the edge of seeing. A haunt to fill them white folk's dreams with fear.

And if a snake get him? Maybe a cottonmouth or copperhead? That be a different story. The poison would start to work on him. Slow his muscles. Maybe make him crazy. Leave him witless. That? Well, Mam, that be bad. They catch up with him then. Hang his whip-scarred black body from a high tree. But, oh, you could bet. They'd make it as hard as they could. Maybe drag him behind the horses? Let the hounds at him for a while? Take a sledgehammer to his hands and feet? Burn him until he screamed his lungs out? Then they'd hang him. Hell, maybe they wait 'til after he be long dead to string him up.

No way to die.

Even Master get an easy death. After all he done. Simple comeuppance, 'specially given that Master, he call himself a Christian man, good Catholic. Go to mass twice a week. Well and fine, he be standing 'fore the throne of God now.

When his foot caught in the roots, Baptiste staggered for balance, trying to find a way through. Didn't matter if he searched left or right, he couldn't find footing.

The baying of the distant hounds drove him to half swim, part crawl over the labyrinth of submerged roots. They shallowed into a protruding cypress knee. Clinging to it, Baptiste sucked air into his hot lungs. The excruciating pain in his back kept sapping his will.

The hounds went still, any sound of them hidden in the buzzing of the insects and chorus of frogs. A big male gator bellowed that gut-stopping mating roar off to his left. Some night creature made a whizzing sound as it darted around Baptiste's right ear. He didn't have the energy to swat it away.

Why had the dogs gone silent?

Had to be where he'd entered the water. Dogs couldn't track through water. How far back was that? Baptiste had no idea which direction he'd been headed. East, he hoped. The river was east. But in the black swamp? He might have been going round and round.

5

"They gotta know which way I's headed," he told himself between panted breaths. "They be thinking they circle 'round. Maybe take a pirogue. Send a part 'o that posse to search the water, huh?"

Baptiste blinked at the sweat-mixed swamp water trickling down from his forehead. He'd a died for a drink. Might have even traded back old Master's life for a tin of water. Instead, he smacked his lips, sucked at his tongue, and got a faint imitation of a swallow. He started forward in his awkward half crawl as he crossed the cypress roots. His hold on the axe made it all the more awkward.

He wiggled his way through shallows of thick mud. It took all of his sagging energy to get his feet under him. Standing up, water and filth drained down the ruin of his once-white cotton shirt. Almost tripped when his feet tangled in grass, but he stumbled up on dry ground. The insects whizzing around his ears would have driven a stronger man than him to madness.

Didn't matter that his legs were on the point of buckling, somehow he made himself plant one foot ahead of the other. Using the axe handle for balance, he waded through the knee-high swamp grass. Clawed his way past the tangled web of hanging vines. Heard something slither away through the thick stems. The owl hooted again. Behind him this time.

He tripped. Fell. The impact sent a numbing wave of agony through his tortured back. Left him half dazed.

"Can't let 'em catch me." Sniffed. Realized tears were leaking from his eyes. Wasn't none of it fair. What they done to a man. What they done to people.

Baptiste fumbled his feet under him, used the axe to push himself up in the crushed grass.

Maybe Master was right. He be a big dumb animal what don't know no better. If'n he be nothing more than a brute, than a brute he be. And with that, he started forward again, wishing for water, wishing for the river.

Gotta keep the axe.

That be his only hope. If'n he run inta that posse, he gotta have enough left inside to charge them. Swing that ole axe like it be a scythe. Make them white devils shoot him dead on the spot. Make them remember that Baptiste died fighting.

He fell again. Lay there panting in the cool grass…

The swamp sounds brought him back. Somehow penetrated past the agony in his back, through the exhaustion.

Where…? Swamp. That's right. They be after him.

He lifted his head. Still black as pitch, the sounds and smells of the swamp all around him. How long had he slept? How much ground had he lost?

Panicked, he grabbed up the axe, fought to his feet. Peering around at the night, which way did he go?

And there, off to the right, a flicker of light.

But whose?

Baptiste rolled his dry tongue around his mouth. Did it matter? He tightened his grip on the axe. Well, if it be a white man, what of it? Thing about having an axe, all it took was one swing. And, if they's anything Baptiste was good at, it was swinging an axe.

Wasn't nothing to killing a man with an axe. But if there be more? Got to swing at the first, chop, and turn. Then swing at the second. Hoping he have enough surprise, take out the third. But being the middle of the night, they probably be asleep and never know what hit 'em.

———

The stick cracked in the night, bringing Travis Hartman wide awake. Most likely a deer, or maybe a raccoon that tripped the warning branch. He'd laid a couple of them across the approaches to the camp. Set each one low where an unwary foot would snap it and give the alarm. Once he might have gone right back to sleep, but that Travis Hartman had paid mightily for his carelessness.

Instead, he snagged up the scarred McCormick .60 caliber pistol from beneath the blanket and wiggled his way snake-like behind the trunk of the ancient red cedar. There he crouched in the shadow and slowly scanned his little camp. The fire was burned down to flickers that danced in the ash. Two tall bald cypress trees, their lower branches draped with thick beards of Spanish moss, stood to either side of the narrow landing. Beyond, the Mississippi River ran in dark silence. He'd driven a stake into the bank and tied off the painter, or bow rope, so his pirogue couldn't drift away if the river rose in the night. His two packs lay to either side of his now abandoned blankets.

Long brown hair falling around his shoulders, Hartman cocked his head. Not that he could hear much over the crickets, frogs, night birds and other chirring insects. All seemed still. Only a flicker of distant lightning was visible far off to the south where the big river ran toward the Gulf.

He considered his blankets. Damn, he was tired. T'was a hellacious bit of work paddling that damn big pirogue upriver. Tuckered a man right to his bones. Come morning, he'd cuss hisself up one side and down 'tother for acting like a scared cat. But then a man being hunted shouldn't be taking chances.

Travis allowed himself a deep yawn, blinked to clear his vision, and fixed on the darkness between the two trees. It was a trick he'd learned at sea on the night watch.

Pick a point and let the side vision see what the eye couldn't directly.

A distant owl hooted.

Something big splashed out in the river.

Hob take it, he was being a fool. Wasn't any way they could have caught up. Still, Captain Avery had been an important man, powerful in the maritime society that flourished in New Orleans. Travis Hartman was nothing more than the illiterate sea dog who'd stuck eleven inches of knife blade into Avery's side, spilled the captain's guts, and left him for dead on the *Avangeline*'s polished deck. He'd paused only long enough to pull the captain's favorite McCormick pistol and fixings from the man's belt. Why, that very pistol had shot his friend Kundakindu dead but a few days before.

Travis rolled the pistol in his hand, the smooth wood conforming to his palm. He could still see it. Good old Kunda, stepping between Travis and Avery at the last instant. Maybe Kunda thought he could talk Avery out of it. Maybe he thought he owed Travis. Or maybe, after two years of Avery's brutality, Kunda just didn't care anymore.

The sound of that shot, the puff of smoke, and the way his friend, Kunda, jerked at the impact of the ball, it was all just as clear in Travis Hartman's memory as that day off the Louisiana coast.

"Shoulda kilt that scoundrel then," Travis whispered. But he had been stunned, staring down at Kundakindu's quivering body. At the blood pumping out onto the polished deck. Seeing his friend's eyes roll back and how the sun gave a sheen to the black skin stretched across his broad cheekbones.

By the time Travis got his wits around him, Smith and Baley had grabbed him. Dragged him away before he could retaliate. Second time someone saved his life that day.

Justice had been Hartman's three days later after the *Avangeline* tied off at the docks in New Orleans. He'd come up on that black-hearted Avery from behind. Drove the knife in from just below the ribs. Odd, how easily the blade had sliced into the man's guts.

Oh, yes. The hue and cry would be out for Travis Hartman. They'd still be scouring the city for him. Checking the ships along the wharf to be sure he didn't ship out on one of the other merchantmen.

Let them look.

No one knew he'd stolen the pirogue. The owner might be hot in pursuit, but by damn, it was a big river with a slew of bayous, backswamps, and creek mouths. Not to say that maybe the thief might have headed off across Lake Pontchartrain or turned downriver toward the delta.

In the distance, over the sounds of the night, he could hear the baying of hounds. What kind of crazy fool hunting party would be out on a dark night like...he grimaced, swallowing hard.

The kind that hunted men.

Like him.

The collywobbles laid hold of his gut. Time to push off, take his chances on the water at night when...

Something moved at the margin of his vision. Stealthy, big. It crawled low at the edge of the river, easing behind the thick bald cypress trunk to the left. From the shape of it, this was a man.

Travis bit off a chuckle, his heart starting to race. Tarnal hell, the rascal was trying to steal Hartman's stolen pirogue. Sure as sun in the morning, Travis could barely make out the mud-stained sleeve, the dark hand that reached for the painter.

On silent feet Travis ghosted forward, circling the dying fire so as not to pass between it and the thief. His life as a boy, growing up on the farm, had given him the skills. Now he put them to good use. Easing around the thick base of the bald cypress, he extended the pistol. Thumbing the cock back, the crisp click of the lock might have been thunder in the night.

"How do, pilgrim," Travis said coolly. "Reckon I wouldn't touch that rope if'n I was you."

———

At the hard words, Baptiste froze, his arm still extended. He turned his head slowly, stared up. The light was good enough that he could see the man silhouetted in the faint light of fire. Long brown hair, wide shoulders under a stroud shirt, lean-waisted, and holding a cocked pistol not more than a foot from Baptiste's face.

The baying of the hounds could be heard again, closer.

With the axe tucked low, Baptiste couldn't swing. Wouldn't have time to strike. Not before that cocked pistol blew his brains out the back of his hard skull. He exhaled as he slumped down in the mud.

"Go ahead. Pull dat trigger, mister."

"Reckon yer a trying ter steal me boat, Doodle."

Baptiste squinted an eye. "Doodle?"

"Ain't ye got no larning? Doodle. Means some igner'ant fool as would try and lift a solid jack tar's pirogue in the middle of the night."

"What language you talkin'?"

"Reckon it's English. Ain't got no other in this hyar noodle."

The hounds were louder now. The white man backed

a half step, head cocked, though he kept is eyes on Baptiste. "They's after ye, ain't they?"

"I ain't going back. So you shoot me now, mister." Baptiste nerved himself, stood on his exhausted and wobbling legs. Doing so, he raised the axe. "I mean it. I'll kill you 'foah I let you hand me over t' the likes of them."

The pistol, held level and steady, would shoot right through Baptiste's heart.

Again, the hounds. Closer still. Somehow, they'd circled the swamp. Found a way across. Figured where Baptiste would head.

He chuckled wearily, pulled the axe back. He'd have to force the damn white fool to kill him. Every muscle in his body was trembling as he raised the axe for the strike. His chest squirmed in anticipation of the bullet. Couldn't think of a better way to die.

The white man, however, stepped back another step as the fire flared up, lighting Baptiste's face. "Hold up, pilgrim."

"I said, you gotta kill me. Ain't no other way. Now, shoot, damn you. Pull dat trigger and set me free."

The white man chuckled under his breath, muttered, "Now, don't that take all? 'Scaped slave. Gotta be."

"I said, I ain't going back!" Baptiste tightened his grip, the axe trembling in his exhausted grip. "You gonna kill me? They give you a reward, white man."

"Name's Travis. Travis Hartman." He reached out with a booted foot and kicked a couple of branches into the fire. "Who're you?"

"Baptiste." Damn it, struggle as he might, the weight of the axe got heavier, so hard to hold up. Did he even have the energy to rush, to swing it and force Hartman to shoot?

As the flames caught and leaped from the new wood, Hartman glanced toward the approaching posse.

Chuckled again, and turned his eyes on Baptiste, taking him in. "Reckon yer a wee bit more'n a 'scaped slave. Looks like old blood mixed in with the mud in that shirt."

"I kilt Massa," Baptiste cried. "You hear? I kilt a white man! And I's a gonna kill you! Now, you gonna pull dat trigger?"

To Baptiste's astonishment, Hartman lowered the pistol. "Kilt a white man, ye say? Well, that's some, it is. No wonder they's tearing up the swamp ter catch ye."

"You hear what I say?" Baptiste asked again, a feeling of desperation in his chest, the axe dropping as he stumbled in exhaustion. "Ain't no crime worse than killin' a massa."

He could see Travis Hartman now that the fire was growing bright. Long-faced, strong jaw, a thin and straight nose between sun-browned cheeks with a full beard the color of bark tea. The eyes were blue and oddly twinkling with amusement. The kind of man Baptiste had hated his whole life.

"What if they was 'nuther way?" Travis asked. "Ye willing ter take a chance on the river?"

"Whatchu talking about?" God, was his mind playing tricks? Too exhausted to understand?

Hartman turned, gestured to where the pirogue was tied to the bank. "Reckon that boat's too big fer me. Hard t' paddle against the current. Looks to me like yer as strong a feller as might come along in a coon's age. If'n ye'll help me paddle upriver, I'll take ye along."

Baptiste was using the axe to keep himself propped; his legs threatened to give out on him. "You crazy?"

"Nope. Just almighty curious." At a particularly loud baying from the hounds, Hartman pointed. "You got enough sand ter climb up in that thar oak tree yonder?"

Baptiste blinked at the tree. The leaves left the branches in deep shadow.

"Why you doing this?"

"I just told ye, Doodle. But maybe ye'd better be shinnying up inter them high branches. Them boys and their dogs is gonna be here any second now, and the ship's clock? She's a tickin'."

Baptiste shook his head, let go the axe, and staggered to the tree. Filling his lungs, he reached for the lowest of the branches, tried to pull himself up. Couldn't. Then Hartman was there, arms like iron bands about his waist, lifting. Baptiste was a big man; Hartman almost tossed him up.

The pain in Baptiste's back felt like a thousand wasps stinging away. Were the scabs tearing? The sound of the dogs gave him the energy. Branch by branch, he climbed. Blessed mother, the smell of the bark, soothing, it lent him wings.

At least for another couple of branches, and there, panting, he folded himself over a limb, arms hung, feet braced below. And even then, a dizzy spell took him, almost swooned. It would have to do.

He could see through the screen of leaves as Travis Hartman waded into the river, shoved the pirogue off the bank, and sloshed upriver into the darkness, tugging the boat behind him.

What the hell?

Baptiste closed his eyes, panting. Figured, didn't it? Just another devil white man, gonna slip away in the darkness and leave Baptiste to his fate.

But when he opened his eyes—the baying of hounds louder—here came Hartman from the darkness. The hounds were close now, each howling from the bloodhounds filtering through the trees.

"No matter what, ye'd best keep quiet," Hartman

called softly. "You let on yer up there, this'll be Katy bar the door and bloody as all hell."

————

Travis Hartman sat across from his fire, his pistol in his lap as the first of the dogs on long leads charged into the camp. He rose, holding the pistol at an angle across his chest. He'd taken the time to find his battered felt hat and tucked his stroud shirt into his belt. The knife was now prominently displayed.

"How do?" Travis called as the posse—five of them—entered the firelight. "Ye best keep them dogs away. They get ter pissing on me packs, I'll take it a might poorly."

The dog handler had leashes on three hunting hounds that were sniffing their way along the bank, nosing where Baptiste had been lying in the mud. A big bearded man wearing a slouch hat and dressed in buckskin jacket and leather pants strode up beside the fire, rifle in hand. Two others, younger, carrying shotguns, spread out, circling around, looking here and there. The last man kept back, fingering a rifle.

The dog handler pulled the dogs off, immediately cutting for sign around the perimeter.

The big man told him, "I'm Derry O'Daniels. Constable here abouts. Sheriff sent me out find a craze-mad man-killer of a runaway. Where is he?"

Hartman uttered a bitter laugh. "Reckon yer talking about that feller that come through here maybe half an hour ago? Big black man. Filthy shirt. Looked stumbling weary." Travis pointed with his free hand. "Black bastard stole me pirogue!"

"What pirogue?" O'Daniels stepped around, staring

down at the water and then at the two packs. "Where'd he go?"

Travis nodded his head toward the river. "Reckon he's stumbling along on his last legs. Might'a been a bit hurt, too. Made enough noise to wake this child from a sound sleep. By the time I got shut of me blankets and got me wits and pistol pulled, he's done shoved off inta the river!" Travis spat to one side in emphasis. "Hell, it be too damn dark t' even take a shot."

"Stole your pirogue, you say?" O'Daniels reached for one of Travis' packs.

"I'd not touch that, if'n I was you." Travis tapped fingers on his pistol. "Ain't good manners fingering through an old salt's ditty bag. Might lead to trouble."

O'Daniels straightened, a frown darkening his face. "Stranger like you, maybe he ought not get too high and mighty when a constable's about his duty."

The two youths half-raised their fowling pieces. All eyes were fixed on Travis.

"Maybe." Travis shrugged. "Maybe not. Reckon this child was headed upriver and minding his own business. Seems ter me, yer after some runaway and that's yer business. He ain't here and neither's me boat. So don't you go getting all outta sort, 'cause this child ain't in the mood fer it."

"Careful, mister," the blond-bearded youth laid a thumb on the shotgun's cock.

"Careful yerself, lad," Hartman told him. "What did this feller do anyway that's got yer tails all tied up in a knot?"

"Killed his Master," O'Daniels said, relaxing the least little bit as he turned his attention to the dark river beyond. "Took an axe and most severed the man's head. This one's as bad as they come. Bloodthirsty and crazy. Folks is cowering in fear. Jean Bourgmont was a beloved man in these parts. Château de Bourgmont is the biggest plantation in the parish, over a hundred slaves. He's a family man, dedicated to his five children and a fine Christian. Any black animal that'd take an axe and… and…"

"Bet yer a gonna make that poor bastard suffer when ye catches him," Travis noted, glancing out at the river. "Hope ye do. But listen, boys. He was looking about done in. Reckon if'n yer a gonna catch him, ye'd better be about finding me boat. Morning's coming. Shouldn't be too hard to spot a big black feller out on the water. River like this, whole different beast than the sea. No swells, just flat as far as the eye can see." He paused, shrugged. "Hell, I'd help ye, but I can't leave me ditty and packs."

O'Daniels was watching him through suspicious eyes. "Then you're not interested in the reward?"

Travis worked his jaws, considered. "How much?"

"Figure your share'd come close to a thousand dollars."

Travis rubbed his bearded cheeks. "That's five years wages before the mast and only if the cargo fetched a healthy profit. Hard to turn away from that."

"Then maybe you'll joins us and go a hunting?"

Travis used his toe, scuffed it in the flattened grass. "Tempting, but I reckon this child's gonna fix his sexton on Natchez. If'n I can find another boat. Somebody'll be along what needs a strong hand fer paddling."

"Something's not right about you," O'Daniels said softly. "Not right about this at all. Coming on you in the middle of the night, awake, with a roaring fire. And that buck was here. Like he knew he's coming here all along."

"Careful, matey," Hartman whispered. "Talk like that might run up debts yer not fixed to pay. I'd hate to have to take a capstan bar and knock ye shipshape."

O'Daniels' lips twitched. "Big talk when you're outnumbered five to one."

Travis glanced sidelong at the youths with shotguns, ignored the dog handler who'd been watching from firelight's edge. The rifleman was too far out for a snap shot. "Yer the constable, aye? Takin' that rifle of yourn and shoving it up yer arse ain't bound to set ye right with your men here. Not to mention how the local folk will talk when word gets around."

O'Daniels stepped forward, his right fist knotting, the left holding his rifle. "Why you—"

"Derry?" the hounds man called. "That buck's not here. I can see where a boat was pushed out. Left a groove in the mud, and they's tracks left by whoever took it. He didn't leave this camp by land. Figger that this feller's tellin' ya the truth."

The now-nervous blond shotgun youth was scratching at his beard as he said, "Reckon there's a boat down to Johnson's landing, Derry. We make tracks, we can take to the river. See if we can catch him. And Deacon's dogs will pick old Baptiste up if he made land atwixt here and Johnson's."

Travis held Derry O'Daniels' gaze. Gave him a slight nod. "Outside of the knowing that we don't like each other just on account of, I got no quarrel with you. Come sunup, I'll flag down a boat and be gone, and I ain't coming back."

"What about that pirogue of yours?"

"Leaky old scow of a boat. Warn't worth that much t' start with."

O'Daniels broke the gaze, turned away. "All right. Deacon, if you're sure that neck-chopping son of a bitch ain't here, let's get a move on."

O'Daniels started for the forest, and hesitated. Pointing with his rifle, he said, "Mister, I don't know what game you're playing. But hear me. We find out you been helping that murdering black bastard to escape? We'll hang you both!"

With that, he followed the others into the inky forest, their feet rustling in the vegetation as they went.

Travis let them get far enough and softly called, "Reckon I'd stay up in that tree, Baptiste. Keep yer voice down. And don't ye move a muscle. Be just like them coons to cut back, just to make sure."

"I heah you. But my arms is falling to sleep. Be just like it that I falls outta this here tree like some big black apple."

Travis laughed at that, bending over his pack to pull out a brass pot. From the river, he cupped up some of the murky water. Putting the pan to the edge of the fire to boil, he tossed in a handful of coffee from a sack he took from the pack.

"Gonna make us coffee while we wait. Let it boil. Then I'm gonna take a scout. Make sure them coons is gone. Soon's we know, I'll fetch the boat and we'll catch the tide good and pull anchor."

"What tide? What anchor?"

"Ever been to sea, Baptiste?"

"Never been nowhere but those two times I run. Never made it outta the parish a'fore they catched me."

"Well, if'n yer game, we're going a sight farther than that."

The coffee on, Travis stood, and taking his pistol, faded into the trees. He cut a circle, taking his time. Stopped. Head cocked, he listened to the chirping and buzzing of the night insects and frogs. Somewhere ahead, a bird uttered a mournful call.

Picking his way carefully back to camp, he took one last look at the dark forest. "I'll be damned. Reckon it might have worked."

The heartless branch was eating into Baptiste's arms, turning them numb. His legs kept quaking as he shifted his feet on the branch below. His back was a tortured misery. He blinked against the pain.

Just hold on. This be over soon.

And then what? What was Travis Hartman up to? Why was a white man sticking his neck out for a buck what chopped his master's neck in two? And he be worth how many thousand dollars to the law?

The coffee was bubbling and black.

"That sure smell good." The branch cracked as Baptiste shifted. "I smelled me coffee before."

"Figure we're all right," Travis told him, moving the coffee to the side to cool. Then he rolled his blankets and repacked his ditty bags.

What trick you planning, white man?

"Travis?" Baptiste almost rasped, eyes blurring with a dizzy spell. "I can't hold on. Arms is gone to sleep. Gotta come down."

Down below, Travis shot another worried look at the forest. "Yep, reckon so, mate. Figure us fer all right." Then he positioned himself under the tree.

Through the overwhelming pain, the lack of feeling in his arms, Baptiste felt with his feet. Managed to find the next branch down. Tried to reach for the lower branch, but his hand was senseless. He slipped, fell back, then the world spun as he dropped. Hit a branch, bounced.

Somehow, Hartman caught his weight, eased him to the ground. A broken whimper issued from Baptiste's lips as pain from his ravaged back—like lightning—dimmed his vision.

Can't let myself go faint. I do...I wake up in chains. White men is all devils.

He struggled to rise, the dead meat of his arms failing him.

Travis's gaze was fixed on Baptiste's shirt, fresh blood visible on dried mud stains. "Tarnal hell. What did they do to you?"

"Massa took the whip to me. Twenty lashes foah runnin'." Baptiste winced as he lowered himself back to the ground and closed his eyes against the pain. "Worst was my woman and little son and girl. That look. Like the blackest night of they poor souls. And me, helpless and crying."

Baptiste sniffed. "I ain't never coming back from what I saw in their eyes."

Travis knelt, dipped his tin cup in the coffee, blowing on it. Then he sipped before offering to Baptiste. "Here. This'll help."

Baptiste started to reach for the cup. Stopped. "You… a white man…ain't gonna share yoah cup with no nigger. And coffee? All we gets is chicory and toasted bran."

The hard blue eyes showed no give as Hartman's bearded lips quivered.

"Maybe I'm a notional bastard. Now, drink. And don't scald yerseff. Ain't the fust time I done shared a cup with a Negro feller."

Hartman sighed, shook his head as he gazed wistfully at the fire. "Close to three years before the mast, and through two of 'em, Kundakindu was me mess mate. Warn't a better tar on the brine, I tell ye. And Kunda? Skin so black it looked blue in the sunlight. Said he come from a place in Africa called Angola. Reckon that old salt, he done proved he was more man than any twenty hardies this child ever knew."

Baptiste warily took a sip, skeptical eyes on Travis the entire time. "So, that be coffee? Don't seem like it be something so special."

"Taste any different comin' from a white man's cup?"

"Not that I can tell."

"Funny damn world, ain't it? Sit tight. I gotta slip off and bring the pirogue back. Then we'll be packed and shove off."

Baptiste watched the man rise on cat feet and slip silently into the night.

Didn't make sense. What he gain from this?

Had to be that reward.

Baptiste fought to keep his eyes open, the dizzy feeling and exhaustion leaching the last of his energy. Nodding off, he jerked his head up almost spilling the coffee. And Hartman was there, pulling the pirogue up on the bank.

The man turned, looked thoughtful as walked up to the fire and said, "My grandpap was what they called indentured. Same as a slave. Forty years he worked for a rich planter in Virginia. Lived in a little shack same as the Negroes. Only difference, he turned fifty and got ter walk away wi' the clothes on his back."

Travis extended his hand, pulling the sleeve back to expose tanned skin. "A feller has white skin, he's a slave for a time. Five years. Ten. Forty. But that skin be black, that feller, he's in it fer life. Never cottoned to the difference 'til Kundakindu signed onto the *Avangeline*. But he warn't no slave. Just an able seaman. Paid as such."

"Why'd you go to sea?" Baptiste sucked down the now-cold coffee, closed his eyes, and cradled the cup as if it were a gold chalice. God, he couldn't think through the fog of fatigue and numbing agony in his back. Thoughts kept flying off like thistle down on the wind.

What was that reward? Five thousand? More?

"Huh! This coon? Wanted ter make a season's wages on a coastal sloop. Figgered I'd make me pay, buy an outfit and rifle, head west to the wilderness. Maybe

Tennessee. Maybe the wild lands in Illinois. 'Cept this child figgered ter make a night of it first. That was in Boston town. In a tavern just back from the docks. Cain't remember nothing past that first mug of rum. Then I come back to me wits, and I'm in a swinging hammock aboard *Avangeline*. When I staggers up on deck, there's Captain Amos Avery wavin' a paper at me. Says I signed on fer crew. Paper's got a blotch of ink what he says is me thumbprint, proving I signed on."

Baptiste frowned through the fatigue. *He could pull that pistol on me. Don't make sense what he be after.*

Travis kept poking the fire with his stick. "And that black-hearted bastard kept adding crew that was brought in by press gangs. What they call crimping a seadog. Haul him on board drunk or senseless. Then he used us like dogs." He paused. "Shot Kundakindu down like he's a dock rat when he stepped a'tween us."

Hartman tapped fingers on the butt of the pistol. "Used this to do it."

"That why you doing this?" Baptiste caught his head as he started to nod off. Tired. So dead weary tired.

"Doing what?"

Baptiste forced himself awake, fought the sudden vertigo that made his head spin. "I heard Derry O'Daniels. I gotta be worth five thousand dollars. Takin' me gonna make you a rich man."

Travis took the cup from Baptiste's fingers and scooped more coffee. "Hell, what makes a man do anything? Maybe I didn't like him trying to finger me ditty bag." He pointed at the pirogue. "Maybe this child needs another hand at the paddles ter head up Natchez way."

And there was another reason not to trust the white bastard: "They's a law against helping a runaway. They catch you, they gonna hang you."

Travis sucked down the cup of coffee, then poured the last of it for Baptiste, handing the cup across. Standing, he collected the brass pot and started kicking dirt over the fire. "Well then, Mister Baptist de Bourgmont, maybe us coons better shove off and battle our way upriver afore those damn idjits figger out we sent 'em on a wild hunt for an albatross."

Hartman turned his back, fiddling with the small pot. The double-bitted axe lay there right where Baptiste had left it. His fingers were working well enough now that he could grip the smooth wood. Maybe the coffee gave him strength. Using the axe Baptiste struggled to his feet. Dizzy. Almost lost his balance. Baptiste lifted the axe high.

Gotta kill him. Strike hard. Right in the middle of the back. Ain't no white man gonna sell me back into slavery. Send this child off to have a rope put…

The world spun. His exhausted legs buckled, pain fogging his thoughts. Everything went gray, and he barely felt his body hit the ground.

For the moment he lay there, broken, hurting, and empty. What the hell had happened to him? The spinning wouldn't stop. When had he ever been this exhausted?

White bastard's gonna win.

Frustrated, defeated, tears welled in his eyes to spill down his cheeks. Wasn't no hope…

His last memory was the look in Lizza and his children's haunted eyes.

And that, too, faded into the eternal haze of gray…

———

Baptiste fought his way out of shattered dreams. In them, he was tied to the whipping post, his weight hanging painfully in his stretched shoulders and raw bound wrists. He knew he hung on the post because his back still ached and hurt, but not as badly. He couldn't look to the side. Couldn't stand to see Lizza and their two children staring, hollow-eyed, tears streaking down their faces. Maybe because deep down in his soul, he was too much of a coward.

To his surprise, his arm was free. With a hand, he scrubbed at his rheumy eyes, blinked, and realized he lay on his stomach. That some sort of blanket or tarp covered him.

"What d' hell?" he whispered through a dry throat.

"Hold still, coon," Hartman's voice said softly. "And keep quiet. They's a boat close."

The tarp was tugged away and Baptiste turned his head, taking stock. He lay atop packs in a plank-hull pirogue. Willows arched overhead. Birdsong filled the muggy air and insects buzzed. Inhaling, he filled his nose with the scent of river, mud, and green vegetation. He could hear water lapping against the hull.

"Where we be?" he asked, tried to rise, and grunted at the pain in his back.

"Creek mouth," Hartman said. "You been out fer two days, matey. Figger me fer a fool. Yer s'posed t' be helping me paddle this hyar pirogue, and all I been a doing is paddling fer both of us."

Baptiste shifted, and in so doing, realized his shirt was missing. And what looked like green paste was falling off his back. "What's this?"

"Poultice I made from crushed pine needles mixed with fat. Not that this child's any physician, but she's supposed ter stop infection. Now, gotta be quiet. Shhh!"

Baptiste straightened enough to look through the screen of willows. Beyond lay the river stretching forever to the distant trees on the far Louisiana bank; the murky water glowed silver in the afternoon sun. And just out from their hiding place, two flat boats were passing. Men wearing hats and homespun clothes worked at the poles to keep the craft straight in the current. Packs and barrels were piled high amidship.

After the craft passed, Baptiste crawled to the side, reached down, and cupped water from the creek.

"Tin cup's thar by yer elbow," Travis offered as he used his paddle to back them out of the willows and into the river.

This time, Baptiste gave no thought to it being a white man's cup but used it to drink his terrible thirst into submission. Blinking, he stared out at the river, looking downstream to where the flat boats disappeared around a bend and out of sight behind the water oak, cypress, and ash that lined the bank.

"Why we hidin' from them? Where we at?"

Hartman was stroking, eyes on the riverbank ahead as he drove them upstream. "Reckon we're some north of your parish boundary. I been keeping a weather eye. Been a couple of canoes come up from behind. Both times, I got us out of sight afore they could get a fix on us. Armed men. Rifles at the ready. Not the sort of coons as would be out on the river fer fishing. They's hunting us."

Travis indicated the vanished flat boats with a nod of the head. "Reckon it wouldn't do no good fer that bunch t' be spoutin' no stories of you and me passin' 'em on the river, neither. Better if'n we's ter jist up and disappear."

Baptiste winced as his belly made a gurgling.

"Thar's a half a catfish boiled in corn in the pot down by yer knee. Cooked it this mornin' and figgered ye'd be a sight gaunted when ye catched yer wits again."

Baptiste reached down, pulled the familiar brass pot up, and sure enough, it was half full of flaked fish and corn meal. With his fingers, he scooped the mush out, almost frantic as he choked it down. All the while he wondered if that wasn't the finest eating he'd ever known. Slurping the last of it, he wiped the pan down to its bright, licking the last bits from his fingers.

In the back, Hartman laughed. "Figgered yer stomach was rubbing on yer backbone."

Baptiste forced himself to struggle up on the seat and pulled his feet under him. The tight pain in his pulled back made him wince. He braced his arms on the gunwales and slowly shook his head.

"Hartman, we really runnin' and hidin'? Why you didn't turn me in?"

"Reckon I need help paddling upriver. Maybe I figger you'll work cheap. 'Sides, cain't neither of us go back. Law's lookin' fer us both. You fer chopping yer master's head off, me fer stickin' a knife in ole Capn' Avery. We's two of a kind."

Baptiste turned on the seat. "You know there ain't nowhere I can go. Anywhere upriver? I ain't nothing but a murderin' slave. They gots to hunt me down no matter what it take. Can't never let a buck nigger kill his master. No sin a Negro can commit, not even bedding a white woman, to compare with that. They turn the whole country upside down 'till they run me down."

Hartman's mustache and beard twitched as he worked his mouth into a twist. "Reckon so, mate. Makes it a might of a challenge, don't it?"

"Say we make it upriver past Louisiana? Where do I go where I ain't hunted? Nowhere's free, Travis Hartman. Don't matter that you kilt a man. You can hide, become just another white man. Me, they's always gonna look at me as property. Then they ask whose. And someone start thinking if'n I be a runaway, they's a reward."

"Huh!" Travis was paddling rhythmically, the bank passing with agonizing slowness. "Reckon even the Yankee Doodles up in New England is bound by that

1793 law. Says that 'scaped slaves has got ter be sent back ter their masters." Travis arched an eyebrow, "'Cept you done kilt yers."

"And that mean they send me back to be beat and cut and burned afore they pull me up in the sky with a rope around my neck," Baptiste muttered. "Then they leave me hang 'til the body rots off de rope."

He stared out at the river. "Can't let that happen. Not where my little boy and girl can see. Long as I die free, they got hope. You understand that?"

Travis kept stroking with his paddle. "I's thinking of Tennessee, maybe Illinois."

"They hold slaves in them places?"

"I reckon."

"What about we go west?"

"That's the Spanish lands. They don't cotton to no Americans in their country. Warn't that long ago they throwed out Freeman and Custis, then they took that fella, ole Zeb Pike, prisoner down to Mexico. Heard tell they's just talking 'bout making a treaty with Spain, but that don't hold no water. This child? He don't figger t' rot in no Spanish jail."

"What's next to Spanish lands?"

"Huh. That be Injun lands up north of the Arkansas. Heard tell of them. Wichita, Caddo, Pawnee. And then thar be the Platte. And above that, the Missouri. What Lewis and Cark explored back when Jefferson was president."

"Who?"

"Why, Thomas Jefferson. He done fought in the Revolution. Good Virginian from down east of the mountains. He sent these two fellers, Lewis and Clark, up the Missouri clean over ter the Pacific Ocean. Don't gotta clue what's been doing up in that country since."

"They got slaves? Plantations?"

"Reckon all they got is Injuns and wild country."

"Wild? That be free?"

"Free as thar can be, I reckon. Way I heard tell, a man can be anything he want ter be."

"Maybe I go there."

"And do what?"

"I can swing an axe. Trim logs. Dig ditches and hoe crops. That's why Massa made me jump de broom wi' Lizza. He wanted..." Baptiste bit his lip. "Lizza, she didn't want nothin' to do with me. I's just a bull-strong field darkie. Massa figured we'd make strong babies, so he married us. Overseer, he watch that fust night. Make sure I breed Lizza like a prize stallion breed a mare. She hate dat, laying there, head to the side an' eyes clamped shut, biting her knuckle like it's a rape."

Baptiste let the memories play in his head. "Maybe that's why I run. 'Cause of Lizza. Prove to her that I be a man. Only way a slave prove he got a choice? He gotta run. Figure if I get away, Lizza can be proud of me. My children be proud. If I get away, Massa loses and I win."

"But they caught ye."

"Twice. And this last time? Massa make sure everybody watch so they see me broken and beaten. Shoulda seen the look in their faces. Hope gone dead in my little ones' eyes. Like they's turned to rotted wood inside, all black and hollow."

"That's as good a reason as any t' chop a planter's head off, I reckon."

"Warn't no other choice," Baptiste said softly. "Don't matter that I never see Lizza. Never see my little boy and girl. I give 'em the best gift an' lesson I can. Better, though, if'n I get clean away. Then it always be there in the backs of everyone's mind. Baptiste won in the end."

"They's money ter be made in furs, if'n yer game. Beaver, buckskins, martin and the like. Heard tell that St.

Louis has companies that hire fellers fer the Indian trade. Might be they'd take a couple o' coons like us 'thout askin' questions."

"They take one look at me and know I's a slave."

"Reckon 'til we figger it out, ye can call yerseff my slave."

Baptiste's gut wrenched. He pivoted on the seat, leaning back in spite of the pain from the pulled scabs in his back. He stuck a hard finger in Travis's face, eyes afire. "I's fixin' to kill you back at that camp, 'cept I didn't have the spit and vinegar t' do it. You *ever* call me you slave? I'll drive that axe right down a'twixt yer eyes. Split yoah skull in two."

To Baptiste's surprise, Hartman broke into a wide grin. "Reckon ye might. Or at least ye'll give her a try. But a'fore ye do, it'll be Katy bar the door."

"What that mean?"

"Means ye better wear yer working clothes and pack a lunch, 'cause this child's gonna take a keg full 'o killing afore he's dead."

The deadly earnest way Hartman said it brought a smile to Baptiste's lips. Turning back straight, he grunted as bent and fished the paddle from where it had been stowed. Then, grimacing, he did his best to dip his paddle and propel them upriver. Damn. It hurt. Pulled his back into stitches of pain. But as he did, a smile bent his lips and his heart felt lighter than it ever had.

———

Derry O'Daniels shifted, using the long barrel of the worn Pennsylvania rifle to ease the grape vines to one side as he, Pap Miller, and Quincy Reynolds crept up on the fugitive's camp. Night had fallen; the crickets, moths, and cicadas all started their evening serenade. He could hear frogs in a chorus out in the water. It had been a long chase fueled by a burning rage. Inconceivable! He'd been tricked! Humiliated. Now Derry O'Daniels got to pay the bastards back.

Half the parish had been on the hunt. Families had barricaded their houses, terrified that the blood-crazed fiend, Baptiste, was lurking just outside their door. Folks just knew the fugitive meant to murder the men and rape the women. Outside of Thomasville, a darkie had been shot dead as he stepped out of the forest and onto the road. And Wilber Thorpe's slave, Jacob, had his arm shot off by a panicked white farmer down near Green's Crossing. People had lost their wits with the murderer still on the loose.

In the midst of the growing panic and the demand for justice, Derry O'Daniels had been told by a passing boatman that a pirogue had been seen headed upriver with a white man and buck Negro at the paddles.

Hurrying back to Johnson's landing, O'Daniels had run across a posted flyer from New Orleans telling of a reward for the capture of able seaman Travis Hartman. A man wanted for murdering Captain Amos Avery aboard his own brigantine. And the image pictured from a line drawing looked suspiciously like the man O'Daniels' posse had braced at that riverside camp the first night of the pursuit.

Sending the hounds man, Deacon Adams, to raise additional volunteers for the pursuit, O'Daniels had commandeered three of Johnson's horses, and with Pap and Quincy, headed north along the riverside trace. Knowing the east bank offered more high ground and better access to campsites, O'Daniels had taken the ferry to the Mississippi shore. They'd made good time, the trace cutting off loops where the Mississippi turned back on itself. From the heights, they'd taken time to study the river. Several times they'd spied boats across the expanse of water that might have been the fugitives, but none had seemed right.

And then, on the point of turning back, they'd stumbled into a river trader's camp just down from Natchez.

"Hell, yes!" the bearded Kentuckians had told them. "Passed them coons a day's paddle north o' Natchez Under the Hill. Headed fer St. Lou, they said. A goin' ter the Missouri country what Lewis and Clark opened. Reckon ye could catch 'em in two or three days' hard ride."

Derry O'Daniels had never been much of a horseman. Nevertheless, he'd urged their flagging mounts onward, stopping only for cornmeal, lard, and salt in Natchez before taking the river trace north.

Pap Miller had seen the pirogue that afternoon as it was paddled close to the Mississippi shore. Here the tree-clad bluffs rose high over the river. Thickly timbered creeks drained the orange-and-tan height with its buff soil. On the confluence of one such creek, O'Daniels watched the pirogue being pulled ashore onto a low gravel bar. The sun was setting over the hazy swamp across the river.

"Got 'em," O'Daniels had told his weary deputies. "Picket the horses. We'll sneak down on foot. Give them time to set camp and eat. Soon as it's night, we'll sneak in. Take 'em by surprise."

He reached inside to feel the stiff paper from the arrest warrant in his coat pocket. By God, they'd get their comeuppance for playing Derry O'Daniel for a fool. That's when he stepped on the stick, didn't think much of it when the low crack was drown in the night sounds of the Mississippi forest.

———

The way his heart was beating, Baptiste figured it would batter its way right through his ribs. Sweat tickled its way down his face, and his mouth had gone dry. Seemed all he could do to keep from panting in fear as he gripped and re-gripped the handle of his double-bitted axe.

Peering into the night-shadowed brush, he couldn't see a thing.

"Come on, Travis," he whispered. "Tell me this warn't nothing."

And then the shadows moved, the sound of branches rasping on cloth barely audible over the forest night. The hunched shape of a man eased his way from the darkness; a fowling piece—it's deadly load of shot pointed Baptiste's direction—was held at the ready.

This gonna end bad. The words kept repeating in Baptiste's head. Even as they did, he raised the double-bitted axe. He and Travis had figured out what they had to do. He had to strike just so. If he didn't hit the man just right, they be no way to win.

In his mind, Baptiste could see the hopeless look in Lizza and his little children's eyes.

———

Derry O'Daniels advanced in a crouch, eyes fixed on the dancing flickers of fading firelight. He was coming in from the side. Pap would have circled to come in opposite of O'Daniels, and Quincy, the youngest, would appear from the trail leading down from the bluff.

Step by step, O'Daniels made his way past the last stand of willows, his rifle finally clear of the vegetation. Raising it to his shoulder, he stepped into the small grassy camp. Took in the two bundled blankets on either side of the dying fire. The bow of the pirogue was visible where it was tied off on shore.

The click of the cock as O'Daniels eared it back was like the crack of doom. Taking aim at the closest mound of blankets, he called, "All right, boys, come on in! I got 'em covered."

"Sorry, coon," a voice said softly behind him. Then something hit Derry O'Daniels in the back of the head. As lightning blasted through his skull, his rifle discharged into the bedding. And then he was falling into a soft gray darkness…

———

Jubal Pike waited on his loaded flatboat, arms crossed as he leaned against the cargo stacked amidships and glared at the New Orleans wharves. Boats like his, handmade craft that floated down, in cases like Jubal's from distant Pittsburgh, landed here, upriver from the ocean-going barks and brigantines. Around him, the landing swarmed with people unloading an entire continent's trade, and here he was, Jubal Pike, waiting on the New Orleans parish judge.

He bent around the barrels of molasses, whiskey, dried corn, and stacked lumber to vent his visual wrath once more on his captives. They, at least, got to hunch in the limited shade cast by the manty-tarped kegs of trade goods. A short rope restricted their bound wrists and ankles so they couldn't stand. A twist of rag was tied around their mouths. That had been his doing halfway through the first day to keep them from shouting curses, making threats, and spewing the lies that Constable O'Daniels had insisted would come out of their mouths.

Finally, now, after all this time on the river, they'd given up on mumbling into the gags, fit just to stare woodenly at him through weary eyes. But, true to Jubal's word and the five-dollar gold piece the constable had paid him, Jubal had delivered his prisoners to New Orleans.

Looking back at the landing, a feller in a dark frock coat with black beaver hat, slim wool trousers, and striking white shirt was striding through the sweating slaves and rivermen who rolled barrels, kegs, and crates up onto the riverside. Two men, roughly dressed, booted, and with a brace of pistols in their belts, followed. Both wore wide-brimmed straw hats against the hot sun.

"Ye be the judge?" Jubal called.

"Aye, sir. What is this about a warrant for prisoners?" The judge minced his way across the plank, his deputies following.

"Reckon so," Jubal said, extracting the somewhat worn piece of paper from his pocket. "Not that I could tell ye. This child cain't read. But Constable O'Daniels done give it over ter me. Hyar's his warrant fer the arrest of these scoundrels. Wanted fer murder, they is. One kilt a planter upriver. T'other kilt a sea captain right hyar in New Orleans. I's ter deliver 'em to the law in New Orleans."

The judge had taken the warrant, reading it through. "Says here that it's a warrant for a fugitive slave by the name of Baptiste."

"Don't know about no slave." Jubal swelled to his full height. "Constable O'Daniels, he done claimed that this other feller, he be a Travis Hartman, and that ye'd know his name and crime."

"Hartman," the judge reflected, stepping around the cargo to study the men. All three were now bouncing, tugging against their ropes, uttering muffled cries into their gags. Reminded Jubal of mice in the bottom of a bucket.

"Killed Captain Avery," one of the deputies reminded.

"Of course," the judge cried with delight. "And this third man?"

"What Constable O'Daniels called an accomplice."

The judge turned his attention back to Jubal. "You've done a noble service, sir. And where is Constable O'Daniels?"

Jubal puffed out his chest. "He said he had more fugitives fer him and his Negro tracker to hunt down. That he'd be along, but ye should hold these no accounts 'til he done showed up. Whenever that might be."

Where he lay bound on the flatboat deck beside Pap Miller and Quincy Reynolds—both having been laid out cold by the flat of an axe—Derry O'Daniels screamed his frustration into the gag. By the time they got this straightened out, Hartman and Baptiste would have vanished like the mist.

NO QUARTER

KATHLEEN O'NEAL GEAR

The notion that any groundbreaking fiction could be written about the Alamo seems impossible. Leave it to Kathleen's insatiable curiosity to discover a story too long overlooked. I never gave any thought to the slaves in the Alamo or what their sympathies would be. Of course they wanted the Mexican Army to win. Slavery was illegal in Mexico. Nor did I realize that Jim Bowie —lionized in legend and literature—was such a rapacious scoundrel and grifter. History whitewashes some particularly unsavory people. Turning her talents to the story of Bettie and Charlie, Kathleen not only brings their plight to life, but "No Quarter" won the 2023 Spur Award for Best Western Short Fiction of the Year, won a Will Rogers Medallion Award, and was a finalist for the Western Fictioneers "Peacemaker" Award. (WMG)

After the battle of the Alamo, Bettie told her story to anyone who would listen, but few people believed her. In fact, most Texas historians dismissed her tale out of hand. After all, she was Black, and she was a woman. Only one early Texas historian believed her, and it was his faith in Bettie's tale that led me to do more research. That started twenty years ago. I've wanted to write Bettie's story for a long time. I hope you enjoy it. (KOG)

March 6, 1836. Before dawn.

A cool breeze filters through cracks in the adobe wall and chills my face where I stand beside the bullhide door, listening to the silence. I've been straining to hear voices for so long, it's hard to breathe. Last evening, when the cannon bombardment stopped, I tried to sleep, but my frayed nerves wouldn't allow it. I jerked awake at every tiny sound, and now I'm so afraid of the eerie quiet, sleep is impossible.

Resting my forehead against the wall, I just try to get air into my lungs.

"Bettie?"

"I'm right here, Charlie. I'm not leaving you."

In the back of the room, Charlie lies curled on the floor at the colonel's bedside with his rifle clutched in his hand. He was wounded eight days ago, and I can smell his leg from four paces away. He's a big, strong man, but I don't know how much longer he can last without a hospital.

"What's happening out there?" He sits up with a groan and leans back against the wall.

"Don't know, but it's too quiet."

"Can you look outside for me? Are the sentries awake?"

I pull open the door and peer out through the slit. As clouds pass overhead, moonlight pierces the swirling mist in bars and streaks of dusty silver. The plaza is over 450 feet long and 160 feet wide, with walls up to twelve feet high and three feet thick. To the east a long row of barracks borders the courtyard. My eyes strain to see anyone moving out there, but everything alive seems to have vanished. Then, on top of the north wall, I make out two men standing like black silhouettes. "I see two sentries. One man is pointing out into the darkness, like he sees something."

"How long 'til dawn?"

"Half hour. Maybe a bit longer. Moon is still bright, but it's hard to tell with the fog. How are you? How's your leg?"

He doesn't answer for a long moment. "Awright. Don't worry 'bout me."

I stare blindly out at the plaza. Every building and cannon shines wetly. I'm pretty sure Charlie's dying. The gangrene has gone too far. "You just hold on. I'm going to get you out of here, Charlie."

I can hear the smile in his voice. "Truly? How you going to do that?"

"Once those gates open, I'm packing you right out through the middle of Santa Anna's army."

"Don't think they'll try to stop you, eh?"

"Not if they know what's good for them, they won't."

He laughs. "Awright. Just tell me when to get up."

"I will," I answer, even though I know there's no way he can stand up by himself, and I'm not sure I can hold him up if I manage to get him on his feet. He's a big man, and I'm barely five feet tall.

"Bettie, I—I've lost track of days. How long has it been since the siege started?"

I have to think about it. One day has run into the next like water rushing down a creek. Eleven days? No. Twelve? "Thirteen, maybe."

"Thirteen? That long?"

"I guess so."

Hard to believe we've been holed up in this crumbling fortress that long, while a purgatory of noise thundered just beyond the walls. I ain't never been this awake in my whole life. Every crack in the adobe stands out like a chasm dropping straight into the fiery abyss. I swear I can see the bottom rising up to meet me.

"Ursula?" a weak voice whispers.

Sucking in a deep breath, I find the strength to answer. "She'll be right back, Colonel. Won't be long now."

For days I've been soothing Colonel Bowie's fevered cries for his dead wife by telling him Ursula stepped out to tend the children or to fetch food...laudanum...speak with Travis about some matter that concerned the Colonel. It's been enough that he could fall back into tormented sleep.

"Our voices must have woke him," Charlie says softly.

"Check his pulse for me, will you?"

Charlie shifts. After a few moments, his voice is reverent. "I reckon the Colonel's 'bout done."

When tears rise, I blink them back. The news brings a strange mixture of sadness and relief. The Colonel bought me nigh onto six years ago. If he's dead, and I can escape, I'll run to Monterrey with Charlie. There's supposed to be a beautiful cathedral there. We could get married.

"Charlie?" My voice sounds faint even to me. "What's going to happen to us if Colonel Bowie's dead? Think we'll go to his wife's relatives, the Veramendis? I heard he owes them money."

"Don't know, Bettie. Can't think on it now."

"But they could sell us off to different folks." *No, no, Lord, not that.*

"...Ursula?" Bowie whispers.

I say, "She's coming, Colonel. Went out to fetch water from the well. Be right back."

Charlie exhales hard. "Everything depends on who wins this fight. If the Texians win, then we ain't got no choice. They'll haul us off and give us to whoever they figure is our new owner, less we can escape in the bedlam. But if the Meskins win..." His voice fades.

"You think Santa Anna might let us go?"

There's a pause, and I hear Charlie's bootheels rake across the floor as he shifts his wounded leg. "I've thought on that. It's possible. If *El Presidente* did free us, we might could go up north to the Indian nations."

"No, Charlie, let's head to Monterrey. Please? It's deeper into Mexico. Slavery ain't legal there. It's safer."

"Well," he says gently, "we ain't gotta decide now. Everything, everything depends on this fight."

My traitorous knees tremble. If the Texians lose, freedom might be a few hours away. Need to start planning out what we'll do. First off, run, run hard, before anyone can take it back. Can't help but worry, 'cause another slave told me the Colonel didn't call us slaves. Called us indentured servants, and indentured servants are legal in Mexico. But the Meskins know the truth, don't they?

Hope is tearing me apart. Every slave in Bexar has been whispering about it, speculating on what will happen to them. Texians will make slavery the law of the land. We won't have no chance...

A shout splits the darkness outside, then I hear a Mexican voice call: *"Viva Santa Anna!"* followed by, *"Viva la Republica!"*

"Bettie?" Charlie cries in panic. "Tell me—"

"Colonel Travis," one of the sentries yells, "the Mexicans are coming!"

I open the door wider and stare out at the misty plaza. "Defenders are throwing off their blankets, running for their posts."

Travis' powerful voice carries as he charges for

ramparts. "Come on, boys, the Mexicans are upon us, and we'll give them hell!"

The heart-numbing melody of a bugle wavers. It's called *El Deguello*. Meskins have been playing it off and on for days. Awful and beautiful, the notes seem timed to the blasts of cannons, shotguns, and rifles. Somewhere to the north a long chorus carries through the unholy music —eternal, undying, torn from the muzzles and throats of desperate men.

Dear God, please make it stop.

All I can do is stand suspended like a feather, unable to move or think while the roar shakes me apart.

Propping my head against the cold bullhide door, I close my eyes, but it doesn't help. I can still see them out there, half-transparent in the mist, their mouths wide open as they race across the plaza of this broke-down old mission.

"How bad? Bettie...?"

"Bad as can be. I hear axes banging. I think they're smashing through the wooden doors along the west wall."

When I open my eyes, liquid silver moonlight twines through the shifting smoke, outlining the huge plaza. In the volleys of gunfire, the faces of the Mexican soldiers are lit by unearthly flares of gold as they pour over the north wall and into the fort.

Men scream in Spanish and English. Shotguns blast, then a long volley from the enemy. Hoarse screams. There's a flurry of activity as men everywhere abandon their posts and rush to the north wall to try to hold back the tide of enemy soldiers.

Finally, I manage to say, "*Soldados* swarming over the north wall."

"How'd they get inside?" Charlie cries.

"Must have sneaked through the mist and thrown up

dozens of ladders. Texians are falling back, running for the low barracks on the east side."

Gunsmoke drifts across the plaza in pale blue streamers. The crackle of muskets is constant. In the midst of the haze men stagger or run, coughing, trying to reach a safe place that no longer exists. A defender trips over someone lying on the ground, and when a scream erupts, he says, "Oh, Lord, I'm sorry. Didn't see you."

When I close the door, the soft thud resembles the last clod of dirt hitting a grave. There's a ring of eternity to it.

Charlie exhales the words, "Well, ain't nobody ordering me to fight now."

His rifle clatters as he lets it fall to the floor.

I ease down to sit beside the door. It's a strange feeling. I have to look, as though these final moments are my entire life—all I've ever known, or ever will know. Survivors leap about in a darkness punctured by flashes and screams. Somewhere a man pants like a woman in the throes of childbirth, but I can't see him. Could be coming from the kitchen next door. Claws at my heart. Part of me wishes I'd run off at first opportunity. Left the sick Colonel to die on his own, but I could no more abandon a sick man than I could abandon Charlie just 'cause his leg is wounded.

"Santa Anna might free us, Charlie," I repeat.

"You know what that music means, Bettie? 'To cut the throat.' And you seen that blood-red flag they hoisted from the Cathedral of San Fernando. Means no quarter. No mercy. Even if we surrender, the general ain't likely to spare the life of anyone inside these walls. Meskins want every one of us dead."

Gunfire penetrates the bullet holes in the walls and strobes the room with flares of dirty rose. It's a wrenching, otherworldly color, a color found only on a battlefield, I expect. I turn around when the details of the long room spring into existence: The Colonel's cot shoved against the wall in the back, Charlie sitting on the floor beside it, his long musket close by and his shot-up leg extended. I used a strip of my yellow skirt to bandage it, but the color got soaked up by blood long ago. A few other items appear—a water bucket with a ladle, Colonel's red shirt tossed on the floor, an extra pair of boots resting in the corner. My eyes fix on Colonel Bowie. He's bundled in blankets like a dying skeleton. Looks dead, but I can't be sure. His last act was to prop himself up, lean back against the wall, then draw out his pistols and knife and place them on the blanket beside him. Sometime during the night, his head lolled to the side. Greasy locks of hair hide most of his face, but for a moment our eyes seem to meet through the darkness, and I am filled with fear.

Underneath the cracking gunfire, a low guttural moan rises and wavers over the plaza. Haunts me, for there's a terrible hope to it. A relief. As though each man is grateful to see Judgment Day arrive at last. One thousand years from now in my dreams, I'll hear that moan filtering down through the cold earth that covers me, and I'll be right back here in this goddamn godforsaken crypt, desperate to run off to Monterrey with Charlie.

Look outside. Watch. *Remember*.

I force my gaze back to the door.

Dozens of soldados race across the courtyard, leaping the dead, bayoneting the wounded, heading for their compatriots in the southwest corner who've captured the eighteen-pounder, a big cannon. Are they going to blast the defenders out room by room? Officers wave swords, and the steel glitters, sprinkled with the bizarre diamond fire of pistol shots.

A tall man shouts orders in Spanish. I learned some over the years, but my heart's thumping so loud, I can't understand anything he's saying. When the soldiers swab the cannon and load it up with iron scraps and chopped-up horseshoes, my stomach twists.

It's going to tear people to pieces.

My gaze moves over the rushing soldados and fleeing defenders and fixes on the unearthly blue moonlight that coats the low buildings on the east side where the Texians hide. The pearly gates must shine like that when the moon rises in heaven. If me and Charlie can escape in the confusion, we'll run as far as we can go. We'll find a place to pass the summers rocking on our porch and watch our babies playing in the yard. I can see their little faces clear as day, smiling at us, loving us. God above, the longing feels like slivers of flint in my veins.

"It's almost over, Charlie."

As I stumble to my feet, my legs shake so hard I grab onto the wall to make my way to where I can ease down between Charlie and the Colonel's cot.

Charlie wraps his powerful arms around me and kisses my hair. "Least we're together. That's all I ever wanted. To grow old holding you in my arms. Lord, I had sweet dreams for us. Always thought Bowie would finally give us permission to marry."

I gaze up into his dark eyes. Brightness passes across his face, like spring sunlight off the river—breathtaking, fragile, and swiftly gone. Lifting a hand, I feel his forehead. It's like fire.

"We might not need permission now. Not if Bowie's dead. Not if Santa Anna frees us, and we can run off south or north or anywhere else that nobody can ever find us again."

"If..."

Reaching out, I place my fingertips on Colonel Bowie's wrist. His eyes are wide open, wider than I have ever seen them, and staring blindly at the door. As though even in death, he's keeping watch, prepared for one last battle when it bursts inward.

"Anything?"

"Can't feel nothing."

As though utterly exhausted, Charlie slides sideways, soft as silk, and rests his head in my lap. The heat from his face penetrates my skirt. "Everything's awright," I tell him and stroke his hair. Should I sing to him? He loves it when I sing. His hand moves instinctively toward mine, and I take it in a tight grip. Songs seem to have slipped out of my heart, leaving it unable to remember any of the words to his favorite tunes. "I'm right here," I whisper. "I'm not leaving you. Not ever."

"You have to, Bettie." He nuzzles his cheek against my leg. "If you get the chance, don't you wait on me. You skedaddle. Fast as you can. It will soothe me to know you're out there running free for Monterrey."

I let my fingers tenderly trace the line of his dark cheek, then I desperately reach out to check the Colonel's wrist again. I wait a long time, trying to feel anything, no matter how faint. It's hard. The air itself beats with gunshots, shouts, and long ululating screams.

"I'm pretty sure he's gone," I softly say. "Thank you, Lord. Been too long in coming. Too much suffering."

For days, Bowie crawled out of bed around noon and staggered into the courtyard where people could see him and be encouraged by the knowledge that he was still alive. The defenders needed to see Bowie, and he knew it. His appearance always brought a wave of cheers and hoots. But as the siege wore on, he grew weaker, delirious, and unable to breathe.

Drawing my hand back, I rest it on Charlie's hot throat. His heartbeat is rapid, fluttering like a dying bird's. "I reckon the Colonel would be mad about this. He ain't never quit in the middle of a fight in his whole life."

47

"Well, least they can't humiliate him now," Charlie says. "That's something."

"It is."

Charlie shifts to look up at me. He has the kindest face I've ever seen, though he looks much older than his thirty-two years. Silver glitters through his hair. "If I die, I want you to—"

"You're not dying. We're going to make it, Charlie. Both of us. I know we are."

He just sighs and nuzzles his cheek against my leg. "Maybe. Hope so."

While I tenderly pet his hair, my mind is racing. *Strange, the things you think about at the end. There's a war raging right outside this room, and I'm thinking about my name.* "Charlie, I—I can't recall my name."

He seems puzzled. The deep lines that cut across his forehead crinkle. "What do you mean? It's Bettie."

"No, I mean my true name. The name I was born to. I think it was Khady, though I could be recalling somebody else's name, my sister or mama, maybe."

Dirt and grit—torn loose from the adobe walls— shower us when another cannon blast explodes. Gently, I brush it away from Charlie's eyes and cheeks.

"Never knew mine," he says. "Wish I did. I'd keep it locked up inside me. Nobody'd ever know it, 'cept you."

First thing the slave traders did is take away our born names and give us names from their people: Sam, Joe, Ben, Sarah, Bettie, Charlie. What would it feel like to stand guard over the other's true name, to keep it wholly inside where no one could ever take it away? Maybe we wouldn't even speak our names aloud. Even when we were alone.

"I know the name of my people, though," Charlie says. "The Wolof. I was only three or four when they chained me with the other babes down in the belly of that ship. Don't recall much except the journey. Only 'bout half of us survived. But before he died, there was a—a *griot*, an old storyteller. He kept repeating that we were the Wolof. The great warriors of the Wolof." A faint smile turns his lips. "I'll never forget that. From West Africa, I think."

"Wolof." I taste the word as it moves upon my tongue. It's sweet, like deep well water. Takes a while before I can get the strength to say, "I had dreams for us, too, Charlie."

"Oh," he replies barely audible and tenderly runs his calloused fingers over my hand. "I know you did."

The next cannon explosion deafens the world, and the walls crack and shudder as though about to topple over us. Every breath now tastes like gunpowder.

Charlie grabs me around the waist. "Hold on to me! Don't let go!"

I cling to him with my eyes squeezed closed and my heart hammering like the hooves of a white horse galloping out of the sky, cutting through the smoke and cries for help as it thunders down toward us.

Across the plaza, men and women cry out in terror, then all goes quiet, except for sporadic *goddamns* and *sonsofbitches* that lace the early morning air.

When I open my eyes, the room shimmers with falling dust.

"Bettie, listen to me, you have to get out of here," Charlie whispers. "I want you to sneak down to the kitchen and hide there."

"What for? They'll just root me out of there, same as—"

"Pretty soon now, somebody's going to ask where the Colonel is. Soldados will come and hit this room hard, maybe with a cannon. You gotta go."

"Awright. Let's go."

Rising, I reach for Charlie's hand.

"No, Bettie, I can't—"

"Get up, right now."

I reach down, grasp his hand, and haul him to his feet while he chokes back pain. His wound must have broken open. The strong odor of rot fills the air. Don't want to think too much on it. On what will happen to that leg. On what will happen to the man I'd die to protect.

Slipping his arm over my shoulders, I stagger forward. He's gritting his teeth and limping badly. The four paces to the door seem to take forever.

We walk out into the cold night, and I can't force my feet to take another step. *God almighty…*

Ashes fall from a pale azure sky, white as snow and as pearlescent as moonlight. Their radiance bathes the smoke rising from the cannon and the solemn faces of the soldados who surge, with bayonets fixed, into the devastated barracks. Somewhere, a man bellows, "Meskin bastards, take this!" and a rifle booms. More booms.

Cries lance the smoke as the defenders fight it out hand-to-hand.

"Gotta…hurry, Bettie. Can't stand up much longer."

I stagger forward again with Charlie limping beside me.

From the eastern barracks, soldados drag dead defenders from blasted rooms—by feet or arms—haul them out into the plaza and pile atop one another, then return for more.

Not dead. Not all of them, for I see a hand sneak out of the pile and weakly grab hold of earth as though it steadies him for the journey ahead. Feet kick. These moments go beyond horror. As I watch, men die like falling stars torn loose from the heavens, flying away into a distant darkness I can't conjure. What are they thinking? Are they wondering if they squandered time?

Wishing for the ability to say a few last words to a loved one, maybe to beg forgiveness for a long-forgotten hurt?

When we reach the kitchen door, I shove it open with my boot, and we step into the soft red glow coming from the fireplace. A dead man slumps against the wall to my right. He's curled up on the floor like an infant waiting to be born. The fireplace where I've spent long, hot hours cooking for the garrison stands to my left. Pots and pans hang on the back wall in front of me.

"Awright, let me down now, Bettie. Gotta sit down."

Bracing my feet, I lower him to the floor, where he sags against the wall breathing hard. His face is a mask of agony. "Oh, Lord," he says as he reaches down to rub his wounded leg. "Sit down, Bettie. Ain't nothing you want to see out there now."

"I gotta look, Charlie."

Dropping to my knees before the ajar door, I place my body between Charlie and what's to come. I know they'll cut through me like a hot knife through butter, but if Charlie only lives for another five heartbeats, the world will be a better place for that long.

The scene outside is wrenching. I stare wide-eyed when the undead erupt from the margins of the dust and smoke, the graveyards of destroyed rooms, and throw themselves at the victors. Who are these men? ...Crumbling...crumbling apparitions, heads, hands, gusting away like old leaves blown loose from skeletal trees. Knives flash, swords cleave the smoke, and men screaming in rage and pain grapple with one another. The nightmare...the nightmare...never ends. It's the tips of the bayonets I can't take my eyes from—they shimmer with moonglow where they stab through spines and skulls. This holy ground runs black with blood, and all I can think about is freedom. We might be headed south before noon. Me and Charlie, and Sarah and Joe, and the other slaves locked up in this fortress. We could all head south together, maybe make our own town along some creek in the backcountry.

An odd hush descends over the plaza.

"What's happening, Bettie?"

"The end, I expect."

My gaze lets go of the dead and climbs into the sky, where clouds drift in wispy flames like horsetails that have caught fire. What day is it? Sunday? I—think it must be. Are you up there, God? *Come, behold the works of the Lord, what desolations he hath made in the earth...*

Be still. Be still.

Shapes in blue jackets, sabers flashing, march across the plaza through the unnatural gleam of approaching dawn. They're either our murderers or our liberators.

I ease the door closed.

"Soldados coming, Charlie."

"Then get away from that door, Bettie!"

I slide back and lean against the wall with my shoulder pressed against his. All I can think of is the buzzards that used to roost in the trees at dusk. Tomorrow, they'll be back by the hundreds to wait for the soldiers to leave.

"Everything's fine," Charlie says. "Just look at me. Don't stop looking."

He takes my hand, and I turn to him. Everything I ever wanted is right there in those dark eyes. "We'll go live in peace together somewhere on the frontier," I tell him.

"We will," he whispers. "Won't bother nobody, less they bother us first."

The bullet holes in the walls wink, going dark, then light, as men march in front of them.

In accented English, a man shouts, "I am told this is

Colonel Bowie's room. Are you in there, Colonel? For the sake of God, if you are in there, come out!"

Sabers and spurs jingle, but there's something beneath it, another sound, faint and haunting, like the far-off crackling of a thousand impatient black wings.

Leaning my head against Charlie's arm, I dream of the beautiful little girls we'll have and the brave boys who will look like him...of harvesting our crops while the children chase each other through the tall golden cornstalks, laughing, happy...

When the soldados kick down the bullhide door and rush into the Colonel's room, Charlie clutches my hand harder. Bowie's alone in there, already dead, but a pistol blast shakes the walls, then I hear the Meskins shout, "*Cobarde!*" and "*Marica!*" Over and over, they call him a coward, a sissy, a chicken. Each curse is followed by a muffled thud.

I frown up at Charlie and mouth the words, "What are they doing?"

"Bayonets."

My throat goes tight. *Where's the sense in bayonetting a dead man?*

"Bettie?" Charlie whispers. "Help me stand up."

"Why?"

"Just help me, please."

He slides his arm around my shoulders, and I heft him up while he suppresses groans. "Leave me leaned up against the wall now, and go hide yourself in the back."

"I am not leaving you—"

"Just do it."

I have trouble letting go of his hand. Our fingertips touch until the last moment when they slip apart, and I walk back to duck down beside the old fireplace where red coals flicker. The dirty pots stacked in the corner smell of grease, corn, and fried beef from the last meal I fixed.

Just outside, five paces away, boots pound the ground as the soldados leave Bowie's room. They hesitate outside the kitchen. My gaze is locked with Charlie's. A square of moonlight filters around the door, and I can see him clearly. There's enough love in his eyes to last me a lifetime. Charlie's leg gives out suddenly, and he staggers back against the wall panting.

"Come out!" a man calls. "Is someone in there?"

Charlie closes his eyes but says, "Yes, sir, there's two of us. We ain't got no guns."

"Put your hands up and come out, then."

Charlie licks his lips, doesn't budge, as though he's trying to decide if it's better to fight or die right now or take a chance that we'll be slaves forever. After a while, the door is pulled open and a Mexican head appears and disappears. Soldados burst into the room with bayonets. When a young officer, half Charlie's height, enters, Charlie grabs him to use as a shield.

"Stop this!" the officer cries. "I mean you no harm!"

"I'll kill you if you don't let Bettie go! I mean it!"

The soldados leap forward, trying to stab Charlie with their bayonets. He has no choice but to swing the officer this way and that, using him to block the cold steel that still drips the Colonel's blood.

"Wait! Back away!" the officer shouts to his men in Spanish. "Stop this!"

Grumbling, the soldados step back, but each stands poised to lunge forward and tear Charlie to pieces.

The officer lifts his hands. "Tell me what you want?"

"I want you to promise you'll let Bettie go!" Charlie shouts. "Let her go! She ain't done nothing. She's just a cook! And we didn't have no choice being in here. They made us come!"

"Are you slaves?" the officer asks.

"Yes, sir, Cap'n."

"Then you have nothing to fear! Slaves will not be harmed. You are non-combatants, yes?"

Charlie fought like a bear, 'til he was wounded. Colonel ordered him to. I'm scared to death he's going to tell the truth, but he says, "We didn't do no fighting. Bettie fried beef, and I hauled wood."

"Release me, and I give you my solemn oath you will not be harmed."

Hope is strangling me so that I can barely breathe. Is he telling the truth? Or lying so Charlie will let him go? Does this officer have the authority to keep such an oath?

Charlie glances at me, and I can tell he's thinking the same thing I am.

"Let him go, Charlie," I plead.

Charlie's arms shake as he releases the officer and sags back against the wall with his chest heaving.

The officer gives me a curious look, then says, "We are gathering survivors outside. Can you walk?"

"I can," I say and leap to my feet. "Charlie can walk, too, if I help him."

The officer gestures to his men. "Let them join the others in the plaza. His Excellency will wish to question the man."

Charlie leans on me as we stagger through the kitchen door into the faint gleam.

The sight stuns my senses. Hundreds of bodies lie in heaps. Odd, odd glints...everywhere...the silver buttons on the soldados' blue coats flash as they bayonet corpses or shoot into dead faces. What are they feeling? Does their vengeance taste sweet or bitter?

As I watch them, a sickening mix of longing and terror burns through my body. These men hate us. They hate all Texians. They see us as Texians, too, don't they? How could they ever free us?

A fierce gun battle is going on inside the church. I hear women and children shrieking while men blast away at one another.

Finally, from the smoking church, a half dozen defenders are marched out with their hands over their heads. An officer herds them toward another officer who's just entered the captured fort, an elaborately dressed man with a big official-looking hat. They speak briefly, then soldados draw their swords and wade into the defenseless prisoners, chopping them to pieces.

The air in my lungs goes cold and still.

Barely audible, I hear Charlie pray, "Take care of them, Lord."

Sobbing women and children appear. Soldados with muskets push them out of the church and into the center of the courtyard, where they huddle together. One woman keeps screaming, "You murdered my little boy! You murdered him!"

Sporadic gunfire erupts here and there, inside and outside the walls.

Charlie winces as he takes another step and murmurs, "Must be hunting down survivors who managed to run."

I barely hear him. Dear God, the dark luminosity of the sky fills me up so full that every whisper of spring scent, greening up grass and blooming flowers, penetrates the heavy smoke as clearly as those perfect bugle notes. Above the old church, a pale pink halo pulses through thin clouds. Dawn's coming. I'm going to see it. One last dawn.

The officer turns to Charlie and orders, "March over to where the women and children stand."

"Yes, sir, Cap'n," Charlie answers.

As I support Charlie, headed toward the women, we

pass two cannons, and I see Sarah...I think it's Sarah... sprawled dead between them. It's her blue dress. My friend. She was my friend. A few more paces, and I frown at Mrs. Melton, who stands drawing circles on the ground with an umbrella. The soldados veer wide around her, and I wonder if they think she's lost her mind. I wonder the same thing. What does she see in those strange circles? Souls spinning 'round? Spiraling up toward heaven?

Charlie stumbles and almost takes me down with him. Wrapping my arms around his middle, I manage to brace my feet until he steadies his shaking legs. My arms are all he has now. I have to help him, to shield him from fearful dreams of no tomorrows, no sons or daughters, no smiling at each other when we're old and gray. Dark and holy dreams that whisper, *it was never gonna be.*

Three men run to hoist the Mexican tricolor over the fort.

In English, a man calls, "Are there any Negroes present?"

Slaves start edging from hiding places. Joe—Colonel Travis' slave—yells, "Yes, here's one." When he steps out of a room on the west wall, two soldiers immediately attack him, one shooting him in the side and the other striking him with a bayonet.

A ragged cry of, "No!" escapes my throat. "You liars!"

Charlie hisses, "Bettie, be quiet! Quiet!"

The officer bounds toward Joe, shouting, "Halt! Leave him alone!"

"But, Colonel," a soldado yells, "I saw this one shooting down at us!"

"Lower your weapons!" the officer orders. "He's a slave. *El Presidente* has given strict orders to free all slaves."

For an instant, I can't move. Blood drains from my

head, leaving me floating so high above the ground I can't feel my body. "Charlie?"

"Don't believe it, Bettie. Not yet."

The man in the big hat walks forward with a lordly bearing to speak with Joe.

Charlie's eyes narrow. "Never seen him up close, but I reckon that's Santa Anna."

Can't hear what they're saying. Joe points a lot. Little while later, Joe limps past us without a second look, leading General Santa Anna across the plaza.

When I glance back, I know they're headed to Colonel Bowie's room. Santa Anna and Joe enter. Does the general want to gloat over his defeated enemy? Perhaps to add one final sword thrust to a man already mutilated by his troops?

My whole body starts to tremble. Eventually, one sees too much, knows too much about the way the world works, and every shred of hope cuts like glass. I wish...I wish so hard that I'd...

"Bettie?" Charlie's voice is soft. "Don't think on it. Don't do no good now."

I fix my eyes on the ground at my feet where shotgun pellets litter the dirt like chicken scratch thrown out.

My God, my God, when I lift my gaze, the dawn is so beautiful I half expect winged angels to swoop out of the heavens with blazing swords and avenge the dead scattered across this sacred ground.

"Listen to me now," Charlie murmurs. "I reckon they're going to haul off the men to question them, but if they see fit to set us loose, and we're separated, we need to figure a place to meet up. I was thinking—"

"Monterrey, Charlie. I'll be waiting for you at the cathedral in Monterrey. We'll get married. We'll have a family."

Tears silver his dark eyes.

"I'll be there," he answers in a loving voice. "If I can."

———

October 2, 1836. Nightfall.

Gathering up the hem of my faded green dress, I sit down on the bottom step of the magnificent *Catedral Metropolitana de Nuestra Senora de Monterrey* and watch twilight settle over the pueblo in a soft blue veil. It's been a hot, hot summer. Heat waves shimmer on the sand and make the road seem to dance. I've been sitting on this step every evening for seven months, studying the carts and wagons that rattle up the rutted road that leads north through the white oaks toward Texas.

In the far distance, a coyote howls. It's a mournful sound, filled with sad longing, as though she's begging someone to answer her, to tell her she won't be alone in the coming darkness. The lilting call moves through me. I, too, wait to hear a voice I know, a voice I remember.

The scents of frying tortillas and hot stones slaked with water carry on the breeze. Fragrances always seem stronger at dusk. There's even the faint perfume of flowers wafting from the garden around the side of the cathedral.

People lift hands to me as they walk by. Most are peasants dressed in loose-fitting clothing and wearing floppy hats. I wave back and wonder what they're thinking. Are they loving their children in their minds, eager to get home and hold them? Perhaps they're listening to the boys' latest adventures of catching lizards or field mice. The little girls may have crawled into their laps to inform them they've decided the color yellow is better than blue, or they've grown another inch taller in the past two days.

My children have turned to stones in my heart. Three boys and two girls, all dead infants, beautiful babies that never grew up. They no longer move, or laugh, or love me. It's as though their faces have frozen into the fabric of eternity like dead animals in ice. Each night, their opaque eyes stare up at me through a blue haze.

My gut wants to believe that when Charlie was taken after the siege, the Veramendis came, claimed him, and his wounded leg was tended to. Isn't that what would have happened? Of course, they might have sold him off to someone who hauled him way up north. That's why he hasn't come. He's a slave again.

The only other possible explanation is that Charlie died from his wound.

Even after all these months, the uncertainty is a living thing coiled in my chest. Keep telling myself, I shouldn't have run off. I should have stayed with Charlie until he got well or died, even if it meant I was a slave for the rest of my life. But I suspect that would have broken Charlie's heart. If he's alive, he's dreaming of me walking free, surrounded by open spaces. He's holding tight to those images in his dreams at night. Just as I hold tight to visions of Charlie walking down that northern road toward me, coming to sit with me on this step, and wrapping his arms around me.

Bowing my head, I let my thoughts drift for another hour or so, until darkness has turned the sky sapphire, and the vault of heaven, full of soft, shining stars, stretches vast and fathomless above me, then tears tighten my throat.

This lonely vigil gets harder every night.

When I rise to leave, I hear Padre Ramirez step out of the cathedral's doors. He closes them and trots down the stairs toward me, as he does every night on his way to water the flowers in the garden. "Bettie, how are you tonight?"

"*Muy bueno, padre.*"

He smiles. The priest is a tall man with black hair and blue eyes.

When he reaches the bottom step, he stands looking down at me with a worried smile. "You are finished cooking for the day?"

"'Til first light comes. Then I'll head back out to the Madrigon hacienda and start baking."

"They tell me they love your breads."

"Good to hear."

In the lull, starlight powders his face. He takes a deep breath, and holds it for an instant before he says, "Anything could have happened to Charlie, you know? Seven months is not so long a time. Don't give up on him."

"I haven't." But I wonder if that's true? Maybe I just come here out of habit now, not hope.

As shadows drown the plaza, the breeze turns cooler.

"Peaceful tonight," Padre Ramirez says and hesitates. "Bettie, I know you do not wish me to preach at you." He pauses to judge my tight expression. "But loneliness is God's way of asking you to turn to Him, to allow Him to help. Would you like me to pray with you?"

"No, padre. I'm prayed out, but I appreciate the offer."

"Very well. Then perhaps you'd like to take a walk with me? We can talk while I water the flowers. It's been so hot."

"'Course. Let me help you."

As I rise from the bottom step, evening deepens, laying everywhere like an indigo blanket. The walk around the cathedral is silent and pleasant. When I see the *peon* wandering among the flowers with a water bucket, I smile. The garden is surrounded by towering cottonwoods and oaks and bordered with huge cactus.

"Jose, it's late," Padre Ramirez calls. "Thank you, but please go home to your family. Carmen must have dinner ready."

Jose waves, finishes emptying his bucket on a clump of lilies, and wipes his perspiring brow with his sleeve. "Sí, padre! Buenas noches."

"Via con dios, Jose."

While Jose places his bucket beside the well, I study the bright colors of the flowers. The garden is a patchwork of white, red, and yellow.

As though concerned, Padre Ramirez says, "Do you know that man? He's watching you very carefully."

I frown in the direction he points and notice a man leaning against a huge cottonwood. He's tall and so thin I can see his ribs sticking out through his white shirt. The dark skin of his face has shrunken tight over his bones, so that I'm sure he's starving to death. He stares hard at me.

There is something familiar...

Pain lances through me as my gaze goes over him in detail, noting the way he leans against the tree. Takes me a while to see through the mosaic of shadows and finally understand that he has a wooden leg and can't hurry to me.

A small cry escapes my throat. "Charlie!"

I run as though my life depends upon reaching him. When I throw my arms around him, tears are streaming down his face.

He wildly kisses my face and hair. "Came as quick as I could, Bettie. Sorry it took so long."

WHAT'S OWED THE DEMON

W. MICHAEL GEAR

What strikes me about this story is the rhythm of the words. Sometimes an otherworldly lilt transports you to the past. Other times, a hard-hitting martial cadence pounds you into the dirt like a fist. Michael's words are as sharp and crisp as a perfect sword thrust. (KOG)

Sometimes inspiration comes from interesting places. The science fiction writer Isaac Asimov once said he'd rather walk on his hands all the way to Poughkeepsie rather than write a story in second person. We have used a second-person POV on occasion in our novels, but just as a short italicized punch scene. My good friend, Keith Kahla, who edits Minotaur Books, once said "That kind of story never works...until it does." The gauntlet had been cast, the challenge given. Only time will tell if I managed to pull it off. (WMG)

Rising from the gray haze, your body feels like it's floating on pain. The headache is numbing. Your ears ring. Blink, and it's agonizing. Grit lies under the lids; it grates with any twitch of your eyes. The impulse is to take a deep breath. You try to wipe at your face. For a moment you wonder why your arm doesn't rise, doesn't bend. That you can't move it confounds you. But that was...?

Before...before the demon.

As you regain your senses, it's not just the sand in your eyes and the splitting headache, it's the demon down in your belly that really burns. The thing twists slowly, sort of rips its way through your guts.

You saw something like it. Once. Long ago. When you were just the boy gutting a cow. Back then it was a gob of wire. All twisted up and brown from rust and gut juices. The stench of it had been overpowering. The boy had backed away, sleeve over his nose and mouth, and came close to puking himself. The whole family was gathered around, staring, wondering how the cow had managed to choke that rude ball of wire down in the first place. But she had, and the swallowing of it must have been terrible. Once down in the gut, the wire had twisted, broken, and the sharp ends had cut through the stomach muscle, needled their way into the liver and guts. Not just in one place, but all through that part of the cow's stomach. And with it came the infection. So much so that the whole inside of the cow gave off that bilious odor.

Remember how Pa's face looked? All puckered with disgust. How his lips had curled in and his eyes slitted. His gorge had risen. Looked like it might have been choked off given how his throat swelled full, and the veins in his bulging neck stood out. And him, just home fresh from the Civil War in Tennessee.

Something changed for the boy that day. Standing there, the knife in his hand, the stench of the freshly opened cow on the clear morning air. She'd been doing poorly, which is why Pa made the decision to put her down. Better to cut her throat, butcher her, and put meat on the table.

Little Sister, Sally Mae, had cried. She had just turned six. Didn't matter that Ma wrung the head off an occasional chicken or Pa would take a hatchet to one of the pigs before gutting, boiling, and scraping it, Sally Mae loved that cow. Said she had "pretty eyes."

"Can't eat pretty eyes," Pa would retort with a soothing wink. But he started to mean it when the cow dried up and stopped milking. Not that a milk cow ever had much in the way of condition on her frame, but she just kept losing. All the while, that ball of wire was eating away in her belly.

Funny how Sally Mae—dressed in a dirt-stained cotton jumper with frayed ruffles, her feet in hand-me-down brown leather shoes—couldn't stay away that day. For whatever reason, she'd appeared in the barn door, her dress tainted with yellow in the slanting sunlight, to watch. What stuck in the memory was how large her eyes had been, the worried O that her pink lips puckered into.

"Don't think you want ta be here, sis," the boy had said.

"Ah, let 'er see." Pa had rejoined after stepping back to catch a whiff of fresh air so as to settle his stomach. And him, reacting like that after what he'd said he'd survived in the field hospital after Franklin and Nashville. Pa still cradled the stump of his left arm.

Maybe the boy had a mean streak. He'd been looking right into Sally Mae's eyes as he reached down, grabbed that ball of wire, and tugged it loose. Seen the horror in her eyes as threads of wire pulled out through the dead cow's liver and guts. Reminded him of perverted worms that conjured themselves from pockets of black blood and yellow pus.

That sight of the slime-rusted brown wire bundle had never gone away. Even now, here, you can smell the stench. A shift of breeze carries it, overpowering before it fades. And you know it's the demon's scent.

Here.

That it's your smell.

That the demon down inside is as terrible, as painful, and as inevitable as the cow's wire ball, brings tears. You blink, and the pain in your eyes lessens. Some of the grit washed away.

You gasp from relief, aggravating the demon. And draw too much air in response.

The demon only desists when you take shallow fast breaths; it retreats, huddling heavy and ugly in your gut.

Your vision has cleared. But nothing makes sense as your thoughts drift and shimmer like the heat waves that dance above a dry desert playa. But no, this is a canyon. Sheer sided, narrow. And you're at the bottom. Sort of wedged against the rock.

It's almost a sitting position, half reclined, head propped in loose dirt that trickles down around your ears with each movement. Your elbow and forearm are mostly buried. The soil covering it is red, filled with gravel and marble-sized rocks. It cascades a little with each breath. Tilting your head back, you can see the cliff rising above you; rock outcrops protrude, blocking your view of the heights. Your left leg sticks straight out into a dry wash dotted with head-sized cobbles. Not more than six feet away, the red sandstone wall rises. The layers of rock look like the tilted insides of a rich man's wedding cake.

Rising high, the muddy ocher of the stone contrasts to the hazy blue sky far above.

You look down, frown. Takes a while to realize that your right leg shouldn't splay out at an angle like that. It's laid out with the precision of a carpenter's square, stark on the threaded gravel of the wash bottom. Ninety degrees. But it's bent backward and stuck way off to the side. The why of it just doesn't make sense. Funny, you can't feel it. Or your left leg either.

Back's broke!

Why?

The ringing in your ears won't let you think.

A flicker of sunlight from above dances on the gravel-threaded sand. Fixes itself there just beyond the outstretched fingers of the left hand. It shimmers, glares—a bit of pristine sunshine caught in the moment. Just beyond it lies a splintered piece of wood. Rifle stock. Snapped at the wrist. And there, over by that boulder, the rest of the broken Sharps has landed against the stone, barrel driven down into the sand. The wood exposed in the broken wrist is pale in contrast to the stained and sweat-darkened grip.

You stare at it, just there, beyond the golden glare of the sunlight trapped in the sandy gravel. You see the broken white wood as the boy did.

Had to be a fox, maybe a bobcat. The boy wasn't sure. Only that Pa had told him not to come home until he'd killed the varmint that had taken six of Ma's prize hens. The boy had done it before: Once it had been a stray dog. One that had been seen around the Illinois River bottoms outside of Kampsville. That had been a gangly red mutt. A bone-rack of a dog that walked with a limp. Some said it was a hydrophobia. But had that been the case, the hydrophobia would have killed it months ago. Man with one arm couldn't use a shotgun, so Pa had handed it to the boy. He finally got on that mangy mongrel down in the willows and killed it dead.

Then there was a red fox. That had been winter. Pa had handed him the shotgun and said, "Don't you come back without that varmint's hide, boy."

It had taken all day, but the boy tracked the chicken killer through one thicket after another. Managed to catch the beast just at sundown when it emerged from its den. Arriving home a little after midnight, the fox over his shoulder and a bait of fleas in his hair, the boy had laid the raider's body on the table where Pa was still up waiting.

The last time, the boy was just turned fourteen. Fact was, he coveted Pa's shotgun. Wondered, if he was successful, if Pa wouldn't just up and say, "Well, boy, you're fourteen now. Maybe you oughta just hang on to that shotgun." But that meant he really needed to bring home whatever was killing Ma's chickens.

It had been two hens killed the first day. Then, last night, another four! And the killer continued to evade the boy's diligent hunting. Night was falling, the shadows where he hunted in the deep woods up from the river had darkened, gone somber. Evening birdsong filled the branches overhead, the distant chatter of a fox squirrel carrying.

That's when he saw the sign: a paw print. Bobcat for sure. Not that he could tell that close, but it looked mighty fresh. Didn't have that softened and feathery look of an old track. The boy knelt down. Fingered the damp earth. Noted how it dimpled under his fingertip. Nope. Not long past at all.

Rising, the excitement built. What Pa called "hunter's fever," that heating of the blood, the rising beat of the heart. Every sense grows acute, vision narrowing with anticipation. It's all a body can do to keep from panting in anticipation.

A patch of gray flashed beneath a stand of sumac. There! It slipped silently behind a thicket of thorny raspberry bushes. The boy held his breath, the shotgun at his shoulder. Where would it come out? From the corner of his eye, he caught movement by the base of a hazelnut tree.

"Gotcha!" He whirled. Swung onto the patch of gray in the shadowed light. Pulled the trigger. Fire and sparks danced, smoke billowed, the *bang* shattered the silence.

The boy charged forward through the smoke. Stopped short. His heart skipped in his chest. It didn't make sense. Couldn't be!

Sally Mae staggered sideways into the hazelnut tree, sort of melted against the rough bark. Her mouth was working, trying to speak, and no words came. But it was her eyes, so wide and disbelieving. Large, brown, and watery, she fixed on him. Started to raise one arm, the other clinging so desperately to the tree. As she did, dots of crimson bloomed on her too-small gray dress. Like dark flowers, the red spread in the coarse fabric.

Sally Mae struggled to keep her feet, gave up, and slid slowly to the ground.

The boy rushed over, some whimpering sound in his throat.

"Ma wants you home...for...supp..." The rest of the words faded with her breath. She just stared at him, her eyes growing ever larger and darker until they swallowed the whole world.

You stare at the broken Sharps. Snapped at the wrist the same way that you broke that shotgun all those years ago. Swung it against that hazelnut. Remember how the wood inside the shattered stock was just as pale? You left Sally Mae in that copse of woods and traveled all night.

"Couldn't go home," you whisper, reliving that empty horror. "Couldn't look Ma in the eyes. Just…couldn't."

The next morning, you found that barge tied to the bank on the Illinois River. You'd wiped Sally Mae's dried blood from the hand you offered the burly, bearded river man. Lied when you said, "My name's Tom Oliver, and I got no kin left. But I'll work for food and found."

Took pity on you, they did, shoving off into the murky and roiling waters.

You could never go home. And now you are here. Half buried in the bottom of a desert canyon. With broken legs, no feeling below the waist, the demon slicing away in your guts, and liquid sunlight gleaming in the sand just out of reach of your fingers. The demon shifts; tendrils of pain—like the wires in the cow's gut—pull and slip fire through your belly.

From instinct, you try to extend your left arm. To reach for the gleaming sunlight beaming up from the streambed gravel. What was once a dull ache shoots a scorpion's sting of pain through your shoulder.

What?

More dirt trickles as you turn your head to look.

Somehow knobby and misshapen, the top of the arm has been dislocated back and up from its proper location. Funny that you never noticed 'til now. Not that you would with the demon raging down in your guts, cutting, chewing at your very core with needle teeth.

Dropping your head back against the gravel and stone, you smack your lips. Dry. Dry as your tongue. Try to swallow. Can't. Thirst should be making you crazy. But maybe the demon is keeping it at bay. Or was it some sense the body has? An unwillingness to reward the demon. A way to punish it for what it's doing down inside.

You think of the years you spent on the rivers with

their roiling, swirling, and sucking surfaces. Sometimes green and clear, sometimes muddy and churning. Often with frothy curls of scummy foam.

All that water.

The young man never knew thirst. Not back then. Six years he worked on the boats. Started on the barges, then moved on to steamboats. Began as a deckhand. Worked up to cargo boss. Got hard. Got tough. Learned to use his fists and got mean. Beat a man to death with his bare hands in Little Rock one time when low water stranded the boat, loaded as it was with bales of cotton.

"Better get out of here," the bartender in the water-front tavern told him. "Not that Old Jack Nicholson, here, was much of any good, but the law don't ask no questions about river riffraff such as yerself. You're worth more to 'em hanging from a tree. Proof they's tough on what they calls 'the criminal element.'"

You remember that flight west to Fort Smith and the Indian Territory. About how the old farmer offered you a day's work for a night's dossing and a meal of...

The breeze shifts and the demon's stench fills your nostrils. God! Rank, cloying, it makes you stiffen. Try to shift away from the smell. Dirt from above trickles through your hair and around your right ear. Movement sets off the demon; it flicks its knives back and forth in your gut. No way to stop yourself from making that little whimpering cry. Hurts too damn much even to think. But from the new angle, you can see your stomach.

The shirt was once red-and-white checked. Store bought. Expensive. But bought where? The thought rises, seems to flicker, and whirl away. That was this shirt, wasn't it? Hard to recall now that it's black with old blood, covered with dirt and filthy. He'd bought lots of shirts before the demon ended up in his guts. The man hadn't counted on the demon.

Not that any man ever did.

The man who'd bought that long-ago shirt had stood proud before the mirror, decked out in new stroud pants, and...

You look. Yes. Down at the bottom of the broken leg. It's dusty, scuffed, and stirrup-polished, but those were the boots. Same fancy hand stitching. But the boots and shirt came later. Was it in Durango? Or maybe Ouray? The memory, slippery as a trout, escapes your teetering mind.

You think back to the first boots, to the docks. Riding boots. For horses. Yes. He could remember the horses. It never would have crossed the young man's mind that he'd have to become a horseman. His skills lay on the rivers, with lines, knots, cargo, and the boats. The plan had originally been to lay low until any memory of Old Jack was long forgotten. Meanwhile, the young man had wound his way south through the Nations, crossed the Red River, and hoped to hire onto another boat at the head of navigation. Work his way back to the river and keep shy of any vessel heading up the Arkansas toward Little Rock.

Was it something about Texas? The young man had heard that Texas brought out the worst in any man or beast. That day on the Texarkana docks, he watched a prized collection of ten of the most beautiful horses he'd ever seen being unloaded. Gorgeous mounts, their hides, brown, black, and chestnut, shone in the sun. Unforgiving hooves stamped and hammered on the bald cypress planks as the majestic animals passed.

"Hey, you!" the man in the derby hat called, pointing a fancy silver-topped cane at the young man. "Looking for a job? I'm Patrick O'Neal, and I'm in need of a hand."

"Reckon so," the young man called back. "You own that boat?"

73

"Wouldn't give you two bits or spit in the sand for any damn boat! No, laddie, I'm looking for a wrangler to get these animals to Fort Worth."

"I'm not much of a horseman. My calling is boats."

"Aye, but ye've a look about ye. Like ye've sand in yer craw when the getting' gets rough. And if ye've done any ridin' it'll come back to ye." O'Neal narrows an eye. "What's yer name and where be ye from?"

"Matt Bailey. I grew up in Springfield, Illinois. Not two blocks from where Lincoln lived." The lie came so easily. He pointed. "Just these horses? To Fort Worth? Why not buy horses there?"

"No such horses exist. Race horses, laddie. The finest to come out of Douglas County, Missouri. It's the blood-lines. These be Alsup-bred horses. And they'll make me a fortune."

You remember that trail. Five of you, essentially hired not for riding skills. No, O'Neal took care of the horse cavy. You were there for protection. Three gunmen, including Yancy Bob Farley, who taught the young man the basics of using a pistol, and Terlingua Jim, who imbued the young man with a new respect for his fists.

Your eye catches the gleam of sunlight where it shines just beyond the reach of your fingers. A miracle that, that sunlight could be so captured by mere sand. If only you could reach out, grasp that wonderous warm light and clutch it to you. It would be to hold the sun. To press it close. To feel the beams, warm in your blood and bones. You could just close your eyes and savor it...

...The way the young man had the whiskey in Fort Worth.

O'Neal had paid off in honest gold coin. And the saloons, brothels, and dance halls south of the stockyards were waiting in anticipation. To this day, your memory of what happened next is cloudy and filled with faint images that might be real or fantasy. But waking up in that alley stinking of urine, shit, and vomit? Your head was in enough pain that it might have been split with an axe.

Maybe the young man should have staggered off, gotten a job in the pens pushing cattle up the loading ramp with a pole as they crowded into cattle cars and the locomotive belched black smoke. But he woke up with memories of Sally Mae. Was staring into her eyes as she died there on the forest floor. Sick to his stomach, head pounding, he forced himself to his feet, rammed his body into the back door, and broke in.

Two men in their thirties, dressed in nightshirts, had clawed their way out of the single bed. Screaming, they'd barely untangled from the sheets. Shouting obscenities. Stumbling as the young man launched into them. When it was all over, it came to him. He had no idea if the two men who lay dead and bleeding on the floor were the ones who'd rolled him. Maybe he'd just been left in the alley behind. Could be that it didn't matter.

You stifle a grunt. The demon is moving inside. Moving so loudly that you hear the gurgling down there below your ribs. It's as if the bundle of wire has come alive, and the impossible image fixes in your head: that brownish slime-covered mass. It squirms, the tendrils of wire wavering and slipping through the ropes of intestine, wiggling corrupt fingers into smooth liver.

When the young man stumbled back into the alley, he had taken a couple of pistols, a wad of stained cash and a sack of coins—ninety-six dollars worth—and a brass-bodied Winchester rifle he'd found behind the disheveled bed.

Then, just because he knew he might have to ride fast after the bodies were discovered, he walked into the pens at the stockyards. Three of O'Neal's last Alsup racing mounts remained. He called her Applesauce, a sort of play on "Alsup horse." And he was putting a halter on the bay mare with the white blaze when the night watchman called out.

"Hey! What are you...oh, it's you."

The young man turned, smiled. "Mr. O'Neal sent me down. He's got a buyer for the mare. Wanted me to bring it by. Oh, and he asked me to settle up what we owe for board for the week." Walking over to the night watchman, the young man pulled out the wad of bills. "Will five cover it?"

"Reckon." The watchman gave him a skeptical glance but didn't hesitate to take the greenback. "Can't give you no receipt."

"Mr. O'Neal didn't say nothing about no receipt. I'd 'spect if'n he needs one, he'll be by come morning."

It had been that easy.

You smile at the memory. Worked slick as grease on a pig. Taught you a lot. About men. About yourself. And maybe about God. The way it was told in church, God was always watching, and he'd make a man pay for his sins. Just didn't seem to work that way in the everyday world. What else could you say? Damnation should have fallen like a crack of doom that day Sally Mae died. And if God hadn't been watching when she passed, He'd sure had chance after chance on the river. Could have been that Old Jack might have stuck that Bowie knife into your guts instead of letting it work the other way around. Or a bolt of lightning could have struck on that long trek to Texarkana. But God always looked the other way.

Like he had in Fort Griffin.

Never averse to hard work, the young man sought employment with some of the last buffalo runners working out of Fort Griffin. Told them his name was Daniel Potts, from Memphis, and he'd work for four bits a day. Hired, he rode west with the wagons, but they found few buffalo. For nearly two months of hunting, camping, and searching, their total take amounted to seventeen hides. All but two of them from old bachelor bulls.

What they called "The Flats"—a jumble of dilapidated buildings on the floodplain between Clear Fork and Fort Griffin up on the hill—was just as depressing as the weather when the barely laden wagons made their return. The heavens had opened, black, lightning-riven, and drenching the land with a fury of wind-lashed rain. A fit and miserable ending for the buffalo and the man who'd planned to make a fortune killing them.

"Here, Daniel," Hank Angelou told him the next morning after the storm had broken. "I promised fifty cents a day for your services as a skinner. Can't cover it. So take the rifle. Cost me nigh on forty-five dollars new at Conrad and Rath's. But don't never let it be said I don't cover my debts."

So, there he is, mostly broke, holding that heavy Sharps rifle when the Ranger walks up. Studies the young man's mare paying particular attention to the blaze, and then gives him a squinting inspection. "Nice horse. How long you had her?"

"Couple of years now." Some sense of wrong is running up his backbone. "What's your interest?"

"Texas Ranger." The man points at the telegraph line leading off to the east. "Been on the lookout for a horse thief. Young fella like yourself. 'Bout your height and color ridin' a bay mare about like this description."

"Sorry, sir. Bought this horse off of a man from Tennessee a couple of years back. Had a bill of sale, but it got wet and sort of fell into faded pieces. Paper ain't much for wear out here. Thought I'd make a fortune on the buffalo ranges." He squints off to the west. "Reckon like so much I done, that didn't turn out like a daisy."

"You got a name?"

"Hank Angelou," he lies.

The Ranger scuffs the dirt with a boot. "Just an idle question. Got a trip coming. State's sending me up to Springfield. Anything a Texas galoot like me oughta see?"

The young man almost speaks, catches himself. Shakes his head. "Never been to Springfield. Had a cousin from over west of there. Town called Joplin."

The Ranger's hard eyes fix on his. "Thought you was raised in Illinois? You got that sound to your voice."

"Different Springfield." The smile comes easily, as smoothly as at the stockyards. "No, sir. Missouri. Up 'round Hannibal. Illinois is just across the river. Guess we talk the same. You got any questions about there, I'll talk your ear off."

The Ranger takes a deep breath, gives the mare another inspection. "Yes, sir. Well, y'all have a good day." And then he turns and walks away.

Couldn't go back east. Not with them looking for me. The words sound hollow in your bleary mind. You blink again. Tongue thick in the dust of your mouth. The swallow sticks in your throat. Causes you to gag, which sends the demon into a paroxysm of agony.

When the world stops convulsing, you blink the tears from your eyes, breathe shallowly to get your wits about you. God, it's so hot. Shouldn't be. It's October.

Hot. Takes you back to the time the man was in El Paso. According to one of the few thermometers in town the temperature was hovering around one hundred and ten. The sun scorched the sere and rocky hills. Heat waves shimmered and danced over the block-like casas, jacals, and ramadas across the river in Mexican El Paso del Norte. Didn't matter how much of the murky local water a man drank, it sweated right out of him.

After El Paso, hot, dusty, and tormented as it was by wind-blown sand, nothing would be the same. Chalk that up to Frank Manning. Or maybe Frank's brother, Jim. They'd never got completely quit of the rustling business. A neighbor, Johnny Hale, had once orchestrated the movement of stolen cattle and stock through the *bosques* on either side of town. But too many killings had centered the interest of Captain George Baylor and his local Texas Rangers. Baylor called the Manning-Hale bunch the "Canutillo gang." But after Marshal Dallas Stoudenmire blew the brains out of Johnny Hale's head, the Mannings distanced themselves from the hands-on aspects of the business.

Which was where you entered the picture.

New to the squalid little town of adobe buildings, the man found El Paso to be a mecca at the end of the world. Across the river lay Mexico, while just to the west and north easy escape could be made to New Mexico Territory. Stolen property could be moved in any of three ways. A perfect place for a man willing to work in the shadows for those like the Mannings.

Problem was that Hale killing. It stirred and fed bad blood between the marshal, his good friend "Doc" Cummings, and the Mannings. Something about the dust-laden air in El Paso maybe, it seemed to brew trouble.

The man was in the Manning Saloon on San Antonio Street when a fellow by the name of East entered, calling, "Doc Cummings is gonna kill Jim Manning over at the Coliseum! I know it, 'cause he just damned near killed me!"

"I got it," the man told Frank Manning, who was in the middle of negotiating a price for some Mexican cattle being held out in the *bosque.* "Cummings don't know me. He'll never know what hit him."

Despite the demon squishing acid through your guts, you can't help but smile as the memory runs in your aching head. "Was that really me? Cold, steady as a rock?"

Like smoke, the man slips through the door to the Coliseum Saloon. Several men are seated at a table in back. Cummings stands at the bar, one hand resting on the polished wood; the other is on his holstered pistol. His attention is fixed on the hallway that leads to the ticket booth. Behind the bar, Dave Kling is nervously wiping a glass clean.

That's when Jim Manning appears in the hallway. Cummings draws his pistol. Probably figuring to shoot Jim down as he steps into the room.

Cummings is too fixed on Jim. He doesn't hear the man approach. The man strikes, smashing his pistol down on Doc Cumming's head. Should have laid big old Doc out cold. It only staggers him. He is turning, swinging his gun around...

The man shoots Doc through the side, and the big man twists right into Jim Manning's shot as it blasts fire, sparks, and smoke. Doc blinks, his jaw dropping down to expose brown teeth. Then he drops his pistol with a clunk to the tobacco-stained floor. Almost falls as he staggers across the room, tumbles through the door, and collapses in the dust and manure on El Paso Street.

At Jim's questioning look, the man tells him, "He'd a killed you when you stepped out."

The bartender, Kling, crouches down, picks up Doc's still-cocked pistol, and shoots a hole in the abode hallway wall. "Can't have a man's gun unfired."

Manning turns on the room, and points. "This man

was never here. Story is that Doc drew first, I shot him."
Then to the man, "You better make tracks."

The man plucks the pistol from Kling's hand, saying,
"Better if they find it on his body."

With that, he pulls his hat down low, steps out, and
tosses the gun into the dust at the dead man's side.

A soft rasping accompanies each exhalation. The pain
is worse, like the demon is squeezing your guts with red-
hot fingers. The canyon walls seem closer now, glassy in
your vision. You always thought that one of those men at
the table would let drop to Marshal Stoudenmire that
you'd been the man who killed his best friend. And,
maybe in the end, one of 'em might have, but Manning
put a final bullet in Stoudenmire's brain a little over a
year later.

Oh, you could have made quite the name for yourself.
Others did. But you always figured you were smarter
than the toughs who drank, bragged, and shot up the
town. Sure enough, you watched them. Like Stoudenmire, that Billy the Kid, "Tom Cat" Selman, Dirty Dave
Rudabaugh, Vicente Silva, or Johnny Ringo, the ones
with reputations all ended up dead.

Meanwhile, El Paso, Mesilla, Deming, Silver City,
Lordsburg—after Doc Cummings, they all offered a
living for a man who didn't mind killing and keeping his
mouth shut. You were nothing if not good at that. And
you always had your big Sharps buffalo gun to keep you
at a distance. Out of sight. Away from witnesses.

Old Applesauce was part of your success. That
remarkable Alsup-bred horse just never seemed to run
out of bottom. As long as you could keep her watered
and fed, she'd cover the miles like an express locomotive.
On those occasions when a posse was put together,
they'd ride out on their scrubby little desert-bred horses

only to call it quits as their mounts gave out a day or two later.

You remember when you heard the first rumor. Word that somebody local who fancied a Sharps buffalo gun would put the fix on anyone for a price. After that, it would only be a matter of time before someone took notice. So you pulled stakes and followed the trails north, winding up through the New Mexican mountains to Santa Fe.

A puff of wind comes gusting up the canyon. It hisses and bats at the branches in the pinions, sighs as it scours the red sandstone outcrops, and whips up a curl of thick dust. After blasting you with grit, it dances up the sandy drainage bed. The way it twists and whirls, you see her dancing. That red skirt whirling as her slim legs follow the music, her hair flying.

Her voice is on the wind, the sibilant words so close to your ear. *"Come with me."*

"Helen?" Her name rises cracked and rasping from your dying throat.

Oh, yes. Santa Fe. And Helen. The man so loved her.

Her hair fell in rings and waves of yellow to lay on her delicate shoulders. That miraculous blue hinted of constant surprise in her eyes. See that smile, bending those perfect pink lips to expose her small white teeth? Helen might not have been a striking beauty, but her mere presence filled a room with charm. She had that aura about her. You could see it in her walk, in the movements of her arms, and flounce of her skirts.

She was the storekeeper's daughter, just turned eighteen. Young and filled with optimism, she'd never had a hard thought cross her mind. Maybe it was that sense of innocence, something fresh that appealed to your soul, gone rotten and dark ever since that day when Sally Mae died in your arms.

As you lie broken at the bottom of the canyon, looking back, you can admit what she meant to you. Yes, she offered that one chance, and had you shown but a trace of basic decency, trusted yourself, you might have found redemption through her.

Then again, maybe God finally started paying attention.

A soft autumn night, late September, wasn't it? The cottonwood trees lining the Santa Fe River rattled in the breeze, dotted here and there by the first spots of yellow. Months had passed since the Sharps had been leaned in a shadowed bedroom corner in the old adobe the man had rented. It perched on a lot up the hill from where the new capitol building was being built. And it had been a week since the man had taken Applesauce out for a ride. Something about Helen absorbed every moment. As it did that night as they'd walked along the banks of the Santa Fe River, feet rustling in the grass, arm in arm.

She'd laid her head on his shoulder, saying, "You have a future here. We could build it together."

That night had been heavenly, a swelling joy fit to burst his breast.

The following day, Helen's father had told the man, "There's not much to running a successful store." A curious hesitation had built behind the dry goods dealer's eyes. "It's all in inventory and accounts. Developing that special sense of what to order and have in stock." A pause as the gaze narrowed slightly. "Assuming a man like you would want to finally settle down and build a solid life."

Any retort died on the man's lips as Helen burst in from the plaza; a sunflower on the wind, she seemed to dance and bob between the dry goods shelves and canned victuals stacked across from them. "I just made the most wonderful trade," she announced breathlessly.

And holding up a coarse-cotton sack, added, "Look at all these *pinones*! I got them for that old red ribbon bow!"

That afternoon had been spent on a bench out front, cracking pinions with your teeth and sharing the sweet nuts. Funny, looking back. Not that every moment with Helen hadn't been magical, but your heart had been filled with peace and contentment.

Ruined it at the dance. Fandango, they called it. As the bands played, you'd whirled Helen around, seen the glow of enjoyment in her eyes. Should have opted for lemonade from the big bowl in front of the Governor's Palace. But someone handed you a bottle. Said it was a for sure sour mash. One swig had turned into three or four on an empty stomach.

Helen had caught that scent on your breath. Stopped short, her eyes going wide. "You're drinking!"

"Man does that of an occasion."

"Not *my* man!" And she'd flounced off, grabbed her father's arm, and pointed right at you as she'd railed. Oh, yes, you'd seen that look in her father's eyes. The old man had never really cottoned to you. They'd stalked off with stiff-legged purpose.

So, in your pique, you'd found more whiskey.

After that, things went a little hazy…

Until you awakened in that dark little room with its low viga-and-latilla ceiling. The bed wasn't much, the mattress just sack cloth filled with straw. A stiff wool blanket lay heavy and scratchy over your thighs. The naked woman wrapped around you snored softly, her raven black hair spilled across your chest. Your head hurt as badly as it does now. And you weren't thinking much better that morning either. As you stirred, the woman reached down, her fingers stroking, kneading, and you never thought twice as you rolled over to cover her.

Wasn't until nigh onto noon when you stepped out

into Burro Alley to squint in the afternoon sunlight. Disheveled, you staggered out onto San Francisco Street. You were scratching your privates when Helen rode past in her father's freight wagon. Her shocked glance went from you to Burrow Alley, filled as it was with whore houses and shady saloons.

"Hey! Helen, wait!" you'd called.

With a slap of the reins, she sent the wagon clattering up the street, scattering pedestrians. And she'd never looked back.

Finished. Just like that.

Nothing left but that aching hollow in your chest.

Funny what a woman could do. But for a drink, you might have married her. Settled down, delighted to raise a family, distance yourself from the guilt and punishment that started with Sally Mae's death. All you'd needed was a reason. Instead you rode north, following the trails along the Rio Grande into Colorado.

And met Johnny Crackers in that saloon on Blair Street in Silverton. You frown. Trying to remember. Which saloon was it? And how did you and he start talking? Does it matter?

Johnny said he'd just ridden in on the train. That he had arrived on business. He'd been a likable character with his puckish blue eyes, an animated sandy-blond mustache, and deep smile lines around his mouth. They'd spent that evening, swapping stories. You telling of El Paso and Fort Worth. He going on about Denver City and the gold camps up in the Rockies.

Somewhere in the telling of it, you'd mentioned that you were low on funds and looking for something to refresh your finances. Empty pockets were all that remained after six months in Santa Fe. Turned out that being a "respectable" man had been an expensive proposition.

"Got an idea," Johnny had said thoughtfully, a whiskey glass held before his half-smiling lips. That devilish twinkle lay in his noon-blue eyes. His sweeping mustache twitched suggestively. "Assuming you don't mind a little risk."

Ah, yes. You remember standing there at the bar, the din of rough miners talking over themselves, laughter, the occasional shouted cuss word. Cigar smoke hung heavy in the air and cast halos around the coal oil lamps in their sconces. You can remember the light playing in the whiskey that filled Johnny's glass, the question in his eyes.

Most of all, you remember the shock in Sally Mae's dark gaze and the disbelief in Helen's startled blue stare.

"Hell, what's a little risk? Devil's waiting to take us all one of these days." You'd reached up with your glass, clicked the rim against Johnny's. "What have you got in mind?"

Johnny had tossed off his whiskey, droplets of amber glistening in the strands of his mustache. "You ever heard of Columbia? Mining town on the other side of the mountains? Otto Mears just finished that toll road from here to there."

"I have. Hear the good town fathers want to call it Telluride. Something about how it gets confused with some California mining town also named Columbia."

"What's not confusing is the gold," Johnny told him. "Now, maybe you have heard of the Smuggler load? Some of the richest gold in the San Juan Mountains is coming out of that hole. But it's way over on the other side of the mountain. Has to be packed over the Mears toll road."

"Reckon I've heard something. What's the catch?"

"Ain't no catch!" Johnny Crackers gave him a big saucy grin. "Least o' ways, no catch if you figger gold belongs to whosoever can keep it. And it ain't like lifting a load of it is gonna cause no widows or orphans to starve to death."

Remember that knowing wink he gave you? Like he could see right down into your aching and angry heart.

"Now," Johnny said, leaning his head close. "Only a fool would hit the train packing the ingots out. Those bars are heavy. And where you gonna sell them? It'd be a dead giveaway. But the mine pays its workers in coin. And ain't no way to trace coins. Hell, I got forty dollars in my pockets right now."

"It's only one road," you point out. "One end at Columbia, the other here. Makes escape pretty damn slim."

"Yep. Anyone robbing the mule train packing payroll, they'd be expected to keep right on to Ouray, or maybe here, where they could take the train to make their getaway."

"Uh-huh, and what way would you go?"

Johnny sets his glass on the bar and takes yours. He places them a couple of inches apart. "So, here's the mountains with the Mears road running between them. Down here, at the head of the box canyon, is Columbia. Telluride. Whatever. And out here, beyond the edge of the bar, there's nothing. Just red rock canyons, pinion juniper groves, and sagebrush flats running clear over west to the Mormon settlements. Two fellers like us, we can get lost out there for long enough that people will forget."

The sun has shifted until it's passing behind the high cliff behind you, shadow creeping across your broken legs. And beyond the reaching fingers of your hand, what you thought was captured sunlight in the sand dulls. Now you see it for what it is: a gold coin. Looking hard, you can see another out in the sand. And another. All spilled, fallen from above to scatter around your broken body.

Oh, yes. It worked just like Johnny Crackers said it would. The two of you traveled by night. Hid out in the aspens and brush where a creek tumbled down from the heights and crossed the road. Sure enough, Johnny called it square. The pack mules, loaded with supplies for the mine, and guarded by ten heavily armed men, arrived right on time. From a rocky outcrop above the road, your Sharps made the difference. Each booming shot peeling a man from the saddle as they panicked, shotguns and pistols pulled, desperate to fight off a close-up attack.

They were milling, confined by the steep slope on one side and the sheer drop on the other. The shouts carried and died in the breeze blowing in from the west. You drop the lever, extracting a smoking brass case from the chamber and insert another of the long cartridges. Raising the Sharps, you brace on the rocks, sight on the chaos blocking the road below. The mules are bucking, pulling each other where they are tail-hitched to those fore and aft. But which of the packed and mantied beasts carries the gold?

You shoot a big black-bearded man out of the saddle. As he falls, the others scream, some shooting in your direction, blasting the slope to your left where the puff of smoke is carried by the wind. In the midst of the fusillade, you can't tell if Johnny is shooting, but another of the guards is hit. He bends over, dropping his rifle, and clinging to the saddle, sends his mount back up the road, reeling with each pounding stride of his horse.

Ah, there! Four of the riders bunch around a mule in the center of the string. They cast desperate looks in all directions while one reaches down and cuts the lead rope with a knife. Free, the four mules in the lead take off in a ragged lope, headed west and down. Two of the guards follow, shooting up and back over their shoulders, flinging futile lead into the sky.

As the guards separate the mule from the bucking and jostling string, you take aim. Find your sight picture. The Sharps bellows and spits smoke and fire. Through the cloud of blue, you see the mule hunch, hear the slap of the bullet as it blows through the mule's shoulders. The animal drops as you reload.

A bullet from one of the Winchesters smacks the rock you hide behind.

"There! He's up there!" you hear the shout, almost lost as the remaining mules bunch, back away, and one is shoved over the edge. Kicking, bawling, and screaming, the entire pack string topples off the far side, vanishing down the sheer slope amid a snapping and banging of timber and smashing crates.

The remaining riders turn, lashing their horses as they race back up the pass heading east.

In that moment, there's silence. Then a hearty "Yaaa-Hoooo!" as Johnny Crackers steps out from his hiding spot behind one of the spruce trees. He pauses only long enough to shoot one of the guards who sits up, trying to raise a pistol. The man drops at the shot.

You rise, reloading the Sharps, and make your way down the loose scree to the road. You kick a heavy Marlin repeating rifle away from a dying man's grasp. His eyes meet yours, desperate, frightened, and blood bubbles from his lips as he slumps back onto the rutted road.

Johnny emerges from the trees, leading the horses. Applesauce is nervous, prancing, head up, ears pricked as she follows the bit.

It takes less than fifteen minutes to free the packed rolls of gold coins from the dead mule. And then you and Johnny are in the saddle, racing down the road. It's a little more than a quarter mile to an elk trail that will take you up and over the mountain. There you will follow another trail around south. It will lead you to the old townsite of San Miguel, now just a scattering of buildings. From there, it's an easy ride down the valley, following the San Miguel River.

You cry out as the Demon twists another length of your guts out and chews them with its scissor jaws. Damn, but that hurts. Again you try to reach for the gold coin, your arm useless, your fingers numb and without feeling.

God, if the pain in your gut would just leave you a moment's peace. Just long enough to draw a lungful of air. Maybe to let you shift to a more upright position.

The rattle of your tongue in your mouth makes the agony worse. You'd give every one of those gold coins for a drink of cold water. Imagine how it would trickle down your throat to land in your belly. Cold enough to smother the burning pain in your guts.

The sound of bitter laughter echoes in the confines of the canyon, pitching from wall to wall. Johnny's laughter. Hollow, empty of humor.

You shift your gaze, expecting to see him come striding up the sandy bottom, that go-to-hell grin on his lips, merriment in his crystal-blue eyes. Nothing but dull red sandstone, stream-patterned sand, and fallen rock. Even the few pinions and junipers clinging to the slopes look lonely and forlorn.

That smile. Remember how it bent Johnny's lips, curled his mustache and made it quiver.

"Ten thousand dollars!" Johnny had chortled, risen from the blanket where the two of you had laid out the rolls of twenty-dollar gold pieces. Five hundred of them. Enough to buy a new life wherever, however, you wanted.

Not since that night with Helen had you felt that surge of joy that sought to burst your ribs.

Johnny was dancing, hooting, his boots kicking up sand in the firelight. You'd made camp on a ridge top west of the San Miguel. More than a mile off the trail where any pursuit might have followed. And they would be searching. Men were dead. Ten thousand dollars had been taken. An entire community had been upended. Not the sort of thing that could be forgotten or forgiven.

That fact had made you think. Two riders? Headed west on three horses in the backcountry?

The words sounded so reasonable. "I think we should split it now. You take half, I take half, and we go our separate ways. I learned in Texas, one rider is harder to follow than two."

Johnny's hopping dance slowed. He turned, that devilish smile on his lips, the laughter full of merriment. "How right you are!"

And he drew and shot you right in the belly. The blow knocked you back, dropped you flat on your butt in the soft sand. Dazed, you looked up, seeing the smoke drifting yellowish in the firelight as Johnny re-holstered his pistol. "One rider is harder to follow."

It didn't hurt. Not at first. Sort of like a punch to the gut that left you winded. Took a moment or two to realize you'd been shot. Then came that queer runny feeling. Warm and liquid down in your insides.

You'd been too stunned to react as Johnny reached down and pulled your pistol from your belt. He tossed it off to the side before stepping back and giving you a kick that knocked you onto your side on the sand.

As Johnny bent down and began rolling up the gold coins, he spared you a sidelong glance. "Don't think I'm ungrateful. Couldn't have pulled this off without your help. But why settle for half when you can have it all?"

The way that happy smile deepened those lines at the corner of his mouth, the twinkling amusement in Johnny's dancing blue eyes did it. Set off something deep in your soul. Something that hearkened to the knuckle-and-skull days on the river, to that Little Rock fight where you killed Old Jack, or the rage in that Fort Worth back alley.

Seeings as you hadn't moved, Johnny must have figured you for too far gone as he walked out to the picket and brought in the horses. He got so busy saddling Applesauce, he quit shooting you those wary sidelong glances.

Didn't see you pull your legs under you. Couldn't hear you rise in the soft sand. Wouldn't know you'd staggered the four paces over to your Sharps. Wasn't aware that he'd made a fatal mistake until the loud click of that big hammer was drawn to full cock.

You waited as Johnny whirled, pulled for his pistol, and took the step necessary to be clear of Applesauce. He was thumbing the hammer back on his Colt when you shot him through the chest. That big lead bullet blew right through his heart and took out his spine. Never knew a man could fold up that fast. Almost as fast as the bullet itself.

But there you were. Left with the Demon down in your center. Didn't matter that it wasn't bleeding much. You could feel it start to grow. Eating its way.

"Ma wants you home for… supper…" Sally Mae's voice is a melody rising and falling in the breeze that blows up the canyon.

You try to swallow. Tongue doesn't work. Can't. It just sticks in your throat.

Tired. So very tired.

Can't get a full breath. Just want to close your eyes and drift.

You tried. Took all of your strength to pick up those

rolls of coins. Got them into the saddlebags. Packed them full. Applesauce stood there, patient as always. Good horses, them Alsup stock.

But try as you might, the Demon was already sucking you dry. You had to lean against the fender, use two hands to get your foot in the stirrup.

When you tried to swing up, you couldn't. Damn near tumbled into the sand. So you stood there, one foot in the stirrup, breathing hard, the Demon starting to burn hot in your guts.

Thought you'd rest. Drink some water.

So you took out a roll of those gold coins and staggered over to the fire. Drank from Johnny's canteen. As you lay there, wincing at the unfamiliar feeling of the Demon, you rolled those coins between your fingers and stared at Johnny Crackers. He lay there in a flopped-out sprawl, his half-open eyes and blond mustache dusted with sand.

The Demon brought you awake as it twisted around inside you and sent the first tendrils through your guts. You were hot, fevered, and through glassy vision, realized that the horses were gone. All that remained was a burned-out fire, a blanket covered with coins, your Sharps and Johnny Cracker's stiff body, buzzing now with flies.

One by one, you reached out for the coins and stuffed them in a pocket. Each time you did, the Demon repaid you with pain.

The scream was muffled as you endured the Demon and got to your feet. Taking up the Sharps, you fought for air. Picked up the horse tracks and started off. Damn, you could barely walk. Each step fed the Demon.

Like that gob of wire so long ago, you could feel it begin to thread through your guts.

The tracks sort of went misty as the world began to

shimmer in your vision. One foot after another. Just follow the…

You came to on a mat of juniper duff. Blinked, the Demon happily chewing in your guts. The tree's rich odor is in your nostrils, the wind sighing in the branches. Twilight. But is it morning or evening?

You use the Sharps for a prop, yipping at the pain, as you struggle to your feet and work free of the juniper branches. In the half light, you see no horse tracks.

Turns out, it's morning. The horizon grows brighter. Thirst is your first concern. Funny that you didn't bring a canteen. Just a drink. That's all that matters in your fuzzy head as you stumble forward through the endless forest of juniper and pinon pine.

At midday, the riders pass. Not more than a hundred yards away, they ride in single file through the thick stand of pinions and juniper. The only sound is the faint creak of leather, the snuffling of the horses and clinking of tack. They pass almost ghostlike, five of them carrying rifles. And behind they lead Applesauce, Johnny's gelding, and the pack horse.

You stand, propping yourself on the Sharps for balance. Filling your lungs, you call out. It's a croaking, "Hey!" More of a rasp. The riders do not hear.

You would run after them.

But you can't.

A step at a time, you take out on their trail…

You blink, back in the canyon. The shadows are deep now, painting the rocks and streambed in a soft purple. A flock of pinion jays chatter and cackle in that laughter-like jeering as they flutter from tree to tree up on the canyon walls. The breeze has dropped to a soft sigh as night falls.

You are not chasing horses. You're lying here, in the bottom of the canyon. Broken. Paralyzed and covered with dirt. The last of your coins are scattered just beyond your reach.

If you could, you'd crawl over to the Sharps. Use it to…

Laughter is beyond you now. You never jacked the spent case out after you shot Johnny Crackers. You couldn't blow your brains out even if the gun was in your hands.

So, what happened up there? You were stumbling along, using the Sharps for a crutch trying to catch that posse that took Applesauce.

Ah, yes. You'd seen them on the other side of the canyon. Thought that maybe you could wave, somehow catch their attention. That they'd come back.

And…what?

But then, hope, too, is dead. Even if they could have saved you, it would have been for a most public hanging. You standing there, weak, looking frail, while all those people watched some sheriff drop a noose around your neck.

Did you know that? Did you make a misstep? Or did you let yourself fall on purpose?

What motivates a dying man who has ruined everything?

As you close your eyes, the Demon takes another bite and begins to chew.

RUINS

KATHLEEN O'NEAL GEAR

Some stories reach up off the page and grab you by the throat. Images from "Ruins" play with my imagination, taunt me, and send shivers down my back. Here is a stark reminder that in the dark twists and turns of the human mind, grief and love are often interwoven. And sometimes a broken mind sees with such clarity that reality trembles. (WMG)

We all struggle with darkness, especially when we've suffered an unbearable loss. I've never considered it my duty to kill the darkness so that light can shine, but rather to allow readers to enter into the darkness, to travel the same road as the character, in the hope that the darkness will bring illumination. (KOG)

RUINS

KATHLEEN O'NEAL GEAR

Scents of moss and wet earth fill the night.

I hurry along the overgrown trail that leads to the ancient burial mounds beside the river. It's been raining off and on all day. The storm has temporarily broken, but the thunder and lightning are not finished. Flashes blaze in the southern sky as the storm continues to push northward.

I don't have much time.

My only hope is that the storm has shut down the ferries and flooded out all the roads.

As I step over a toppled maple that blackens the path, I try hard to remember when it happened. It's so difficult. A month ago? A year? The countless days have fallen into a meaningless rhythm, passing as though contrived by God to torment me.

I should have looked. Why didn't I look at my son? Didn't I owe him at least a few moments of love?

As the moon edges over the trees, the clouds part and the moonlit air takes on a silver shimmer.

There's a crackle behind me.

I stop dead in my tracks and listen intently to the darkness. Probably an opossum or a raccoon. But…

It sounds like someone walking on the dark trail, tiptoeing on soft leather soles. Rain begins to fall again, drifting down in wavering veils. The soaked branches drip, creating a constant patter. Is that what I heard?

It requires an act of courage to turn around and scan the depths of the dark forest. Moonlight shines through the distant gaps in the clouds and silvers the falling rain. Wet leaves bob.

There's no one there. *Breathe. Just breathe.*

I must have imagined it.

Turning back to the trail, I break into a trot. The path is clear now, a serpentine line that cuts through the mist, heading for the tallest of four burial mounds on the river bank. As I get closer, moonlight haloes the rounded shape, forming a glistening cavern that plunges into a dark underworld. Sooni, my Osage midwife, told me that some tribes believe each person has two souls, one that travels to the afterlife at death and another that stays with the body forever. The souls in the mounds still hear and see.

Tears blur my eyes as I run to the base of the mound and take the washed-out path that leads to the crest. How many grieving parents have taken this trail over the centuries? It's a difficult climb. The mound is sheathed with vines, and covered with a strange litter of feathers, shells, pieces of copper, and empty medicine bottles. Each artifact is a moment of grief, a failed weapon in the war to hold back eternal night.

Vines curl around my boots as I climb, trying to trip me, to stop me.

But this is the ritual. I come. I sit. I talk to him.

By the time I reach the mound top I'm breathing hard and my legs tremble. The view from up here is stunning. Tendrils of lightning-silvered fog drift over the dark river and twine through the trees. The first fireflies have emerged and net the branches like twinkling stars. To the south, an indigo wall of clouds moves toward me.

The river has become a torrent. I try to imagine how Sooni could have drowned him. Beyond the bank, the current is terrifyingly swift. But perhaps it was not on that terrible night. Perhaps it was slow and languid, sheathed in brilliant starlight.

"Don't—don't think about it."

I claw vines out of the way and kick aside rocks... until I find him.

The little skull is half buried, resting on its side, facing west. I've never been able to locate the rest of the bones.

"Hello, son."

Lowering myself to sit beside him, I dig away the dirt and use the hem to my red shawl to wipe the mud from his eye sockets and tiny misshapen skull. "Shh, don't cry, Bobby. I'm here."

While I rock the skull in my arms, I gaze around. The medicine bottle shines in the moonlight that penetrates the thinnest clouds. It's a reminder of the last month when Sooni poured a constant stream down my throat to ease my pain. I pick it up and hurl the bottle as hard as I can, then watch it splash into the river where it's swept downstream into oblivion.

"Bobby? Bobby, listen to me. We have to go. We have to get home before he does. If he catches us..."

My voice fades when I think I hear someone breathing out in the forest. Heavy breathing, as though he's tracked me and is enraged.

Leaping to my feet, I clutch Bobby to my chest and rush down the trail to the bottom of the mound. The first twenty steps are easy, but when clouds move in again, the moonlight vanishes, and I have to slow down.

He could be standing ten feet away in the dark under-brush, watching me, and I would not see him.

But...but maybe by now his anger has faded, and I'll find him at home sitting by the fire reading a book. When I open the door, his face will light up and his eyes will shine. He'll rise, take me in his arms, and examine the changes in my face since he's been gone. Then I'll make chicory coffee, and we'll talk long into the night, smiling like children as we watch Bobby sleep in his crib.

I break into a panicked run, trying to get home.

The log cabin emerges just as the heavens open up and rain pounds the forest. When lightning flashes, I desperately look at the shattered windows, praying to see a figure waiting for me, worried about me.

But they are dark.

A few paces from home, I stop to stare at the cobwebs that drape the porch like thick gauze curtains, then I charge through the rusty gate. The garden has gone wild. Were it not for the fence around it, no one would know it had once been crowded with corn, beans, and bright yellow sunflowers that swayed gracefully every time the wind touched them.

I leap up the rotten wooden steps and shove my way through the cobwebs to get to the door.

"We're safe now, Bobby. We're home."

When I grip the doorknob, the wind rips it out of my hands and slams it back against the wall. Rain drums through the forest, sounding like hooves chasing me down. I grab the door and pull it closed behind me, then I barricade it with my body—and listen to the darkness.

Wind shrieks around the corners of the cabin.

No breathing. No footsteps.

He's not here.

My heartbeat slows.

Pulling off my wet shawl, I hang it on the peg by the door and feel my way across the room toward the fireplace. Bobby has grown oddly warm where he rests against my chest. For a fleeting instant, I swear I feel him nursing my breast. The sensation is perfectly clear.

"Are you all right?" I ask as I stroke his skull.

There's no answer.

Darkness hides most of the details, but I see the faded curtains that hang in shreds around the broken windows and the rocking chair where I sat manically rocking for hours on end. Old autumn leaves are piled in the corners.

Happiness fills me, and I sing Bobby a soft lullaby while I do a little dance around the room, barely noticing the glass shards that grate beneath my boots. Bobby's empty eye sockets are like twin holes in the world. What color were they? Blue and sparkling?

"We're all right now. Everything's going to be fine."

Outside, the creak, creak, creak of the old windmill competes with the roar of wind. It's unnerving. Leaves gust by the windows.

"You feel cold, Bobby. Come on, let's build a fire."

Gently, I rest the skull on the hearthstones and pick up the fire steel. The char cloth and branches I left in the fireplace are covered with dirt that's blown in through the empty window frames and sifted through the gaps in the logs. It doesn't catch right off. But finally, the cloth flares and orange flames spring to life amid the tinder.

With a sigh of relief, I slump down on the hearth and pick up the skull again. "You'll be warm soon."

I was lonely. After Fernando left.

We had neighbors for a time before the war, but they all drifted away to find jobs in town. Most of their houses are toppled heaps now, though a few still stand. On occasion, when I can get free, I meander through those ruins, examining the broken furniture and moldering books they left behind.

I try to force myself to relax. Golden light flutters over the walls, but I'm strangely upset, as though my body knows something my mind refuses to believe.

I'd forgotten how pleasant it felt to be among my own things. The plants on the windowsills are dead, but the patchwork quilt thrown over the back of the rocking chair will look beautiful once I've shaken out the dust. Maybe I'll carry the quilt and the grimy cast-iron pans down to the river and wash them tomorrow. I'm not sure what to do about the shattered plates that cover the floor.

Perhaps I'll boil pine pitch and glue the pieces back together? They won't be as pretty as the day my grandmother gave them to me, but at least they'll be functional. And the rocker crib across the room will be fine once I've washed it down.

I get to my feet. When I start toward the crib, Bobby whimpers. "No, no, shhh. We're all right. I promise you we are."

Filthy mouse-chewed blankets fill the crib. I gently place Bobby atop them and kneel to stare at him for a few moments. I can see him. His silken hair is coal black. I hope it stays that color as he grows up. It has a bluish gleam in the dancing firelight. It's a stark contrast with his pale, pale skin. Dirt squeals beneath the rockers as I rhythmically shove the crib back and forth.

When his eyes close and he finally falls asleep, I quietly wander the house, touching things, smoothing my fingers over my great-aunt's crystal vase, and my mother's porcelain figurine of an angel. It's a miracle they survived the night of violence. The heavy wrought-iron mirror on the wall has been in my family for generations. I wipe it clean with my sleeve, then stand stunned at the reflection. The woman staring back at me has gaunt cheeks and sunken blue eyes. When did my face become so wrinkled? The long days of tending the fields without a hat have taken a toll, just like grandmother told me they would. I wish I'd listened.

A sudden gust of wind thrashes through the forest.

I wonder where Fernando found lodging? Perhaps Miss Eve's House of Happiness. I've heard that he goes there often, though he does not know that I know.

He's a strange man—very tall, very thin, cadaverously pale with thin hair as colorless as his eyes. There's an odd air of finality about him, the sort you might feel if you found a man standing alone in a cemetery with no reason to be there.

Doesn't matter. All in all, he's a good husband. He built this cabin and gave me a precious child. If I'm not happy, it's my own fault. He says I ought to be grateful for the small joys in life, and he's right. I'm selfish and shrewish. I nag him far too much.

When thunder booms, lightning flashes and rain cascades from the roof. Something darts by the window. A shadow.

I hold my breath.

The worst of the storm must be sitting right on top of us for the thunderous booms explode at the same time lightning flashes.

Was that a face? A small face peeking in through the bottom right corner of the window? It's gone now. But... the huge eyes were fixed upon me.

I continue to stare, not breathing.

I'm such a fool. With each flash of lightning, I see different shapes out there. Branches tumble by like dancing skeletons. The cobwebs on the porch resemble a flapping white cape.

"Bobby? Did you see that?"

A small fist waves above the crib, drawing my attention, then it lowers. His movements must have affected the crib; it's rocking faintly. In the wavering firelight, I think I see a shadow climb out of the crib and drop to the floor.

My fingers tighten to fists.

Even in the beginning, he was only a shadow. A small blackness that continued to live inside me despite the fact that his heartbeat had stopped months ago. Sooni told me I was carrying death in my womb. I told her that was impossible. I knew blood pumped through Bobby's veins. I could feel it. He was *with* me.

My eyes narrow when the shredded window curtains swing in a wind I do not feel.

I don't like the rustling sound. It's more than the curtains. Something else is moving in the room.

From the corner of my eye, I notice the strange darkness drifting across the floor. Firelight seems to bounce off it. I have the urge to flee, but running will only prolong my terror, draw out the suffering. I know how this goes.

The darkness haltingly moves around the wall, and I realize he's holding on, steadying his feeble steps. Coming into the world again.

The first time was unbearable.

I remember lurching to my feet when I felt a small explosion in my belly and a rush of fluid soaking my shimmy. It was the beginning of saying goodbye.

Bobby did not cry. He came out in silence as though he knew there was no reason to announce his arrival.

Fernando shouted, *"What is it?"*

"Shh," Sooni's soft voice answered. *"It's alive"*

"Alive? It can't be alive. It's not human."

"It's moving, sir."

"Then take it outside and kill it!"

I squeeze my eyes closed, just as I did that day. I shut my eyes and never saw my son. I should have held him until he died. But I did not ask for him. I did not demand that Sooni lay him on my chest so that I could stroke his back until it was over. He had the right to die in my arms. I think I was afraid Bobby would know I gazed upon him in horror, not love.

I remained mute while Sooni wrapped Bobby in a blanket and carried him out into the darkness.

Footsteps echo, faintly at first, then louder. The small shadow moves around and around the room until its legs are strong enough, then it totters across the filthy floor and passes me, showing me that he can walk now. He looks so happy as he grabs hold of the dusty rocking chair and grins at me.

There's a deafening roar in my ears.

None of this is real, is it? I'm dreaming. Hallucinating. Conjuring monsters out of firelight.

I'm still huddled in the darkness of that locked room where the curtains are never drawn. Why does this feel so real? I'm here. I swear I'm here. Bobby and I live in this warm cabin, enveloped by fluttering firelight. Every morning, I go outside to sit on the porch step and feed him as the sun rises.

Bobby totters across the floor and hugs my leg while he rests his chin on my knee. His face is alight with kindness. Forgiveness.

From a great, great distance, a bubbly little boy's laugh rises and lilts in the air high above me, and suddenly the cabin is filled with a wash of sunlight.

I blink as my pulse speeds up, trying to figure out what has...

Outside, a little boy's voice sings, *"Amazing grace—how sweet the sound—that saved a wretch like me."*

I look at the window. The sun-drenched forest is alive with swarming bees and birds flitting from branch to branch. The air has changed, as well. The smell of the fire in the hearth is gone, replaced by the strong fragrance of flowers and summer grass.

Nerving myself, I walk to the door and fling it open.

I see Bobby. He's trotting around the garden, smiling. He sings the same verse over and over in an absent-minded sort of way, as though they are the only words he remembers from the song. I sway on the crystal-clear notes and watch his black head bob just above the young cornstalks. His sweet voice is the sound of safety. No one will find us way out here in the wilderness. Fernando will never find us.

The maples and elms down along the creek create a dazzling mosaic of bright and dark green. I walk out into the garden and pick up my spade from where I left it yesterday. The scent of rich, damp earth encircles me.

Bobby trots out of the corn and into the grape trellises, where he appears and disappears among the vines. ...*uh-uh wretch like meeee*...

I smile with tears in my eyes as he holds the note and gazes down the line of fruit trees. By fall, we'll be harvesting and canning over the old wood stove in the kitchen, lining the panty shelves with jars of colorful vegetables and fruits. The fragrances of cinnamon and nutmeg will fill the cabin as I cook and can the apple pie filling. The last thing to be harvested will be the potatoes growing down on the far end of the garden. I'll dig them and load them in burlap sacks to hang from the rafters in the root cellar alongside dried stalks of corn with the cobs still attached. I hate grinding corn, but the cornmeal makes the best cornbread we've ever eaten.

I marvel as Bobby trots by. He's growing tall and straight and faster than I'd ever have imagined. It's as though time has rushed past, and I don't know where the moments went. For a few disconcerting heartbeats, I can't recall what he looked like at the age of two or four, then the thought vanishes like icicles in sunlight. I'm just really tired, and it's a hot day.

It's a comfort to know that winter isn't too far away. When the first flakes of snow start to fall, I'll wake Bobby up early and laugh while he rushes to pull on his boots and coat, takes my hand, and drags me outside into the white world. "Come on, Mommy! Hurry it up!" He loves the snow. We'll play and build a snowman and won't come inside until our faces are so frozen we can't laugh anymore, then I'll make hot chocolate and we'll snuggle together in front of a roaring fire in the old stone fireplace. My son will fall asleep across my lap while I stroke his dark head.

Intense despair fills me. I don't understand. This is a happy memory. Why is it tinged with the awful smell of blood and distant shouting?

My son's sweet voice rises: *"Now I lay me down to sleep, I pray the Lord my soul to keep, if I should die before I wake…"*

Bobby abruptly stops praying and looks at me with wide eyes.

"Mommy, am I gonna die?"

The words are like slaps. "Oh, no, honey, no, you're not going die. I won't let you die."

Bobby starts crying. Suffocating, pitiful cries. "I feel like I'm dying."

There is something wrong with him. I know there is. He's such a weak boy, forever tripping on his own feet and falling face-first into the dirt, and I have the awful feeling it's my fault. What did I do? Did I drop him on his head when he was a baby? God, how could I hurt that precious little boy? I love him more than life itself, and we have only each other to ease the terror of the dark locked room where we usually…

Is it raining? I hear rain.

"Mommy? Are you back? I've been talking to you."

My son's voice is so, so faint.

He runs through the garden with his hands outstretched, fingers moving in a 'take me, take me' gesture. I crouch and allow him to run into my arms. "I'm right here. You're all right."

"But you were gone. I couldn't see you." Tears flood his cheeks as he throws his arms around my neck and hugs me tightly. "Don't go away again. Stay here with me. My back hurts. Can you rub it?"

Darkness swallows all the light in the world. Everyone is against us. Fernando and the doctors all want to forget the problems we're causing. I know they want us both gone.

I rub Bobby's back in slow circles, whispering—as I have done a thousand times—that everything is going to be all right. Inside, I'm stars and stripes snapping in the wind. I'm ready to crawl out of the trench and rush into the face of certain death and kill anyone who tries to put Bobby in the cold, cold earth.

Resting my chin on top of my son's head, I close my eyes, waiting for a sign from God that I'm doing the right thing.

…It is raining.

"Mommy! No! Don't leave me."

I snap back to the garden. "Bobby, let's pray. Come on, let's get down on our knees and beg God to forgive us."

Bobby drops like a rock to his knees and clasps his hands beneath his chin. "Why, Mommy? What did we do wrong?"

"I don't know. I…I don't know." I'm crying, and I can't remember when it started. "Let's just silently ask God to guide us."

I feel like I'm sinking, plunging deeper and deeper into a gossamer shadow play where Fernando walks hunched over behind me with a knife. In the play, Bobby must kill the monster that wants to murder his mother.

Bobby whispers, "I can't, Mommy. I'm too sick and scared."

"I'm scared, too, but if we want to stay together, we must fight."

In a pathetic voice, he says, "All right."

Hidden in the darkest recesses of this little boy's heart, I know a great hero is waiting to be born. Like all shamans and wizards before me, I would prepare him if I could. But I have no magic wands, or silver keys, or secret words. I can't even help him wage war against the forces of evil trying to take him away from me. But I must. I must save him.

When horses whinny, I lurch to my feet. I don't see anyone in the garden. Scared, Bobby's tiny fists clutch my skirt and hold on as though he knows the truth. I can feel his chest rising and falling against my leg, and I can't bear it.

He never took a breath.

From faraway, a voice cries, "Dear God, she is in there. I can see her through the window."

When I look down, Bobby's eyes have gone dead and white. Wet hair slicks down around his face and hangs in curls over his forehead.

"Sir, you want me to bring the rope?"

"No."

I grab Bobby and lift him into my arms. His body is slippery, oozy, like the body of a drowned child that's been lying at the bottom of a river for a year. Phantom fingers reach up to touch my throat, and Bobby nuzzles close to me.

I hug him hard. "Mommy loves you. I've always loved you."

I can feel it. He is *with* me. He's still with me.

The world goes dark and cold, and thunder rumbles through the forest.

The cabin door flies open and Fernando steps inside. A strange mixture of sorrow and rage line his thin face. He barely glances at me. Instead, as though he's done this over and over, he walks straight to the crib, pulls the small skull from the blankets, and turns to stare at me.

"How could you do this to me again, Maria?"

I reach out with shaking arms. "Please, let me have him. He needs me."

A burly man with red hair rushes through the door. He wears a pistol on his hip. Horror widens his eyes as he surveys the decaying remnants of lives ruined by the imagined patter of a dead child's feet. For a year, Bobby's bubbly laughter trailed me through the house, following me everywhere I went. He crawled into bed with me at night and hugged me in the darkness, breathing deep between me and Fernando. We moved to another house, but I could never shake the feeling that my son was still alive.

"Do you want me to grab her, sir?"

Fernando lightly shakes his head. "No. Just take the skull outside."

The man hurries across the floor and wipes his hands on his wet pants before lifting Bobby from Fernando's hands. "Good Lord. Why is it so grotesque?"

"Born that way. That's why it died."

"Why does she keep digging it up? It's macabre."

"I don't know, John," Fernando replies. "I've never known."

"What do you want me to do with it? Rebury it?"

"For now, I just want it out of my sight."

As though the thing in his hands is loathsome, John holds Bobby at arm's length and walks through the door onto the rickety porch. I see him pass by the window and disappear into the rainy darkness.

Fernando dries his face with his sleeve and exhales a long breath. His eyes drift around the cabin as though trying to remember a time when we were happy, then he turns to me and frowns. "Are you all right?"

"Fernando, just leave us here," I plead. "We'll be all right by ourselves. You don't have to stay."

"You'll starve to death, and I won't have that on my conscience."

He hesitates a moment, then walks to the fireplace

and stamps out the flames. When he's finished, he bows his head and shakes it. "You've forced my hand, you know? Now I'll have to chain you to your bed at night."

Stalking across the room, he grabs my arm in the hard careless grip of a stranger and drags me toward the door.

Lightning illuminates John where he stands in the rain by his horse. "Sir?" he calls, holding up the skull.

Fernando stops and tightens his grip on my arm.

"Find a rock. Smash it to dust."

THE OLDEST PROFESSION

W. MICHAEL GEAR

On that cold January night, we took Uncle Joe to the "wild game feed" at the Casper VFW. Uncle Joe, in his eighties and mostly blind, could still navigate to the free bar like a homing pigeon. Loading him into the truck later was a major feat, but Joe didn't want to call it a night. It didn't matter that Kathleen, my fiancée at the time, was present. Joe kept insisting that we "find a lady" shall we say, down on the Sandbar. We got Joe home and put to bed, and Kathleen married me anyway. But the Sandbar's past is only a shadow's length away. (WMG)

Reading the above made me laugh. Uncle Joe was a character. At the age of sixteen, his father indentured him to pay off his debts. Joe used to say, "Can you believe a father would do that to his son?" When Joe was free, without a cent to his name, he hopped the first train he could find and started riding the rails to see the country. Later, at a time when it could get you killed, he worked as a union organizer. Joe was downright heroic —including shady ladies at the age of eighty. (KOG)

I watch the cockroach as it scrambles across the smudged white paint on the jail cell wall. Legs milling, the long antennae in frantic motion, the little beast zips up the wall and vanishes into the gap between the concrete ceiling and the angle iron that holds the bars. They say cockroaches didn't exist in Wyoming before the coming of the railroads. That the little pests arrived in boxes of fresh fruit carried in freight cars from the tropics.

But "cockroaches" come in all kinds and all species. Like Ted Twillacker. Two days have passed since Ted walked out my Natrona County jail cell. He's a lawyer, you see. One of Casper's most unsavory. His usual beat is defending the drunks, whores, bootleggers, and gamblers who parade through the Natrona County court system on various charges of vice.

The jail I'm in was built in 1909, before the petroleum boom. Just the row of cells in the Courthouse Building on Center Street. It's 1923, for Pete's sake! The city is booming with oil, murders, robberies, brawls, and prostitution. You'd think with the funds pouring in, that they would build facilities to handle the traffic. As it is, being the only woman behind bars, I have the six-by-eight cell to myself. And probably will until Friday night. Unless one of the girls on the line shoots, stabs, or beats another of the girls, or breaks a bottle over some unruly john's head.

I am in serious trouble. If they were going to charge me with anything, it should have been simple prostitution. I'd pay my twenty-five-buck fine for moral turpitude and flounce out the door. Instead, it's an arson charge? I rack my brain over and over. What made me stand out when that damn police chief, Davis, was questioning me at the scene? I looked perfectly miserable, huddling there in my shimmy, shivering, as the fire hoses sprayed water.

People like me are supposed to think that we're smarter than everyone else—and to be honest, most of them do. Even after they're caught because of some ridiculously simple mistake. Not me. When it comes to brains, I know I'm not the flashiest dress in the wardrobe, so I plan. And plan again. Like I have been doing since I arrived in Wyoming. I have made it a habit to always pave my way to a way out.

Looking back at the last couple of weeks since the Lavender Palace burned, I can't figure it out. The trail had been perfectly laid to a dead end. All the loose ends neatly tied up, the clues left in place. They should have cut me loose. None of it made sense until I heard the jailer say that Chief Davis was supposed to meet a woman at the depot today. That she was coming in from back East.

Damn it! It has to be her.

Having nothing else to do, I perch myself on the vile-smelling mattress atop the squeaky bed springs and chew my lips. I don't even have the cockroach for entertainment anymore. It's two days now, that Twillacker is gone. What the hell is he doing in Cheyenne? He should have already cabled. Money always buys favors, and Wyoming is cheap in comparison to someplace, like, say, Philadelphia, where corruption costs you an arm and a leg.

Come on, Twillacker. How long does it take you to bribe a bunch of politicians?

———

The west wind gusted around the Chicago, Burlington and Quincy depot's brick walls and sent tendrils of dust scurrying down the platform and between Police Chief Harney Davis's boots. That afternoon he waited for the train and fought shivers as he scuffed his feet on the gritty concrete. Another gust whipped around the depot and Harney pulled his collar up. Wind was a constant this time of year. Not only was it cold, promising a miserable winter, but it carried the nose-burning stink from the two big petroleum refineries on the Platte River terrace just west of town. The refineries, along with the two railroads that served them, had turned Casper, Wyoming, into the boomingest boom town in America.

Already, 1923 had set a record for murders; violence, arrests, and shootings took center stage. While the "city fathers" considered the fines, licenses, bribes, and fees to be a financial gold mine, the more settled and prosperous elements of the population—the family and business types—wanted the town cleaned up. Harney had stepped into a hornet's nest.

He turned at the sound of the approaching steam engine, its pending arrival announced by the locomotive's whistle. People—those smart enough to huddle around the coal stove inside the depot—emerged from the two-story red-brick building. Most were dressed in warm coats, but this was Casper, after all, so some were wrapped in blankets or shivered in threadbare jackets. Harney stood to the side, taking note. The wealthy ones —and Casper had more than its share—mixed with the merchants and refinery workers. The ranch folks, sheepherders, and cattlemen, kept themselves separate from the townsfolk as well as from each other based on mutual dislike.

Excitement built as the locomotive chuffed into sight, steam clouding around the pistons. Another shrill whistle caused some of the women and children to clap hands to their ears.

Harney exchanged nods and smiles with those he knew and made note of the ones who watched him with wary gazes. The current police force wasn't uniformly well-liked by the townsfolk, good or bad. For one, Prohibition had never been popular, Wyoming being Wyoming. Second, when as much money flowed through a community as it did in Casper, not all police officers were above adding a little outside income to their meager finances. That was one of the reasons Harney's predecessor, Bert Yohe, had turned in his resignation.

Harney stood his ground as the heavy locomotive hissed, puffed, and squealed its way past the platform. The passenger cars rolled by at a groaning crawl, stopping as the lead reached the end of the platform. People crowded forward as the doors opened, the first of the passengers climbing down. What ensued was a bedlam of greetings, hugs, smiles, and backslapping, while down the line, the porters had opened the freight cars, rolling out luggage on the carts.

Harney resettled his hat, an old gray Stetson that he refused to surrender despite his appointment as chief of police. The mayor had even suggested the city would cover the cost of a new blue uniform—one just as sharp as you'd see in New York, Boston, or even Philadelphia. Harney had had enough of uniforms to last a lifetime.

The woman he waited for was the last to emerge. She stepped out wearing a fashionable Burberry's pattern dark-blue dress under a long wool coat belted at the waist. Below the hem he could see expensive-but-sensible lace-up boots. A dark cloche hat sat low on her curled black hair. The beaded-and-black-sequined purse she clasped in both hands probably cost as much as Harney made in a month. He'd seen the like among Casper's well-to-do; she might have been dressed for a stroll down Fifth Avenue in Manhattan.

The effect when her startling green eyes met Harney's, however, belied anything her fashion might communicate. She fixed him with a competent and penetrating stare that sent a quiver through him. He'd seen eyes like that—but they'd been looking at him over the battlesights of a Mauser rifle.

She stepped forward, offering a gloved hand. "Police Chief Davis, I presume?"

Harney took her hand in his right; his left doffed the battered old Stetson. "Yes, ma'am."

"Eleanor Williams Clark, sir." Withdrawing her hand, she reached into the purse and produced a business card. "Private Investigations. As I stated in my cable, Mrs. Willimena Bourke of Baltimore has retained me to ascertain the whereabouts of her daughter-in-law, Eudora Jenson Bourke. I believe you are familiar with the details?"

"I think I've got the general idea from the wires you sent." He gestured. "Do you have any luggage?"

A hint of smile bent her lightly rouged lips. "Thank you, but I've already made arrangements to have it delivered to the Henning Hotel. My first priority is to see the crime scene. If you have other obligations, I can make my own arrangements for transportation."

Harney gestured toward the arched entrance to the depot and held the door as they stepped in out of the wind. "I'd be happy to drive you." He bit off a wince. Hoped he hadn't been too forward. "If you have no objection."

They crossed the bustling depot, her heels clicking on the wooden floor. "Well, Chief, I assume that I'm as safe with you as anyone."

At the slightly mocking tone, he chuckled, figuring

she was one of the most formidable women he'd ever encountered. God help the man who might cross her line. He led her into the wind out front and down the steps. Being chief had its perks. The Cadillac Type 61 was parked front and center. He stepped around, opening the door for her. She eyed the big touring car before sliding onto the seat.

"Somehow, being in Wyoming, I half assumed you'd travel by horseback or buggy." She settled back on the leather cushions, breath puffing in the air.

Harney slammed the driver's door, set the choke. Clutch in, he toed the starter button. The V8 turned over twice and caught. "It was brought to the attention of the last town council that our rattly old four-cylinder Fords couldn't keep up with so much as a fast horse, let alone the new automobiles the bootleggers are driving. And, at times, it was deemed necessary for city's lead law enforcement officer to make his presence known post-haste."

He paused to back up, then shifted into first. "And Casper, for the moment, is one of the richest cities in the nation." He gestured where construction on six new brick multistory buildings was in progress. "It's like this all over town. We're literally rising from the plains."

As he drove down C Street, she asked, "What makes Casper so rich? On first impression, outside of sagebrush, dust, and endless wind-swept emptiness, I don't see much."

"Oil," he replied. "Remember all those tank cars on that train you arrived on? That stench and haze in the air? We have two brand-new refineries working round the clock to serve three major oil fields, and they're begging for workers to come to make their fortunes. Young men, making high wages, seem to have a reckless compulsion to spend it."

She nodded, staring toward the forested slopes of Casper Mountain, its heights buried in scudding gray clouds. "It's always the money, isn't it?"

"Miss Clark—"

"Eleanor, please. And it's Mrs. Clark."

"Sure. As I was saying, oil is remaking Wyoming. Before the war, the economy ran on livestock and a little mining. This was a dusty little railroad town that was home to a thousand people. Then the Stock brothers struck oil just north of here, and then they found the Muddy Flats oil field, which meant refineries. Then came the war. Demand for petroleum keeps growing, and people keep flocking here."

He nodded at the brand-new five-story Henning Hotel. "That's where you are staying. Best in town." Then pointed up Center Street. "Not a mile from here on the terrace, they're building million-dollar mansions for the wheelers and dealers. The kind of people who own mineral rights, drilling leases and production companies, trucking firms, bankers, oil field supply companies, lawyers, and the like. Money like Wyoming has never seen."

He took a right, heading west on B Street.

"Understand." He paused. "Wyoming has always had predators. Wolves, bears, coyotes, and cougars for the livestock. Now it's gamblers, thieves, prostitutes, and whiskey-and-dope peddlers for the oil patch."

She gave him a knowing glance. "That sounds promising given what we know of Eudora's proclivities."

"We cross the line as we drop off the hill. In less than a block, we're down on what is called the Sandbar. Think Sodom and Gomorrah enhanced with all the invented vices of the twentieth century. A separate world from Center Street."

The change was immediate. Casper's new fast-rising

multi-storied brick buildings and recently paved avenue gave way to a rutted and wind-blown dirt street littered with broken bottles, flattened tin cans, and other trash. Either side was lined with plank shanties, occasional two-story commercial buildings, frame and brick boarding houses, saloons, billiard parlors, and small squat dwellings. In the distance to the west, the refineries' towering smokestacks and condensate stabilizers thrust up from the horizon. The flame towers with their flaring fires and the acrid smell added to the illusion of hell broke loose on earth.

As they passed the line of weathered shacks, scantily or provocatively dressed women leaned out of doors. They were waving, gesturing, and calling as they struck seductive poses. A few, recognizing the Cadillac, showed the better part of discretion by ducking furtively back inside their shabby little cribs. From the corner of his eye, Harney noted that Eleanor didn't so much as bat an eye.

"Not exactly demure," Eleanor said dryly. "But Eudora wouldn't be a lowly streetwalker like these."

"Reckon not," Harney agreed, turning south onto Ash Street. "Like I said, there's a lot of money in Casper. Means you get every kind of clientele. This part of the Sandbar caters to the refinery workers, roughnecks, hod carriers, truck drivers, pipefitters, and the like."

Crossing West First Street, he followed Ash up the hill to the top of the terrace. Pulling over to the curb, he set the brake and killed the engine. To the left lay the fire-gutted remains of a building. Three of the burned-out rickety walls still stood, windows broken out like empty eyes. Charred timbers, ash, bent metal, and blackened rubble was mounded over the remains of both heat and cook stoves. Skeletons of beds and springs had fallen in soot-blackened twists. Shattered porcelain from sinks, crockery, and fire-cracked toilets scattered here and there.

Stands of twisted pipe protruded from the ash. What had been a fancy copper tub lay partially crushed under burned-through floor joists.

"They called it the Lavender Parlor House." Harney said. "Unlike most of the bordellos, I never had the opportunity to be inside. I hear, though, that they named it for the color of the wallpaper and the scents they used. They built the brothel up here on the terrace so the upscale clientele didn't have to venture into the less savory parts of the Sandbar. But close enough that the whiskey, opium, dope, and other vices were close at hand."

"In your cable you said that it was arson?" Eleanor opened her door and stepped out, drawing her coat tighter against the plucking wind as she crossed the street.

Harney opened the driver's door and followed, pointing to what was left of the collapsed and burned-through stairway. "A couple of the witnesses saw the smoke. Given it was nine in the morning, they broke in. Said that the stairs were engulfed in flames. Trapped the folks upstairs. Said that they could smell the gasoline. And, believe me, in Casper we know what gasoline smells like before and after it burns."

Eleanor picked her way around scattered charcoal and ash, peering at the wreckage. "And where was the woman's body?"

"By that, I assume you mean Eudora?" He pointed. "We recovered eight burned corpses in all. Their remains indicate that five were huddled against the second-story back wall. Probably to avoid the fire.

"You can see that the wreckage here came from an upstairs room, the floor having fallen when the walls collapsed. One corpse was determined to be the suspected Pinkerton, given the security service badge number 4898 found on his body. Another woman lay on the floor by the door. But the woman with the ring around her neck..." He pointed to the large bedframe with the fire-tarnished brass headboard. "She was still lying on the bedsprings, totally unrecognizable, of course. But she had that chain around her neck to suspend the ring."

"Did you ever see her alive, Chief?"

"I didn't. She wasn't around long enough, or in trouble enough, to cross my path. To be sure, it's always news when a new madam comes to town, and this one arrived amid a swirl of rumor. Word was she paid cash for the business. Twenty thousand. All the paperwork was handled by Bernie Benson, a local attorney, and filed at the courthouse. Then Ted Twillacker took over as the house's lawyer. Oddly, Bernie closed his office and was last seen boarding the C. B and Q. Hasn't been seen or heard of since."

Eleanor's lips twitched as if amused by some certainty. Reaching into her purse again, she extracted a photograph. "Look closely, Chief. Have you ever seen this woman?"

Harney took the photo. The woman, thirtyish, was seated on a chair, the wood elegantly carved, the rich fabric upholstery, fringe, and high back hinting of expense. She wore a tightly fitted silk dress of the sort that Harney knew was the rage back east. The neck was cut low and square, and the belt at her thin waist sported an oversized bow tied to look like a big rose. Her posture was perfectly straight, poised, legs crossed at the ankles, and her head tilted.

Something about her expression fixed his attention. She'd cut her hair short, had it tightly curled and close to the scalp. Her wide eyes seemed to mock the camera, a mischievous tension in her small mouth. Even in the photo, Harney could see the thin chain around her neck where it dipped beneath the fabric covering her breast.

"Eudora?" he asked.

"Taken over a year ago," she told him. "Before her husband, Bryce, was killed and she disappeared. It was a fire, you know. Bryce's body was identified by his wedding ring. As was Eudora's."

"Then why come all the way out here? What makes you think Eudora didn't die in that fire?"

She gave him a hard look, glacial green. "The Pinkerton was our first clue. Special Services Badge 4898 was worn by Jasper Lamont. He'd been hired by the family to look for Eudora. Close to a hundred thousand dollars disappeared at the same time that Bryce and Eudora supposedly burned to death out at the country estate. There were suspicions since Bryce and Eudora had been married for less than a year."

Eleanor fingered her chin, eyes slitted as she studied the charred wreckage. "Bryce came back from the war changed, moody, and just couldn't settle into normal life. Eudora was wild, exotic, and just as game for excitement as he was. Apparently, she was an excellent horsewoman and could ride neck and neck with Bryce. That's one of the reasons they stayed out at the estate rather than the mansion in Baltimore. She could match him drink for drink, laugh, and deal blow for blow. The family thought her behavior, not to mention their sexual escapades... shall we say, unseemly. Beneath the Bourke family standards. Which was another reason they were encouraged to confine their activities to the country house and grounds."

Harney stuck his fingers in his back pockets, tilting his hat against the aggravating wind. "Nearly a hundred thousand dollars? So, assuming the woman's body that you found in Maryland isn't Eudora, despite the wedding ring, why would she come here? To a parlor house, of all places?"

The hard green eyes studied him from the side. "That, Chief, is an excellent question. One that perhaps Jasper Lamont might be able to answer were he not a charred crisp. Bryce has a brother, Sanford, who chanced to over-hear Eudora mention that she had met General John J. Pershing once 'when he came through Cheyenne.' The implication being that she was a resident. And there were other Western hints. Things she'd say and then clam up about."

"What do you think?"

Eleanor indicated the toasted bed with a tilt of the head. "That she might have ended up there? On that bed, with that chain and Bryce's Harvard ring around her neck? In the same room as the Pinkerton detective sent to track her down? I think it's too neat."

Harney rocked his jaw, his attention split between the woman and the burned brothel. "Does seem that way, doesn't it?" He took a deep breath. "Now, I've never been in a burning building, but the last place I'd stay is in bed. And I guess my first thought when I got here was why, unlike the girls who died in a clump as far as they could get from the flames, were the bodies found laid out in this one room? Maybe, when the floor fell, they got jostled around. But the fire chief tells me the floor fell flat. Dropped like a pancake."

Eleanor clasped her collar as the wind scoured her with dust. "Why did you hold the single survivor?"

Harney tilted his hat against the wind. "You ever deal with hookers, Eleanor?"

The look she was giving him went colder by ten or twenty degrees.

"That was a rhetorical question," he said easily. "Being just people, they come in all kinds. But you still get types. The hard and calculating ones that life has abused. The innocent victims on their way to eventual suicide. The ones who don't have any choice but to make the best of it. And the ones who just don't have the wits for any other path. Now, the girl I've got locked up doesn't fit, and I'm not sure why. Says her name's Dolly Louise James. That she's from California and Nevada. That she was recruited by Lavender House and arrived a month ago by private auto."

"You buy that?"

Harney shrugged. "C.B. and Q was shut down that month after the Cole Creek Bridge train wreck. The Chicago and Northwestern was the only line running, and they have no record of Dolly Louise James arriving by train. She had to come from somewhere. Private auto is as good as any, and she insists she paid the driver twenty dollars to deviate up here to Casper from his planned route on the Lincoln Highway."

"Wouldn't it be nice to find that driver?" Eleanor asked.

"If he even existed." Harney hunched deeper into his coat. "So, what's your next step?"

Eleanor gave him a crafty squint. "I think I'd better have a talk with Dolly Louise James."

———

I am prepared. I sit with my back to the grimy white wall, eyes closed as I concentrate on the slow and rhythmic beat of my heart. I breathe in, hold it, and exhale through my nostrils. The secret is to be in control, to let no vulnerability show. Until I hear from Twillacker, I am the lowest of the low. Totally vulnerable, without power or rights. It doesn't matter that Wyoming is the "Equality State" and that women were given the right vote, hold office, and own businesses—a female is always relegated to the bottom of the social order. And a whore is the lowest of low women. Basement bottom.

If Chief Davis and the district attorney decide they need a scapegoat for the Lavender House fire, I'm the ready-made sacrificial lamb. And if the mysterious woman from back east is who I think she is, I might as well whet the blade and slit my own throat. Doesn't matter that I'm dressed in a soot-stained shimmy and a discarded man's shirt or that my hair is now back to its natural straw-yellow, she'll…

The heavy door at the end of the hall makes its clunking sound as the bolt is turned back. In the over-crowded cells down the row, men start yelling, banging on the bars. Some calling, "Let me outta here!" "You got the wrong man!" and "I didn't do nothing!"

When he steps through, Chief Davis ignores them. Stops at my cell, and with a long key, unlocks it. "You've got a visitor," is his only greeting.

I give him a wary inspection, climb to my feet and step wide of the modesty screen that hides the thunder mug. Yes, yes, it's just a bucket. I wince as my bare feet hit the cold floor. I can tell you for a fact, that caked black patina isn't the original color of the concrete. I pull the oversized man's shirt tight around my shimmy and step out. The males down the line let loose with howls, wolf whistles, and jeers.

Playing to character, I toss my hair, swish my hips, and call back, "Don't you wish, boys? Save your dollars. In another century or two, you might make enough for a toss in my hay!"

It's like rattling their cages with a stick. They go nuts.

I catch the faintest twitch of Chief Davis's lips as if he's barely hiding a smile. I'm led into what serves as the police and sheriff's offices.

If I'm saucy enough, maybe I can still get away with playing the simple country tart. All I really have to do is convince Chief Davis that anything my woman visitor tells him is insane.

Twillacker? Where are you?

The thought crosses my mind that the worthless sack of shit might have taken the dough and skipped. Maybe learned from Benny's example and lit out for safer climates. Like Cuba or Brazil. That's the problem with boom towns like Casper. Doesn't matter that there's a large pool of immoral riffraff to choose from, you just can't buy reliable help.

I step into the chief's office, my heart beginning to pound. My mouth has gone dry. I see her, sitting, back to me, an expensive tailored wool coat on the chair back. She's in a classy Burberry. Must have cost her close to five hundred dollars, and the cloche hat is a very fine felt.

This is it. Doesn't matter what the rest of me looks like, she'll know my...

The woman rises from the oak office chair. Turns. And to my amazement, it's *not* her. Instead of the tightly coiffed white hair and dowager build, this much taller woman is young, thin. I have no clue who she is. Even as relief floods through me, I meet those hard green eyes. Measure them. I am immediately on guard, drop my gaze. Whoever this woman is, she's a hunter. Every bit as dangerous as any tiger in the jungle.

Chief Davis points me to a seat opposite the woman's as he steps behind his desk and settles into his squeaky office chair. It's a big pale-yellow oak thing set on rollers with curved arms; he leans back to the sound of tortured springs.

I give the woman a sidelong and submissive look, figuring it's best to stick to the original plan. Never make eye contact. Keep the mousy droop to my shoulders.

Then, to my surprise, she slips a photograph from her purse. A slight frown lines her brow as she studies it, and then me. From this angle, I can't see the picture, but I can imagine. After an uncomfortable thirty seconds, she replaces the photo and leans forward.

"Dolly Louise James?" the woman asks, well-modulated voice neutral.

"Ma'am," I reply, massaging my left wrist with my right hand. I tap my bare foot on the worn wooden floor. She's expecting a bundle of nerves.

"I'm Eleanor Clark. Call me Ellie." She shifts. "What day did you arrive in Casper?"

I purse my lips, twist a little harder on my left wrist. "Um, I think it was August...the twenty-eighth. That man Halloran drove me in. Shouldn't have let him drive me. He was...um, not a nice man."

"What kind of automobile did he drive?" Chief Davis asks.

"Oldsmobile," I tell him. "He was very proud of that auto. Said he bought it in San Francisco and that it would do sixty. He cussed every time we hit a bump." I cannily add, "There's a lot of bad road on the Lincoln Highway. Especially in Nevada."

I keep my eyes lowered, fidgeting.

In an almost conspiratorial voice, the woman tells me, "The world is full of not-nice men. What about the one who died up in Eudora's room? Did he cause trouble? Make anyone upset that morning?"

I frown. "Eudora?"

"The woman who wore the chain with the Harvard ring." Ellie leans forward, and I can feel those green eyes as if they're trying to drill right through my skull and into my head.

"You mean Dorrie? Her real name was Eudora?"

"The deed lists her as Dorrie Hamilton," Chief Davis

offers from the side. "Did you ever hear her called anything else?"

I briefly flick my eyes to Chief Davis. "Um, it's a parlor house. I heard her called a lot of things. Probably shouldn't repeat them in front of the lady here."

Davis barely hides the smile again.

"Did Dorrie ever mention Baltimore? Maybe a horse farm? Or perhaps how she got that ring?"

"No, ma'am." I go back to massaging my left wrist and tapping my foot, eyes on the floor. "She didn't talk to us like that. For her, it was all business, and she knew how to run a fancy house. That's why she recruited me. One of the Johnny's bragged to her about what a good fu…"

I clear my throat. "Um, I mean, we'd talk the business. What worked, how to better service the men, how to skim more money from the tricks, things to look out for with certain of the clients. You know, quirks and things that some men have."

From the corner of my eye, I see that Ellie is indeed well aware. I wonder. Who is she? Why is she here? Just from his posture, I can sense that Chief Davis is smitten.

"Did Dorrie ever mention anyone named Bryce Bourke, or how she got his ring?" Ellie doubles down.

"No, ma'am. Like I said, Dorrie was a real private woman. She didn't talk none about her personal affairs."

"Did she have regulars?" Chief Davis asks.

"Yes, sir. Reckon I'd best not mention names, reputations being what they are in this town. At Lavender House we made the distinction between Johnnies, tricks, and, um, 'clients.' Dorrie just entertained the clients."

"Was the Pinkerton a client?" Ellie asks.

I take a deep breath. "I think so. He spent the night in Dorrie's room. Arrived about six the night before the fire. Asked specifically for the madam and was led up the stairs by Hallie. Never saw the Pinkerton, Dorrie, or Hallie again. Not that I'd notice. It was a busy night."

"How did the fire start?" Ellie asks.

"They say gasoline. And, no, I don't know who or how." I keep my eyes fixed on the floor. "If I was to guess? I'd lay it to Mary Lou. If there was a girl there fixing to off herself, it would be her. Just desperate, you know? Always sad and never a sunny word. I know that Dorrie was going to send her down the road. Girl like that, having her around's sort like throwing a cold wet blanket on a room full of joy."

Chief Davis is giving Eleanor one of those evaluative cop glances. Eleanor is watching me through thinned eyes. I slump a little more in the chair and twist at my wrist.

"Miss James, something doesn't make sense. Why did Dorrie come to Casper? She had money. From Baltimore, she could have booked passage on a liner to Europe, taken a train to New York, San Francisco, or Chicago, and lived quite well. What's in this..." She catches herself. "Why Casper?"

I play a hunch, and for the first time, look at her with wide blinking eyes. "Why, for the money." I sound surprised. "Don't you understand? These men...Dorrie's clients, are making millions. It's the West, with all that being western means. And the oilmen are the new kingpins. The new Wild Bill Hickoks and Buffalo Bills who have to strut their manliness with money instead of six guns. And what better way to prove your pecker's the hardest in the pack than by buying your visiting associates a night at the city's fanciest parlor house while you, being the cock rooster, stick it in the madam?"

I pause, sound wistful. "And Dorrie was downright beautiful to boot."

That is as reasonable as I can make it. Chief Davis,

being a Western man himself, has bought it. I'm not so sure about Eleanor. There's something about her that I don't understand, and that scares me.

"Remind me again about your association with Dorrie," she says. "You said that she heard of you through a client?"

"Got a wire at the house I was working at in Carson City. Offered to pay my travel expenses and double my take if I'd relocate to the Lavender House."

Eleanor's eyebrow lifts the slightest bit. I wonder what that means.

She asks, "Do you still have that telegram?"

"Reckon I don't," I tell her truthfully. "Would you want something like that lying around where anyone could read it while you considered another job offer?" Then I decide to take a chance. "Pardon my asking, but why are you here? You a friend of Dorrie's? Come to look after her estate? Surely there'd be insurance and the like to see to."

Then Eleanor takes me by surprise as she smiles, the knowing eyebrow lifting. "Actually, Miss James, like you, I'm here for the money."

For the first time, a cold feeling corkscrews down my backbone.

Twillacker? Where the hell are you?

———

Chief Harney walked into the Henning Hotel's lobby and nodded in response to greetings. At the door to the restaurant, he removed his hat and used a hand to sweep his brown hair back. Looking out over the room, he was suddenly conscious of his dress. Brown duck pants, his duty belt, and checkered flannel shirt under his police coat with its badge, were in contrast to the men in dark suits, ties, and white boiled shirts, the women's fine silk and colorful satin dresses, not to mention the sparkling diamonds, pearls, and lush furs. This was Casper's stunning wealth on display.

"Chief," Huck, the maître d, greeted. "You here for business or pleasure?"

"Uh, there's a woman, Eleanor Clark. I was supposed to meet her here for…oh, there she is. In the back."

"Ah, pleasure then. She's quite a looker. This way." Huck threaded through the elegantly appointed tables with their white cloths, sparkling porcelain, and polished silverware. Again, it was a gauntlet of greetings, waves, and nods. These were, after all, Casper's movers and shakers. The men, and their ladies, who powered the oil boom. And, of course, the parasites who, like ticks and mosquitoes, feasted on it.

Harney was sure that Eleanor had picked the location for the table. Rear of the room, in the corner. She sat where she could watch everything, her back to the wall. As he seated himself, she cradled a cup of coffee, those striking green eyes evaluative.

Harney ordered his own cup of coffee, shoving his hat under the seat and unfolding his napkin.

"Find your car thieves?" she asked.

"Nope. Sorry to be called away like that, but we had a tip. Casper, can you imagine? They're stealing expensive cars like Pierce Arrows, Packards, and Cadillacs in New York, and driving them here, of all places. By the time we got to that warehouse, it was empty. But you could see the tire tracks in the dirt floor. And they left a bunch of parts they didn't have time to haul away."

"What do they do with the cars?"

"Refinish them and drive them on to Los Angeles and San Francisco." He fought the urge to tuck his napkin under his chin. Left it self-consciously in his lap. "It's a whole new class of crime. You can't trace an automobile. How would a buyer in Los Angeles know about a car stolen in Manhattan?"

He switched topics. "So, what occupied you this afternoon?"

Her lips twitched, that little tell he'd come to associate with amusement. "I walked back to the burned brothel. I wanted to see it through Dolly James' eyes. As I did, I read her testimony. Said she was downstairs early, having been awakened by what she termed 'female complaint.' Said she was in the kitchen starting breakfast."

"I remember."

Eleanor braced her elbows on the table, rocking the china coffee cup so the drink swirled. She drank it black. "She testified that her 'complaint' had her in the bathroom. Maybe fifteen minutes. Said she'd been on the toilet when someone cried 'Fire.' That by the time she could extricate herself, the stairway was encased in flame.

"I assume that the toilet in question is the cracked and blackened porcelain piece just to the left of what would have been the downstairs parlor."

Harney leaned back as a waiter placed his cup of coffee along with sugar and cream.

"Do I dare order the salmon?" Eleanor asked, "Or is the steak the way to go?"

"Steak," he told her, and they placed their orders.

Leaning forward, he explained, "Lavender House was the only brothel in Casper with running water. It was built where it was because that was at the terminus of the new water and sewer line that Henning was laying. High class, remember? You don't want the president of Standard Oil to inconvenience himself by walking out back to a four-hole jakes."

"If we buy that Dolly is on the pot, who does that leave us as the potential arsonist?"

Harney rocked his jaw, scratched at his chin, and realized that on top of the way he was dressed, he desperately needed a shave. God, she must think him to be a total hick. Swallowing his embarrassment, he said, "That's why I held her. But if she set that fire, she burned up everything she owned. She came out of that fire barefoot. Doesn't make sense. The woman doesn't come across as the stupid type."

Eleanor took a deep breath and in a gulp, finished off her coffee. "So, that leaves us back at the beginning. Who set the fire?"

Harney's cup made tinking noises as he stirred his coffee. "You said that the family hired the Pinkertons to investigate Eudora. That they did so because there were questions about the burned woman's body found beside Bryce Bourke's at the country estate. That the identification was initially made because of the woman's wedding ring. Now, we have a second woman's body being identified because she has another of Bryce's rings? But what I want to know, is why were the Pinkertons brought in originally?"

"The missing cash," Eleanor told him. "The big safe out at the mansion house on the estate survived the fire. When it was opened, the cash was gone. As was jewelry. Diamonds. Necklaces, and Bryce's Harvard ring. The same ring found around Dorrie's neck. Though why she'd keep it remains a mystery."

"Trophy?" Harney shrugged, sipped his coffee. "Maybe she actually cared for the fellow."

Eleanor's expression pinched. "The family—that's Bryce's brother Sanford, his sister Louise, and their children—hired the Pinkertons to look into Eudora's background. I mean, she literally came out of nowhere, swept Bryce off his feet, and married him in a whirlwind romance. A woman without a history. That, along with the missing money, raised the red flags. And now, evidence points to a whorehouse in Wyoming?"

He cocked his head. "Can I ask you something?"

"Of course." Her green eyes were fixed on his.

"What does your husband make of you running around the country, let alone your consorting in jails, poking around burned brothels, and interrogating soiled doves like Dolly James? Seems remarkably open-minded, even in this day and age."

She looked down at the gold ring on her finger. "He's dead. Killed at Belleau Wood. He was a spy, you see. The Germans caught him behind their lines with a radio. At the time, he was broadcasting details of how they were deploying to attack. According to the reports I found in Berlin, he was bayonetted in the back. Never had a chance."

"So you decided to go into detective work?"

The look she gave him was dry, slightly mocking. "Chief, I was involved in 'detective' work, as you call it, when I first met David. We were both 'in the business.' I spent the Great War hunting German and Italian spies. And, you must understand, not all spies are men. Sometimes it takes a woman to catch a woman. Let's say I was very good at it."

"Are spies that much different than criminals?"

"Spies are usually much smarter." She stared thoughtfully at the ceiling. "But not this time. It's a feeling I have."

Harney allowed himself the pleasure of watching her, admiring the lines of her face, that perfect long neck. Something had changed down inside him when she admitted her husband was dead. What would it be like to share time with a woman like this one? To be able to gaze over the table into those competent green eyes on a daily basis?

He hated to break the spell, but said, "We have another option, you know. You said the family hired the Pinkertons, but you were hired by Bryce's mother, Willimena. She obviously was uncomfortable about the situation. Let us assume that Dorrie is Eudora. That the Pinkerton, Agent Lamont, did indeed track her down. What if it's someone from the family? Someone who follows Lamont upstairs to Dorrie's room? Someone who takes revenge on Dorrie, removing Lamont and Hallie as witnesses? Perhaps tortures Dorrie into disclosing where the remaining money is, and burns the place on the way out?"

Eleanor considered. Still thinking as the food was placed, she began cutting up her steak.

Taking a bite, she shook her head. "Not their style. We're talking old East Coast money. They're more the type to have her arrested, brought back to Baltimore, and very publicly tried and executed. The family wouldn't settle for anything less than a public vendetta with all the attendant drama."

Harney turned his attention to the steak, trying to concentrate on cutting and chewing so that he didn't embarrass himself by staring moon-eyed at the striking woman across from him. She looked so poised, every movement spare, precise, right down to the small cuts of meat and the way she used her fork. A perfect example of a high-bred lady in the old sense of the term.

She glanced up, caught his worshipful gaze.

"You're a lot like him, you know? My David? You have that look about you, Chief. Like you've seen the worst of men, been shot at, and gutted your way through. You were in the war, weren't you?"

"Third Infantry, Fourth Regiment. Started at Château Thierry. And they never let us rest until the armistice. Some things...I guess they change a man."

Her gaze went vacant. "They do. That's what Willimena thinks made Bryce Bourke such an easy mark. She said he was fragile when he came back. That he was tortured by the nightmares. That he'd awaken in the night, sweating, crying. Sometimes, she said, he was back in the trenches, talking to men who'd died on the wire, or been blown apart. Easy prey for a woman who..."

"What?"

Eleanor nodded. "I was thinking about how easy it would be. A psychologically vulnerable vet. She snapped him right up. Played to his weakness, his need for excitement, and to prove he was alive. You hit the nail on the head, Chief: Prey. The reason she came to Casper. She's *hunting*."

"But hunting whom? Sure, we've got our share of vets. Most of eastern Wyoming is being settled by vets who've been granted stock-raising homestead entries, but—"

"Miss James told us," Eleanor leaned forward, and Harney would have offered his foot to be cut off just to enjoy that steely and victorious look that filled her green eyes. Call it rapturous. "Like she said, it's all about the money. Millions of dollars. Casper is filled with ambitious men, most of whom travel here alone. Some of whom might be looking for an exciting young and very beautiful woman willing to engage in their fantasies. A woman who might not be above using blackmail or guilt. The kind who might drug or intoxicate a man into marriage. And where better to pick a victim than in Lavender House?"

"A brothel?"

"Maybe it was more involved than just snagging a client." She arched a slim eyebrow. "Maybe she just uses the first man to get her introduction into the society, plays the field, and snags a second or third down the road.

Maybe she doesn't even snare her victim in Casper, but does so in Houston or Anadarko? Someplace that's never heard of the Lavender House."

"That's an awfully long game to play."

She raised an eyebrow. "How long would you be willing to play for a crack at a million dollars, Harney?"

Despite her fancy fifth-floor suite, Eleanor didn't sleep well. When she'd close her eyes, she could see the burned ruins of Lavender House. That curious way Dolly James kept rubbing her left wrist. How the woman refused to meet her eyes.

She's a whore. Women like that don't expect respect from decent women.

Eleanor tossed and turned, thinking. She, herself, had come within a hair's breadth of using her body to gain a man's confidence. What if it had come down to that?

"Yes," she admitted, sitting up in the bed. The stakes in the case would have merited such a decision. Even David would have agreed, for in the end she'd broken the spy ring. Hundreds of American, French, and British soldiers were alive as a result. What was a woman's chastity worth in comparison?

The image came back of Dolly rubbing her wrist. Then the thought of the ring, still suspended by its chain from the burned Dorrie's neck. Dorrie, Eudora, Dolly?

Eleanor had compared the photo of Eudora sitting in the chair. Pert, perfectly postured and dressed, black hair neat as compared to the unwashed straw-blonde woman in a sooty shimmy and oversized man's shirt who slouched and bent her head.

Eleanor flicked on the light and retrieved her purse. She studied the photo again and then reached for her watch, flipped the cover open. Damn. It was barely three o'clock.

But she'd wait.

Chief Davis had said that due to the nature of the case, Lew Gay, the coroner, still had the bodies on ice.

Interesting man, that Chief Davis. Subtle, strong, and self-possessed. He had that look so familiar with veterans home from the Great War. Like he'd seen into Hell and in doing so, had wounded something in his soul. But unlike so many, he had not let that wounding destroy him.

Yes, an interesting man.

———

The jangling bell on the telephone brought Harney upright in bed, his heart racing. He rubbed his face, winced, and pulled back the covers. Walking over, he picked up the earpiece and leaned close to the mouth tube. "Harney, here."

"Sorry for the hour, Chief." Eleanor's voice sounded tinny. *"I've just got off the phone with Lew Gay. He's meeting me in an hour to look at the bodies. Says that given the pittance the city is paying him to keep them on ice, they're going in the ground. Well, all but the Pinkerton's body. The Pinks have paid to have him sent back east."*

"Right. See you there."

He hung up. Worked his tongue around his fuzzy-feeling mouth and rubbed his eyes. Were it anyone but Eleanor, he'd...okay, if it were a murder, or a...hell, didn't matter. He was the chief of police. And he'd never shirked a duty in his life.

Fumbling on the wall, he found the switch, pressing the button that turned on the lights.

———

Eleanor was waiting outside the coroner's when Chief Davis drove up in his Cadillac, the engine purring. She stood by the door to Dr. Gay's office, her coat pulled tightly against the October morning chill. Casper, she thought, was at its best just before dawn. The air was still, cool, with a bite. And in the distance, she could hear roosters crowing.

The city was silent, missing the daytime rattle and banging of hammers, the churning of engines, as every-where the eye roamed, another building was going up. Come daylight, the place swarmed like an anthill.

Harney stepped out, his hat pulled down tight; she could see the stubble on his jaw was darker. She approved. Harney Davis paid more attention to doing the job than looking presentable.

"Morning," he called, stepping over.

As he did, the lights came on inside, and they could hear the lock pulled back before Gay opened the door. Silhouetted in the light, Gay was an older man, an apron over his suit.

"My apologies for the hour," Eleanor told him, offering a gloved hand. "I'm Detective Eleanor Clark. I really appreciate your kind consideration."

She could see Harney grinning as Gay bowed, taking her hand. "Oh, odd hours come with the job Mrs. Clark." He turned, leading the way through his office and into the back. "The Pinkerton, Mr. Lamont, goes out on tonight's train, so I have to have him prepared anyway. I brought the three you asked about from the cold house."

In the back, the rather gruesome sets of remains were laid out on the tables. Blackened, grotesque, each might have been a horror-monger's caricature of a human being. The eyes were desiccated, lips pulled back and powdered, scalps cracked and tight across skulls.

Eleanor stepped over to the first woman's body,

noting remains of large breasts. "This is the woman who wore the chain with Bryce Bourke's ring?"

"Yes, ma'am," Gay told her, stepping back. "You can see the imprint on her chest and the charring where it lay at between her breasts. I took it off myself before handing it over to the chief."

Eleanor pulled her photo, trying to find any hint of resemblance between Eudora's image and the blackened ruin on the table. Then, stepping over, she saw nothing that might link the second woman's remains to the photo. "What is this grease covering the woman?" Eleanor asked.

Gay shifted uncomfortably. "She was, shall we say, rather corpulent, Mrs. Clark. The body's adipose tissue, well, when heated, it runs. Like when you put a well-marbled steak on the—"

Eleanor raised her hand. "I understand." Then, "They look better than I thought they would."

"Fire department got there in excellent time," Harney told her. "They pumped enough water on the flames to keep the bodies from total cremation."

Turning back to the first woman, Eleanor leaned forward, staring at the ruined face from her new angle. Again, she compared it with her photograph. "The damage is too extensive for a solid identification. Something about the breasts and mouth might be wrong. But it could be the photo. I can't be sure this is Eudora."

———

Harney sat in his office, his feet up on his desk as he nursed a cup of coffee. He'd always been a cream and sugar kind of fellow, but something about Eleanor drinking hers black and strong, encouraged him to do the same. Hell of a woman, that Eleanor. That image of her in the coroner's office just stuck. He'd remember that cool expression, her complete concentration as she studied those bodies. How could a man help but admire her strength of character, and…

The phone rang.

Harney resettled himself and pressed the speaker to his ear. "Harney here."

"It's Lew. Listen. I had to prepare that Pinkerton for shipment. Found something under his skin just below his right shoulder blade. When I cut it out, it's a 380 auto slug. And I'd say he was shot through the body and it lodged under the skin. The front's too burned to really determine an entry wound, but I want to cut him open and see if I can trace the path of the bullet."

"Do it."

Harney sat back again, took another sip of his coffee. Eleanor had excused herself to have breakfast, write up her report, and wire it off to Willimena Bourke. She said she'd drop by when she'd finished.

A bullet in Pinkerton Agent Lamont? Now, there was a new twist.

Eleanor arrived as he finished his second cup of coffee. She more or less blew into the room like a self-contained tornado, announcing, "Willimena got the ring. She confirms that it was Bryce's."

He swung to his feet, opening his drawer and pulling out the key ring. "Lew just found a bullet in Lamont's body. So, given our new understanding, I think it's time I brought the lovely Miss James in for another palaver."

Making his way to the jail hallway, he opened the door and was greeted by the usual hoots, curses, and pleas. Dolly James sat on her bunk, legs pulled up, back to the wall. She fixed those knowing eyes on his, taking a deep breath. "What now?"

"New facts in the case. And, suddenly, you're a most requested witness."

He led her out, listened to the jeers from the men, and wished, like in real big cities, that the jail had a women's wing.

Back in the office, Harney gestured to Dolly's previous seat and settled into his squeaky desk chair. Dolly dropped limply onto the oak, head down, twisting at her left wrist. She might have been a little girl who'd been caught stealing sugar cookies.

"We need the answers to some questions," Harney announced. "Turns out the Pinkerton has a bullet hole in him. You know anything about that?"

"No, sir. I never saw him after Hallie took him upstairs. And, it was, um, a bit raucous that night. Some of the Johnnies were celebrating a gusher. Said they were looking for a different kind of wet hole to…" She glanced worriedly at Eleanor. "Um, it was pretty loud. None of us heard any shooting."

Eleanor leaned forward, elbows on her thighs, keen anticipation in her eyes. A crouching lion might have looked like that. "I think you know a lot more than you're telling us, Dolly. Come on, girls in a house like that…"

The thunderous knock at the door was accompanied by one of the patrol officers outside yelling, "The chief's in the middle of an interrogation! You can't *go in there!*"

The door burst open, Ted Twillacker, charging in. He wore a gray suit, rather more flashy than his usual ten-years-out-of-date, moth-eaten and shiny-elbowed attire. His florid face beamed in triumph as he waved a sheet of paper like a regimental guidon.

His eyes swept the room, fixed on Dolly James, and his smile exposed yellow teeth. "I see I'm just in time!"

Handing the paper to Harney, he stuck his thumbs into his vest, proclaiming, "I have here a writ, signed by the governor, granting Miss Dolly Louise James full pardon for any activities she might have undertaken, been part of, or under coercion to perform while in the employ of the Lavender House. Further, she is to be released into my custody at this time and allowed to freely pursue her normal endeavors without hindrance or harassment."

Harney swallowed hard, taking the paper. He skimmed the legalese, read the wherebys, and fixed on the governor's familiar signature. Then he leaned back, sighed, and flipped the paper onto the desk.

Eleanor was watching silently, her expression mask-like, her back rigid.

Dolly James broke into a knowing smile that thinned her lips, her eyes having taken on a hard satisfaction.

"Well?" Twillacker thundered. "How about it?"

Harney licked his lips, forced himself to stand, and woodenly said, "Miss James, you are free to go."

———

As we hurry down the stairs, my bare feet slap the cold tiles. "About goddamn time," I muttered just loud enough for Twillacker to hear.

"You got no idea, babe," he taunts from the corner of his mouth. "I had to put the squeeze on two of the state senators and a couple of the big wheels on the governor's staff. The money was fine, but they'd have never flipped but for your threat to rat them out for their butt-screwing and dick sucking at the Lavender House."

He gives a big sigh. "Glad you could hold out 'til I got back."

"Barely. Fortunately, I'm a member of the world's oldest profession." I pause. "Storyteller! And I spun 'em a whopper."

"Yeah, well good for you. Got your trunk out of storage. It's in the back of the Olds," Twillacker tells me as he steps out on the sidewalk and raises his hand to beckon.

I watch the blue Oldsmobile take off from the curb, putter its way up, and stop. I can see that my trunk is indeed in the back, a rope tying the lid tight to the bumper. It's still locked, so the remaining cash from Maryland is safe. Opening the door, Twillacker climbs in back. I slip into the passenger seat. Looking back, I say, "Oh, and Ted, if you ever call me 'Babe' again, I'll put a bullet through your heart."

As Halloran pulls away from the curb, I stretch over just far enough to kiss him on the cheek, then flop back into the seat. "Now, let's get the hell out of here."

———

Eleanor stared woodenly at the photo in her hands as Twillacker's heavy steps faded beyond the door. "In the photo, Eudora's rubbing her left wrist. I've seen that somewhere…"

"Well, hell." Harney's frustrated gaze fixed on his empty coffee cup.

Then came the sound of running steps, Lew Gay burst in the door. "That woman? The one you think was Dorrie? Those buck teeth…they should be heat-cracked, almost have a blued tone. So, I took my forceps, grasped an incisor. Porcelain! Whole thing came free. It was a bridge. She'd had extensive dental work."

Eleanor straightened. "I know for a fact that Eudora Bourke didn't have dentures,"

Gay cried, "But one of Dorrie's girls, Edith McShane, did. I just talked to Doc Arthur. He not only knows the dental work, but it's his."

"And it's no doubt that the other woman is Hallie."

Harney shot to his feet. "So the only body missing from Lavender House is Dorrie's."

"And we only had Dolly James' word that she'd come in from Nevada." Eleanor, too, was on her feet. "Eudora, Dorrie, Dolly? One and the same?"

Harney was jamming his hat down tight as he headed for the door. "She's barefoot! In a shimmy. And Twillacker doesn't own an auto. We've got her!"

Like a herd of impatient horses, they thundered down the stairs, across the lobby, and pushed through the doors. Looking up and down the street, the only thing to be seen were trailers of dust driven by the wind.

———

"Oklahoma, boys," I tell them as Casper disappears in the dust welling behind the Olds. "We'll have to up our game, play to a higher class, but there's millionaires by the dozens. And one or two of them are bound to be looking for love."

WOLF BAIT

KATHLEEN O'NEAL GEAR

Good fiction is dangerous. It opens those forbidden doors in the mind that we would prefer to leave closed. What happens when those doors open? When the neural pathways of the brain are triggered and past and present mix? Flashback melds with reality. Perhaps the theoretical physicists are right, and time is meaningless. The question is posed: Does the brain ever really heal itself? Or is the wounded soul condemned to endless loops? Kathleen's story is timeless. Two and half millennia ago, "Wolf Bait" might have been penned by one of the great Greek tragedians. (WMG)

A soldier once told me that seeing every moment against the horizon of death was the only way he could feel fully alive. He suspected that's why he fought the same battles over and over in his nightmares...that and the fact that he couldn't forgive himself. (KOG)

David dropped the fresh elk hide in the back of the wagon, braced his elbows on the box, and let his gaze drift over the Big Horn Mountains. The highest peaks above the tree line rose like snow-capped granite giants against an impossibly blue sky. Lower on the slopes, golden eagles circled, flapping their sunlit wings as they rode the air currents. This time of late afternoon the world started to cool down, and the long, enormous shadows cast by the mountains stretched out like dark hands reaching across the plains, grasping for the last rays of golden light.

His chest expanded with relief. He'd brought his family here less than a year ago. It was a wild, hard land, no doubt about it, but as he breathed in the scent of newborn grass and spring's first wildflowers, he thanked God that he'd lived long enough to see this vast country.

"Big brother, you going to stand there gawking at eagles or come help me?"

David turned and smiled at Charlie where he stood knee-deep in the grass, straddling the dead elk while he carefully severed the muscles in the hindquarter. Sweat soaked Charlie's blond hair and dripped from his pointy nose, but his blue eyes danced. As boys, they'd always been mistaken for twins, though David was two years older, forty-five next month, and gray had pretty much taken over his blond hair.

Before he started back to help Charlie finish quartering the elk, he stopped to gently pet the old Sharps rifle that leaned against the box. The stock was scratched and pitted in a dozen places, but the barrel was free of rust and oiled to a shine. Softly, he said, "You're glad to be here, too, aren't you, old friend?"

The rifle seemed to warm beneath his calloused fingers. He patted it and exhaled hard. By the time he neared his brother, he noticed Charlie's gaze shift and saw his mouth go tight. Charlie brusquely tossed his knife on the elk carcass and stood up to stretch his back muscles.

David followed his brother's glare and saw Suzanne, David's young wife, pull the battered old Army canteen off the wagon and walk away with it. Charlie seemed to be focused on the long black braid swaying against the back of her yellow dress.

"Where's she headed?" Charlie asked. "I could use a drink myself. We're the ones been working all day. All she's done is pace through the grass with her arms folded."

"Probably just wants to sit in the shade of the trees. Give her some time."

"That's the last of the water, Davy."

"She's not going to drink it all."

"You mean like she did yesterday?"

David gave him an unpleasant look. "She wasn't born to this life, Charlie."

"Don't have to tell me that twice, but you'd think after eleven months on the ranch..." Charlie's brows pinched over his nose. He closed his mouth, picked up his knife and went back to work, slicing through the muscles of the elk's hind leg, neatly severing the quarter from the body. "We ain't making it home tonight. You know that?"

David looked up at the clear blue sky. "Not a single cloud up there, little brother."

"Not yet, but there will be. You can smell it on the wind same as I can. It's a good three hours back to the ranch. You cogitate on the possibility of camping here tonight. We could hang the elk in a tree and head home in the morning. I know Suzanne ain't going to like that, but—"

"She'll be awright."

David's gaze moved across the Big Horns, noting where their two horses grazed in the distance, then climbed higher to a long grassy valley that ran up into the mountains. It was a mosaic of yellow and purple wildflowers. The winter of '86-87 had been brutal. Thousands of cattle had starved to death in the deep drifts, but folks said they'd never seen a crop of spring grass like this. The few cattle they had left ought to flourish.

"We'll make camp at the top of that pretty meadow ringed by pines. We can drag up some deadfall and make a big fire. I think Suzanne will be warm enough."

"Do you? I figure she's going to start complaining at the sight of the first flakes, and it ain't going to end until—"

"I said she'd be awright," David cut him off.

Charlie took a deep breath, said, "Yep," and focused on the elk.

David watched his wife. She was slender and frail, and seventeen years old. Her father was a prominent lawyer in Boston. No matter how hard David tried, he'd never be able to give her the kind of foofaraw she'd grown up with, and he knew she missed it.

"Just prepare yourself," Charlie said without taking his eyes off the elk. "You and me'll be warm enough, but that Sunday soldier has no idea what real cold feels like."

David's lungs filled with cool air, and he slowly exhaled a breath. "Sunday soldier" was an insult for a man of little merit. "She ain't a soldier, Charlie. Neither am I. Nor you, for that matter."

Charlie's mouth puckered, probably realizing he

should have stopped his tirade five minutes ago. "You're right."

Suzanne slumped down beneath a newly leafed-out cottonwood tree and took a long drink of water from the canteen. Her shoulders were hunched forward. She wasn't crying, was she?

He'd been hoping, when he got enough money put aside, to buy glass windows for their cabin, but the glassworks in Paola, Kansas, had closed its doors last year. When he'd told Suzanne, she'd stayed in bed for three days. Said she just couldn't stand their tiny dark cabin a day longer.

Charlie wiped his knife blade on his blue pants and changed the subject. "You 'member the stories ole halfwit Jonas used to tell about the Big Sandy River freezing over in Kentucky in '63? He said icicles the length of his arm decorated the trees that December. You believe that?"

"'Course. That's Kentucky."

Charlie grinned. "I swear my teeth started chattering in April of '62 and didn't stop..."

Without warning, David's body went rigid, and he couldn't breathe. It was like a punch to the gut. *Dead everywhere.*

When his fists clenched and started shaking, Charlie froze. "Oh, Davy, sorry. God, I'm an idiot. Forgot what day it was. Wasn't thinking."

"Don't—fret it."

From that locked door inside him, faces rushed up until all he saw were eyes pleading with him. Then they popped like soap bubbles and more took their places. *Cap'n, I'm over here!*

Squeezing his eyes closed, he struggled to blank his mind. Breathe. Finally, he blinked. "Guess I better go check on Suzanne."

"You go on," Charlie said apologetically. "I'll get the

elk meat in the wagon, fetch the horses, and haul the quarters up to hang 'em."

"I'm coming right back to help you. Won't be long."

"I'll be here."

David walked to the wagon, grabbed his Sharps, and trudged through the fragrant grass. The whole world smelled green and lush. High over his head a flock of sandhill cranes curved in a wide arc, sailing down to the river in the distance. Their melodic calls were the stuff of dreams, too beautiful to be real.

When Suzanne saw him coming, she quickly wiped her eyes on her sleeve. "Didn't mean to be gone so long," she called.

David gave her a smile and sank down on the grass beside her, placing his Sharps within easy reach. The canteen was almost buried in the grass between them. He dug it out and started to lift it for a drink but could already tell it was empty. Absently, he dropped it on the grass and propped his elbows on his drawn-up knees.

"You awright?"

She toyed with the long braid that draped her right shoulder. "Fine. I was just watching that wolf out there."

"Where?"

She pointed. "Right there."

He nodded. "I see him." The big animal sat almost invisible in the tall grass about one hundred yards away. "Is there only one?"

"That's all I've seen. What do you think he's doing just sitting there on his haunches?"

David's eyes tightened. He could feel the wolf watching him. "Likely waiting for us to leave so he can get at the gut pile. But he could be a scout for the pack. We'll need to keep our eyes peeled."

Slipping his arm over her narrow shoulders, he pulled her close and kissed her dark head. "And that's why you can't just wander off like this. There could be a big pack hidden in the trees right behind you, and you wouldn't know it 'til they pounced."

She gazed up at him with wet eyes. "David?"

"Yes, ma'am?"

"I want to go home." Silent sobs moved her chest.

"I know you do."

Suzanne buried her face against his shoulder and cried. He stroked her hair. Didn't know what to say. After all these months, he'd run out of words. Nothing seemed to help.

"A week before we left," she wept, "the Bijou Theater installed electric lights. The whole city of Boston is probably lit up now."

"I'm sure it is."

She lifted her head and gave him a hopeful look. "Can you imagine how dazzling that is? Every hill and valley must glitter like an overturned jewel box."

He hugged her. "You're getting pretty good at rendering elk and deer fat to make lamp oil. I like coming home and seeing that soft glow in the windows."

Her eyes were as green as the cottonwood leaves behind her. "But you say my biscuits taste like the hardtack you ate in the war."

"Well"—he bowed his head and looked at his Sharps —"I shouldn't have said that. You'll get the hang of it."

She licked her chapped lips before rushing to ask, "Do you know what we'd be doing right now if we were in Boston?"

"I got no idea."

Her pretty face took on that faraway look of longing. "We'd be dressing for dinner. I'd wear my green watered silk gown and white gloves. The servants would have set the table with the best cut crystal. In the electric lights,

158

each goblet would be a sight to see, shimmering like a star."

The lines around his eyes tightened, recalling how much he'd hated Boston. At the end, he'd felt like he was drowning and there was no one to throw him a rope. "Do you ever think you'll be happy here with me?"

Suzanne grimaced and looked away. "I just don't see how, David. There's nothing here."

As she said it, an eagle screamed and swooped low over the pines on the mountainside, which must have spooked the herd of white-tailed deer that had been hiding in the forest. Six does and two big bucks crashed through the trees and bounded off across the plains with their tails flagging. His heart swelled at the sight. *Nothing here.*

Suzanne folded her arms tightly and seemed to be monitoring the clouds that had just edged over the mountain peaks. Blue-black and coming fast, a gray haze of snow billowed beneath them. "Sorry I upset you," she said. "Let's talk about it later. It's going to be dark soon. We should head home."

When she shoved to her feet to leave, David grabbed her hand. "Me and Charlie were discussing this, and we think it's best to spend the night here. Maybe make camp in that pretty meadow up the slope and wait out the storm." He gestured to indicate the wildflower-strewn meadow. "If the snow isn't too deep, we can head home tomorrow morning first thing."

Suzanne turned to examine the meadow. "You and Charlie? Did you think I might have a different idea? I want to go home."

"I'm sure you do, but it's not smart, Suz." He released her hand and picked up his Sharps. As he rose to his feet, he said, "If we get caught in a blizzard out on the open plains, we'll be in bad trouble. It's best to hole up here in the trees where we've got wood for fire and a bit of shelter."

Her mouth pressed into a tight white line. "David, I know you and Charlie were in the war together, but on occasion you need to talk to me, too. You never talk to me. You're cold and distant. You fly off the handle for no reason." She gestured to the Sharps. "And you love that ugly old gun more than you do me."

Defensively, he clutched the rifle tighter. He was not surprised she thought so. He'd carried the Sharps through the entire war. At home, he was always fussing with it, cleaning it, polishing the wood, whispering to it. When the nightmares came upon him, he did not reach for her. He reached for the Sharps. She'd seen him cradle it in his arms and rock the gun like a precious child until the shakes left.

Suzanne continued, "I hate that gun. It's so heavy, I can barely heft it, let alone aim and hit anything. My shoulder still hurts from the last time you made me shoot it."

Gently, David said, "I'm going to go help Charlie load the last of the elk, then we'll drive the wagon up into that meadow and make camp."

With tears in her eyes, she replied, "I have no idea why my father agreed to let you marry—"

"Because he thought having a war hero in the family would help his campaign for Congress, that's why." He regretted the harsh words as soon as they left his mouth. "And I love you, Suzanne. You're the best thing that's ever happened to me."

Tears filled her eyes again. She sat down hard in the grass and twisted her hands in her lap. In an odd voice, she asked, "Why'd you get that medal? What happened to you in the war? There are times when you jump out of bed shouting orders. I try to talk to you, but you can't see me or hear me. What is that?"

Her words were like a bullet straight to his heart.

"I...I..." The stammer made him feel weak and vulnerable. He took a second to collect himself. "Suzanne, I spent eighteen months in an Army hospital. I'll tell you all about it when we get back to the ranch, awright?"

She gave him a sidelong look. "I suspect you won't, but I'd appreciate it if you gave it a try."

"I will," he answered, and wondered if he would. Opening those doors was frightening at best and dangerous at worst. Besides, how could she ever understand? No one could, 'less they'd been there.

An owl silently flew over his head and sailed into the forest. He watched it flap through the patches of sunset that decorated the trees like shards of deep amber glass. "I don't want you sitting here alone with that wolf out there." He extended a hand to her. "You need to walk back with me."

Angrily, she shoved his hand aside, leaped to her feet, and stalked away from him.

David cast a glance at the wolf. He could just see the tips of its ears twitch above the windblown grass. Gripping his Sharps in both hands, he lengthened his stride to catch up with his wife.

———

Midnight...

Wind swept through the camp and rattled the cook pots by the fire.

The sound barely disturbed the night. David didn't even open his eyes, just shifted slightly against Suzanne's warm body and tugged at the quilts. The cold air carried the smoky scent of campfire and the sweet tang of pines. On occasion he caught a whiff of elk. They'd hung the carcass in a cottonwood down at the bottom of the meadow.

He drifted back to sleep.

At some point, the breeze stirred, carrying the slightest hint of urine and wet fur.

Half-asleep, he blinked his eyes open and saw three elk slowly moving through the snowy meadow, beautiful and quiet, as though nothing was wrong. He wondered when the storm had broken? The sky blazed with a million stars.

Horses whinnied, and he heard hooves dancing.

David started to roll over to look for them, but the elk captured his attention when they suddenly bolted down the slope. Their hooves cracked and snapped on the ice as their legs parted the snow. Halfway through their mad flight, he saw flashes, and a low-pitched moaning, part whine, part growl, rose.

He didn't even register fear. He was calm. Just watching.

Then the wind sighed. The sky tilted.

My gaze...fixes.

In the pines to the north, shadows slink between the smoke-colored trunks.

Rebs.

No, no, don't be a fool.

But my body doesn't believe me. Everything inside begins going slower and slower, freezing up like a winter pond in a sudden cold spell.

Don't move. Don't move. They won't see you if you don't move. They'll pass by.

Five big animals trot out of the trees, and confusion makes me shake my head. Where am I?

Horses scream and hooves thunder away. They must have torn loose from their pickets...

"Oh, dear God, wolves."

When Suzanne leaps to her feet, she rips away the quilts, and my unfeeling body flips onto the left side where I can't see her.

"David, get up!"

My heart is bursting through my ribs, but the paralysis is stealing over me like a thief in the night. I can't... can't recall my wife's name. Senselessly, I stare at the shimmering haze that cloaks the horses as they fly down the valley with their hooves kicking snow high into the air. Flashes sparkle behind them.

Gunfire! Gunfire in the trees. Take cover!

"David, get the rifle!"

Charlie's rifle bangs, and an explosion of light blinds me. Where's my brother?

Branches crash, and feet suddenly pound away. Gasping and screams from ten paces, then twenty. Is he running away?

Goddamn it, I told him never to run. They'll see him! Just lay still, play dead.

"David, help me!"

A woman charges across the meadow with starlit wolves behind her, but somehow it's not real. The distinctive smell of gunpowder fills the night, and I'm choking on smoke.

Cap'n, I'm over here.

The rest of the pack glows as they trot around camp with their ears perked, snarling, jaws slathering foam. Clouds of hot breath escape their muzzles and trail away across the meadow.

There's a scream, and feet pound back toward me.

"Davy, wake up! Wake up!"

I fight to answer Charlie, but I have no air in my lungs.

Something falls on me, and fingernails claw my arms like knives. "This is Wyoming! Davy, you're in Wyoming." He shakes me hard, but I'm a mindless block of wood. My arms flop. Lunging to his feet, he grabs my hand and tries to drag me to safety.

"Come on! Come on!"

A skinny wolf leaps forward like a fanged frost wraith. Flies through the air. Hits him broadside and tumbles him across the snow. He lifts an arm as it dives for this throat, and the wolf clamps hold and shakes furiously until it rips out a chunk of meat, flings it aside and rushes in again. Charlie does not cry out. He's punching like a prizefighter, his fists striking muzzle and furred chest. Each time he connects, the sound that erupts from the wolf's throat is neither growl nor snarl, but something more akin to a high-pitched shriek of rage.

The rest of the pack struts around, teeth clipping, yelping, attempting to lunge in, snatch a bite at legs or arms, before falling back and prancing in frenzied rapture.

I blindly study my hand, the one he grabbed. It rests palm up in the churned snow. Each finger is curled just so, as though still holding on.

There's a term for this: *Rigor.* That's what the Army surgeon called it. *Rigor mortis.* The muscles go stiff as a board. What surprises me is how long it's lasting. Time seems to be stretching out, like a rope pulled too tight, about to fray and break. My jaw has locked, waiting. Waiting for it to be over.

Charlie rolls into my line of sight. He's gripped the wolf by the scruff of the neck and, as they wrestle, he's screaming in its face.

Yelps of pain erupt, followed by a human roar, then a horrific noise of snarling and barking, and finally a shrill cry of agony that soars upward into a high-pitched screech.

Everywhere the dead.

Suddenly, the scent of peach blossoms is nauseating.

Down the hill gray boys charge out of shattered trees, regimental colors flying, and a great wave of terror ululates through the thick haze. Men throw themselves at each other, kneel and fire, run. The constant explosions and cries of friends are deafening. I cover my ears and stare wide-eyed at the battlefield, roaring orders in a voice I don't recognize, while men in blue die all around me. Up along the ridge cannons are lined out. That makes me shake my head. Where…this isn't the Wilderness.

Shell shock. That's what the doctors called it. *The Fatigue.*

When my teeth unclench and the rigor lets go, I have no idea how long I've been lying here in the snow, but the world has gone eerily quiet. Can't hear…anything. The only sound is the hollow echo of my heartbeat in my head.

"Charlie?" My mouth moves, but no sound reaches my ears.

There's a wide swath of cleared snow, the width of a man's body, that leads out into the trees. Wolf tracks chowder the snow alongside the drag marks.

Is he out there?

The silence is bizarre, but familiar. Sometimes I hear, sometimes I don't. I look around the mountains. The horses are gone, their trail little more than a black line of shadow stretching down the valley.

"Charlie, where are you? Answer me!"

Fighting not to panic, I get to my feet and stagger

across the meadow. My wife must be dead, killed by wolves. Tomorrow, in the daylight, I'll discover her bones crushed and chewed and strewn across the ground, the air filled with the sweet fragrance of melting spring snow. Spring. *April. It's April 6th.*

Behind me, panting. Paws crunch on snow.

Coming faster.

I spin around.

A pale silver halo arcs over the trees. As the moon glows beneath the eastern horizon, the pines and spruces transform into dark spikes set against an expanse of stars. Standing in the middle of the trail is a single wolf with one paw lifted. He's an old, old wolf with a gray muzzle. The animal wavers through my tears.

Leisurely, it steps toward me, cocks its big head first one way, then another, as though curious about me. Perhaps wondering why I haven't run. *Never run. Never. Dear God…*

At the edge of my vision, dark shapes filter through the trees, and thick smoke begins to blanket the field. Men stumble through it, visible at first, but then they erupt in black specks and fly away into the yellow blaze of cannons. Thunder rolls over the hills. Heartbeats later, men come staggering back out of the smoke, ragged, coming up slowly, dragging their guns. The retreat parts around me.

When I gasp a breath, the vision bursts and I'm back.

The old wolf hunches, ready to spring forward. Its tail extends straight out behind it.

My chest fills as my heart expands. For a few moments, I stare into the wolf's eyes. The wolf licks its muzzle, stares back, then it backs away and slips into the shadows. What did it see in my eyes?

Hell.

Unsteadily, I walk away.

Before I've made it four paces, bright pewter light floods the sable sky, and the risen moon drowns the stars as serenely as though I'm not falling through the abyss at the end of time.

My feet feel the snow and old pine needles, but I can't hear my footsteps. I'm coming back, but I'm not fully here yet. The windblown trees rock without sound. Up in the branches, birds fluff up and seem to be watching something back in the deepest shadows. What's back there? All I see are black shapes floating between the trunks. Just odd ghosts going about their nightly duties.

The smell of blood and guts saturates the breeze.

Drag marks flatten the grass where dying men have dragged themselves to the bloody pond to drink. The fragrances of blossoms and blood twine together. Tastes like a copper penny at the back of my throat. Pink petals fall upon the broken men, upon the red water, then puffs of white smoke start up, rising through the haze down the valley, and leisurely blow to the west to stretch out across the black cannon standing beneath the limp flag.

Sir? Sir? Pardon me, sir...

A Godawful caterwauling assaults the air as howling rises, and the Rebs lift their voices in a soul-numbing yell.

...shouldn't we entrench, sir?

Charlie. Charlie's yelling. Where is he? Don't see him.

As if I've been struck, I blink awake and stare at the drag marks that flatten the snow and lead back into the dark forest.

"No." The word is barely a whisper.

Is my little brother back there at the end of those drag marks? He shouldn't be back there. He's suffered so much. He should die twenty years from now, lying in warm firelight surrounded by loving children and grand-children.

My fingers clench to fists. Stop this. Stop trembling. If

only I could grasp my heart and stop it from slamming against my ribs.

"Charlie!"

By the time I've stumbled around the meadow again —how many times have I circled?—the moonlight is brighter, and I spy the heap of flickering coals in the middle of the meadow. Quilts lay in shreds near it. Saddlebags are over there. They've been ripped open and the contents strewn around. The pungent odor of wolf urine covers everything. There's a rifle almost buried in the snow. *My rifle.* How did it get there? Did I throw it down and run? No, no, I wouldn't do that.

I need to go pick it up.

Slowly, as if the very air has changed, I begin to hear faint forbidden sounds. Whimpers float amid the black ghosts....paws squeal on snow. Sodden thumps erupt as arms and legs are dragged between tree trunks. Things I cannot bear. That's always the greatest shock, hearing, but not. Not really. I don't hear that. My mind goes on straining for any other sounds. There must be owls hooting and coyotes singing, but all I hear are the dream-like whimpers.

Cap'n, I'm over here. For God's sake, don't let me burn to death!

"Jonas! I'm coming!"

I leap forward before forcing myself to stop and brace my shaking knees. Not Virginia. This stunned tingling makes it impossible to think. What day is it? How long ago was our camp attacked? Moments? Days?

Tilting my head back, I stare up at the crescent moon. The silver gleam has turned the pines into swaying giants. There's a...a story my father tells...about a spectral army that tramps over old battlefields at night.

Nonsensically, I scan the vast mountains that stretch across the western vista, wrinkling it like a colossal blue-white blanket creased with the shadows of valleys and dotted with trees.

"Hello? Anyone? Can you hear me?"

Clouds pass in front of the moon, and the gleam changes, going from liquid silver to a hungry blue that gobbles the trees whole and turns the mountain utterly black.

Lightheaded, I boldly stride for the flickering bed of coals in the center of the meadow.

On the way, I pull my Sharps from the snow and clutch it hard against my chest. I didn't fire it tonight, did I? It's loaded. It's always loaded. This scarred old single-shot gun is my life.

Crouching before the smoldering fire, I rest the rifle across my knees and tug a branch from the woodpile we gathered at dusk. As I place the branch on top of the coals, wind gusts and flames lick through the tinder. The sweet scent of burning pine perfumes the air. I add more and more wood, building up the fire until fantastic flame shadows leap through the dark trees. Will it keep the pack away?

I wait for the yellow eyes to come.

My wife didn't want to move here, but I had to escape. Every time I turned a corner in Boston someone wanted to stop me and talk about the war. I promised her we'd move to Wyoming Territory and build a big ranch. We'd have a dozen children. *What's her name?* She has wavy black hair and green eyes...

"Suzanne!" Leaping to my feet, I clutch the rifle so hard my hands hurt. "Suzanne, where are you?"

A wolf barks, and the shadows in the trees bounce around. Then the snarling begins like an operatic refrain, building to a crescendo, and human whispers eddy through the trees.

"Jonas? J-Jonas?"

No, no, it's not.

"Charlie?"

My knees shake so hard I collapse and stare at the fire until nothing exists except the fluttering orange glow. No trees. No boulders. No cries for help. It's like living inside flame-glow.

A branch breaks in the fire and sparks shower me. When I turn away from the assault, I'm looking down the mountain. Far out on the plains, maybe three or four hours away, lights twinkle. A town? A hunter's camp?

I have to get there. Tell someone. Tell them... something.

Sobs puncture the moonlight, but they are faint and breathless. The harder I listen, the less I hear.

You're imagining it. It's not him.

Rising on shaking legs, I take a step toward the place back in the trees where the wolves move. Jonas can't be back there. He died long ago. Is it Charlie? It's impossible. Unless the wolves are playing with him as a cat does a mouse, chasing him between them, snapping and lunging to drive him in one direction, then another. Dear God, please, make him stop crying?

"Charlie? Answer me!"

All across the mountains, the howling of wolves erupts and echoes. Terrifying and beautiful, their calls are not quite of this world. Three pups trot out of the trees, tugging a heap of yellow fabric, ripping it with their teeth, wagging their tails and growling playfully. Their muzzles are washed to the eyes in blood.

My steps falter.

Like dark phantoms, wolves seep out of the trees, step lightly forward and surround me. Twenty? More?

They are so patient, just closing in, licking their bloody muzzles.

Gripping my Sharps, I back away, then panic and break into a dead run.

Wolves line out like shining gray beads behind me. When the warm breath leaves their muzzles, it freezes into clouds and drifts across their backs, riming their bristly fur with white. They glitter as they trot. Occasionally, one stops and lifts its head to sort through the sea of odors carried upon the wind: Pine resin, smoke, maybe a deer nearby, then it barks and the whole pack breaks into a lope. That's when desperation takes over, and I charge mindlessly ahead.

Run. Run.

My boots keep slipping off roots and rocks, several times I almost drop the Sharps, but vault ahead.

To my right, wolves shoot through the forest shadows, as sleek and silent as arrows in flight. The ground should be shaking beneath so many giant paws. Instead, the earth is quiet and still, glistening in the moonglow.

Is this it? Is it about to be over?

All of my dreams evaporate with the sound of the panting behind me. I'm never going to be a father. I wanted sons and daughters. Not now. None of that now. I'm not going to get to watch them grow up.

Cradling my Sharps, I leap a snow-covered log, lunge down the mountain, and pound past the wagon.

Every glimpse or scent is unbearably intense now. I'm alive. Truly alive for the first time since the war. My God, it's a beautiful night. The moon-silvered clouds cast shadows that roam the snowy slopes. As pine boughs saw back and forth, wind whistles around mossy granite outcrops, and the forest breathes music.

The steep trail gives way to gentle curves, then flattens out and runs like an old mining road. I'm shaking with the need to hurl myself headlong down the path, but if I trip and fall…

The beat of paws picks up. On both sides of the trail now. They're flanking me. The huge old wolf lopes closer to eye me from less than three feet away. I can smell its musty feral scent, heavy and cloying, something more than blood. The animal keeps pace with me. When I run harder, the grizzled guard hairs on its shoulders rise and bristle.

My thumb moves to the hammer of the Sharps and pulls it back, then my finger hovers on the trigger. I might be able to shoot this animal, but then the pack will attack from all sides. I'll have to use the gun to club the beasts back.

Maybe I can scare them off.

I fire my one shot into the densest part of the pack.

Two wolves topple headfirst into the snow with their legs kicking. The rest yip and scatter, thrashing away through the underbrush.

When I lower the Sharps, the boom is bouncing around the mountains, ricocheting from the trees and boulders, rumbling down the valley.

A rush of hope pacifies my terror. The wolves must be hightailing it for the high country.

My ears roar as I look around for any place to take cover. I could climb a tree, but they'd just wait me out, but it's better than nothing. I run for the nearest pine.

At the edge of my vision, gray fur appears and disappears amid the dense weave of the forest. They're back. Like small moons, eyes glow everywhere.

I swing my Sharps up and grab the barrel with both hands to use it as a club. While I watch them closing in, the air fills with faint screams that rise in intensity. There's a rush from the right. A violent blow. The stars swirl around and around, then the canister tumbles down, and I fly straight up over the wall.

The long slow fall through emptiness begins, quiet, peaceful...

Everywhere the dead scatter the blood-soaked ground. Blue uniforms crowd around me. Across the meadow gray boys come on with flags fluttering. Splintered trees waver through the smoke and dust. I leap to the shattered stone wall, and cry, "Follow me, boys! We're going to give 'em Hell..."

BAD CHOICES

A WYOMING CHRONICLES STORY

W. MICHAEL GEAR

Stories like Bad Choices *are fascinating to read because you're never quite sure what's going on, then wham! the unexpected twist sneaks up on you and whacks you. Not only that, I really enjoy female villains and Michael is a master at creating them. (KOG)*

I was asked to contribute a short fiction piece to the Ridin' With the Pack *anthology. The year before, Kathleen had won the Spur Award for best short fiction with her magnificent story, "No Quarter." No pressure, right? I cudgeled my besotted brain about subject and story but could imagine nothing to compare. So, what the hell? I voted to have fun instead of trying to be brilliant. I love the Wyoming Chronicles universe! The character of Thea Salva had been trying to wedge her way into all three of the novels, but just didn't fit. So I turned her loose with every trope in a traditional Western "save the ranch" story. Danged if Salva didn't turn them all upside down and inside out! So, imagine my surprise when I was notified that "Bad Choices" had won the 2024 Spur Award for best short fiction of the year. Maybe pure fun makes up for brilliance after all? (WMG)*

The storms came every afternoon, spawned by the perpetual overcast and acrid haze that covered the Bighorn Basin. The falling sheets of rain—punctuated by strobes of lightning that knotted and throbbed like the veins in an old man's hand—left Annika Clint soaked and chilled. The cracking thunder could have split bedrock. The only upside was that the downpour had washed the faint acrid stench from the smoke-thick air. Some claimed it came from burning cities in California, Oregon, and Washington.

But then, no one had ever said the end of the world would be fun.

Most of the tortured and bruised-black clouds had drifted east beyond the peaks of the Big Horn Mountains. Water dripping from her hat and raincoat, Annika Clint shifted in the saddle. She was riding Jumper along a slick elk trail as she scouted the steep mountain slope. What they called the high pasture.

Horses have better eyesight than humans. Especially backcountry horses used for hunting. Annika was cutting along just below the perimeter fence that marked the ranch boundary with the Forest Service when Jumper's ears pricked; the sorrel gelding's attention fixed on the slim figure. A woman was picking her way carefully down the rain-slick slope.

Annika reined in. Raising her binoculars, she shifted her battered old Bailey hat higher on her brow. Through the glasses, she could see that the woman was tall, wearing a smudged gray hat with a pinched crown. Her rain-damp slicker hung open to expose a fleece-lined Levi's jacket; a polished silver buckle gleamed above faded jeans. Of more interest, a rifle was balanced over the woman's shoulder. Something long, scoped. Awkward to pack.

Annika stuffed the binoculars into her coat before reaching down behind her right thigh. She pulled her battered old Sako .25-06 from the scabbard. As she did, Jumper blew, expecting her to dismount, to take a shot. Just like she would if she saw an elk. Instead she spurred him forward.

The woman had reached the elk trail, stopped, and watched Annika approach. Cupping her free hand, she called, "It's all right! I'm friendly."

Annika took another wary look up the slope—beyond the fence to the thick stands of spruce and lodgepole. Saw no one. A woman alone? Way up here?

Annika's warning bells were ringing.

"I'm Thea!" the woman called. "Thea Salva."

"What are you doing up here?" Annika shifted her grip on the Sako, balancing it over the saddle horn. A flick of her thumb would click the safety off. She had enough slack in the reins she could steady the rifle's forearm with her left as she kicked Jumper around for an off-side shot.

"Hunting. Up on the Forest Service." The woman called. Then she turned, pointing at the timber and the black storm clouds beyond. "Or I was. I was on elk. Working through the timber. I'd tied Moll, my horse, back in the clearing. I loved that mare. Bolt of lightning killed her dead."

As if to make the point, thunder seemed to roll and cascade down from the distant peaks.

"You're on Clint Ranch. Trespassing." Annika stopped Jumper twenty feet shy of the woman. Dark eyes were taking Annika's measure, the woman's face tight-lipped under a straight nose and high cheekbones. She looked to be in her thirties, fit, and athletic. Hard used.

"You Annika Clint?"

"I might be."

Thea nodded, as if fitting a piece into a puzzle. "Heard of you. People say you're a tough woman, but that you're to be relied on when things get a little Western."

"Glad to hear folks think so kindly of me. Now, what the hell are you doing wandering down into our property?"

No give in her voice, the woman replied, "Given my druthers, I'd be hip deep in a gutted elk right now. Like I said, lightning killed my mare." A pause. "Look, down-hill is the fastest way to get off the mountain." She narrowed an eye as she added, "You always this hostile?"

Jumper was shifting, fidgeting over Annika's rifle being out.

"These days? Yeah." Annika kept casting wary glances up the slope. "Wasn't bad enough that the Collapse brought the country down. Or that the government went away. Out here? Foot of the Big Horns, on a ranch? Should be the last safe place." She gave Thea a thin smile. "But we got neighbors. The kind that aren't from here. And, with no government left to speak of, they figured they'd move right in. It's come to killing."

Thea gave a half derisive snort, turning to look out across the ranch, beyond the hogbacks to the haze-obscured basin off to the west. The pastures here were lush, thick with C3 grasses, dotted with lupine, paint-brush, and asters among the sage. And below the slope, red sandstone hogbacks cupped green valleys. In the gap where Taylor Creek flowed, she could see Clint Ranch; the house, barn, and corrals lay astraddle the only water for miles. Call it everything a family would need to survive the end of the world.

Thea, the long rifle with its big scope still propped on

her shoulder, shot Annika a probing look. "So, what are you doing way up here? Wouldn't any threat come from down below?"

"Calvin is keeping an eye on that."

"What's this trouble?"

Annika shifted her grip on the Sako. "Something you'd know about if you were from around here. And since I don't know you, maybe you'd better start talking."

Thea pursed her lips, nodded. "That's fair. I used to outfit for the Shingle Guest Ranch north of here. Up on Shell Creek. I was in Cody after the Collapse. Back when Homeland Security Director Edgewater tried to take over the Basin. The man was the legal federal authority in a time of national emergency, and maybe he did overstep his authority. No matter. Let's just say I made enemies, so a spike camp up in the Big Horns seemed like a smart thing to do."

"A spike camp?" Annika lifted an eyebrow.

"That's what people call a small camp packed into the backcountry so that—"

"Yeah, I know. But where?"

"Sylvan meadows." Thea's lips bent in a sarcastic smile. "Know the place?"

"Uh-huh." Annika squinted back up at the tree line. "But it's fifteen hard miles from here. And you did that by yourself?"

"Why not?" Thea snapped, fire in her eyes. "Like I said, I used to pack dudes into the backcountry. That's a funny question from a woman who's riding a high fence line by herself in a thunderstorm."

"So...an elk's a big critter. Even if you shot one, how were you going to gut it and pack it?"

"Honey, this ain't my first rodeo. Usually I can wrestle an elk around. Get it on its back. The trick is to cut a sharp branch to stick between the hocks, you know, keep the back legs apart. Then I split the pelvis, gut my way forward and use the pack saw to open the ribs. Get the trachea out. I've got one of those panniers that you hook over the saddle horn and cinch under the horse's belly. After that, I just butcher my way down the legs, loading the panniers. It's messy as hell. Bloody…but I get the job done."

Annika felt some of the tension leak out of her bones.

As if an afterthought, Thea added, "And you're frigging right! Fifteen *hard* miles. And packing an elk would have taken two trips with me leading Moll."

"But the lightning strike ended that, huh?"

"Which is why I opted to head down. Follow the slope to a drainage. It's Wyoming. There's always a ranch where water runs out of the mountains. And if there's a ranch, maybe I could buy, rent, borrow, or con someone into the loan of a horse. Maybe bum a saddle. Not only is mine trapped under a dead mare, but lightning's as hard on leather as it is on horses."

Annika eased the Sako back into her lap. "See anyone else? Recent tracks? Any sign that anyone's been up in the forest?"

Thea—still giving her that irritated squint—said, "Only some old horse apples where someone tied off horses in an aspen grove. Might have been a couple of months ago."

"That was us. Killed an elk up there just after the grocery in town closed." Annika nodded to herself as she shifted her Sako to a less threatening position. Jumper must have figured out that no shooting was about to take place. The gelding relaxed to stand hipshot.

Annika tilted her head back, staring up at the roiling dark sky. "I guess if you meant us harm, you could have waited until I rode past. Shot me from ambush. The bastards damn near got Calvin that way."

"Listen, if it's a problem, I can cut south along the forest boundary. I think I hit BLM a couple of miles from here. Work my way down into the Tensleep drainage. Sounds like you got enough trouble as it is."

"Naw. It's okay. Been in a fix myself a couple of times." Annika waved at the dark sky. "Just 'cause it's the end of the world, and we're fighting for our lives, doesn't mean I have to act like an asshole." She grinned. "Might ruin my reputation for being, how did you put it? 'Reliable when things get Western.'"

A satisfied smile curled Thea's lips, and she took a deep breath that might have been relief.

"Follow me." Annika turned Jumper and let him pick his way down the slope. "Need a horse, huh? Well, hell. If there's one thing we're rich in, it's horses."

Thea matched Jumper's pace, descending the slope on light feet; the rifle bobbed where it was propped over her shoulder. "All the cow pies are old. Last year's. Height of summer? Where are your cattle?"

"Mostly run off. Or dead. Listen, it's only fair that you know. You're walking into a nasty damned fight. 'Bout two years ago, this billionaire rap artist from New Jersey called JaXX-EE-JaZZ—"

"Who?"

"Yeah, well, we'd never heard of him either. Anyhow, he decides on a wild hair that he's gonna buy up the whole west slope of the Big Horns for a wilderness retreat. Puts together about sixty thousand acres. Pays twice what the land's worth to do it."

Annika pointed off beyond the hogbacks to the distant bottoms where the Big Horn River was masked by a band of cottonwoods. "Built him a huge twenty-five thousand square foot mansion on the river. Italian marble, soaring roof, enough glass to cover a skyscraper. And, being a rich celebrity, he has a small army of security guys to ensure none of the fans, paparazzi, or curious locals can sneak in to film his pool parties and orgies."

"So, this rap singer, Jacks what's it…"

"JaXX-EE-JaZZ. Lots of capital letters."

"Right. He's causing you problems?"

Annika shifted with Jumper as he descended a steep spot and sent rocks rolling down the slope. "Nope. So far as we know, he was at his compound in New Jersey when the shit came down. Word is the East Coast is gone. Maybe nuked. It's Gaites. Leon Gaites. The guy in charge of old JaXX-EE's security. Him and his team of New Jersey thugs. Used to be twelve. They're down to seven now. All hard cases. When the extent of the Collapse became clear, they started moving on the surrounding ranches, the ones that wouldn't sell. In exchange for political support, Edgewater turned a blind eye."

Thea skipped lightly down through a thicket of currants, barely missing a step. "I guess Clint Ranch is one of them?"

"We're like the key that opens the mountains to Gaites. We've got the only water for miles east of the Big Horn River, not to mention that our valley is the easiest access to the high country. Started out with threats. Then he cut our fences, had his guys drive off most of our cattle while we were in town. We went to drive them back. They shot at us. We shot back straighter."

"What about the sheriff? Don something?"

"Killed in an ambush along with some deputies about a month back. People suspect Gaites. No one's anxious to step into Don's shoes."

"Gaites?" Thea asked. "If he's only the security chief, even if he could force you to sell, does he have the money to buy you out?"

Annika gave the woman a cold glare. "Not to belabor a point, but after everything's gone to hell? After Director

Edgewater tried to turn the Basin into his little kingdom, what makes you think Gaites would pay even a penny for what he can just take? Look around you. It's just us. Town's a forty-five-minute drive. Even if we had a sheriff, the phone's been dead for months."

Thea eased down a section of loose limestone, picking through the low-growing lupine and ground vetch. "So, if you're dead, there's no one to ask questions." She shifted the black-stocked rifle to her other shoulder. "But you said there's seven of them? How is it they haven't taken you down?"

Annika told her, "These guys came from New Jersey. Maybe they're hell when it comes to the mean streets of Newark, but they're dumber than rocks when it comes to slipping around the backcountry. Like I said, there were twelve to start with. And Sophie might have winged one the other night. The guy's flashlight was a dead giveaway."

"Sophie. Your daughter?"

"There's four of us. Me, Calvin, my son Talon, and Sophie."

"That's all that's holding your ranch?" Thea mused. "I heard somewhere that you were from Casper."

Annika reined Jumper around a couple of wind-bent limber pines and onto a game trail that angled over to Taylor Creek canyon. "Easier this way than straight down." Annika barked a bitter laugh. "Casper? Yeah. You might say I got here because of a whole string of bad choices."

"Bad choices?" Thea fell in behind Jumper, following the faint trail worn into the canyon side. "Sometimes I wonder if there are any other kind."

"My dad died when I was sixteen. Electrocuted himself while he was trying to rewire a light socket in our trailer. Mom kind of went a little crazy with the booze and pills. Lost her job. So I married the first guy to come along who acted like a tough stud. Dropped out of high school. What the hell did I know?"

Thea said, "The way you're talking, that's not Calvin, right?"

Annika pulled up at the edge of the canyon. "Take a breather. This is the last high spot. Let me take a minute to glass the approaches. From the hogback, it's seven miles across the flats to the mansion. Gaites and his guys have to cross a lot of open ground. Gives us plenty of warning."

Thea settled herself on a boulder; pulling back her slicker she extracted a CamelBak tube. The woman sucked, drinking deeply.

Point in her favor, Annika thought as she glassed the sage flats beyond the first hogback. The only thing moving were some cattle scattered in the raid. Seeing them out there always soured her stomach.

Lowering the glasses, Annika said, "First husband was Jess. A real piece of work. So there I was, just turned seventeen, pregnant with Talon, sleeping on a worn-out mattress on a cement floor in a crappy basement apartment, married to a drunk-and-drugged twenty-one-year-old piece of shit who'd screw anything with tits. Even when he was sober."

Thea rubbed her shins, and as she did, Annika could see the pistol and long belt knife her slicker had hidden. Well, why not? The woman had been elk hunting, after all. The only oddity would have been if she hadn't been armed to the teeth.

"How'd you get out of the basement?" Thea stood, shouldering her rifle.

Annika gave Jumper a tap with her spurs and started down the rocky trail into the canyon. "Jess didn't come home one night. The next morning he was still passed out naked in bed with some skank when the Casper police raided her place. They found enough meth to send him to the pen in Rawlins for five years. And being desperate and stupid, I hooked up with Woody. One of Jess's best-buddy friends."

Annika glanced back where Thea was picking her way down the steep trail, saw the woman's clamped mouth, read her disgust. Annika told her, "Oh, yeah. It was bad. Jess might have been a worthless loser, but Woody was a full-fledged son of a bitch. Into all the wrong shit with the wrong people. The violent kind. With a temper and right hook to match."

"So, you're not worth a shit when it comes to judging men? Huh?" Thea asked from behind.

"Didn't have a choice. I had a baby boy to feed. And there was generally food on the table. And it wasn't three months after Talon that I missed my period. Like, first ovulation and wham! So there I was."

"You didn't have any other family?"

Annika let Jumper pick his way to the bottom. This was well-established trail that they used to move cattle to the slope pasture. With the good footing, Annika had to hold Jumper back, Thea almost trotting behind. Granted, it was all downhill, but the woman was barely breathing hard. Maybe she was a jogger?

"Dad's family was in Denver, and I barely knew them. As to Mom's...well, they weren't the type to go to. Had a ranch outside of Douglas. Let's just say that asking for help from the 'holier than thou' would have come at too high a price."

"So...how'd you get out of Casper?" Thea finally was starting to pant as the trail wound through tall sage.

"Funny thing, that. There's a cowboy bar just outside the Casper city limits on the road to Shoshoni. Big thing. They have concerts, bands...country western hangout with a dance floor. So it's Saturday night. I'm home with the kids, and one of Woody's scarier friends shows up at the shabby apartment where we're living in North Casper. Says Woody owes him a couple thousand bucks over a car he stole, and if he don't pay by the next morning, it's gonna be nasty. Says he'll start by having his way with me, and it won't be kind and gentle."

Annika shook her head, leading the way down the narrow bottom where the chokecherry, currants, and willow-lined the trail. Taylor Creek burbled over the rocks to her left. High canyon walls, thick with trees, added to the almost claustrophobic feeling; too easy to ambush a person down here. A raven lay by the side of the trail, dead, its wings outstretched as if in desperation. They'd begun to find a lot of dead birds since the Collapse. Ants swarmed the carcass, marching in lines across the ash-coated feathers.

"I had this ratty old Chevrolet Impala, burned and leaked oil by the quart, but I grabbed up the kids and drove to the bar. It's, like, after midnight, and I locked the kids in the car at the edge of the parking lot."

"Sounds like…trouble," Thea called between puffs for breath.

"We'll stop here. Take a breather." Annika pulled up as they reached the mouth of the canyon. Jumper got his moment to nip at the thick grass that grew in the narrow floodplain. "Yep. I had to argue my way past the guy at the door 'cause I didn't have money for the cover charge. I find Woody with a bunch of his friends. Totally wasted, you know?"

"I'm starting to get the picture," Thea agreed, immediately dropping to a deadfall. She pulled out the CamelBak tube, drinking again.

Annika slouched in the saddle, staring up at the lacework of narrowleaf cottonwood branches overhead.

"Band's playing, so I yell, 'Vince says you owe him two thousand bucks. Something about a car you stole! You got till tomorrow!'"

Annika laughed bitterly. "The whole table heard, and these guys, they turn, looking at Woody like he's touched a live wire. He's out of the chair like a shot. Grabs me by the arm, pulling me out of there, screaming in my ear, 'You effing bitch! You don't never humiliate me like that again!'

"And we're outside, in the dark, where Woody slaps me hard enough to bring tears, drags me over to the car. He shoves me down. Kicks the wind out of me. Pulls me up by the hair. I'm pleading, crying, saying I'm sorry. And smack, he clocks me on the side of my head. Once, twice, then I don't know how many times. My head's ringing, and I'm seeing stars and blubbering..."

Annika glances at Thea—a thunder darker than the just-passed storm behind the woman's eyes.

Annika grins. "Suddenly, it's like Woody's yanked up into the sky. The sound's like a breaking oak tree. This loud *crack*! Meaty, you know? And Woody hits the ground like boneless meat." She sniffs. "I look up. There's Calvin. Standing there, feet spread, fist knotted. This big, raw-boned cowboy in a Stetson, a snap shirt, and pointy boots. He reaches down, helps me up, and asks, 'Ma'am? You all right?'

"I'm bleeding, ears ringing, and hurting too bad to think. In the car, Talon and Sophie are bawling in terror. All I can think to say is, 'He's going to kill me and the kids.'"

"So what happened?" Thea had her wind back. The woman was in really good physical condition.

"Calvin asks, 'Can I take you someplace safe?' And I say, 'I've got nowhere to go where Woody or Vince can't find me.' Calvin gets this real serious look. 'If you don't mind helping me with a fence for a couple of weeks, I'll put you and the kids up in the bunkhouse.'"

Annika shifted in the saddle, stared at the soot rings where puddles had dried. Sometimes it did that, rained black drops from the sullen sky. She wondered what it was doing to the grass and the animals that ate it, and pulled Jumper's head up.

"Hey, I didn't even go back for my things. I just grabbed the kids out of that brokedown Chevy and piled them in the back of Calvin's crew cab. Drove half the night to get here and never left."

"Moved right in, huh?" Thea got to her feet, propping the long-barreled rifle over her shoulder.

"Took a while." Through the trees, Annika could see another black patch of clouds building overhead. Going to rain again. What had it been? Two months since they'd last glimpsed the sun? And sometimes the smoke was so low-hanging, thick, and stinking, they couldn't see past the hogbacks.

"Calvin's folks had died the winter before, and he was alone here. All he wanted from me was help stringing wire on a fence he had to build, and he was smart enough to know what a damned mess I was. He took to the kids a hell of a lot faster than he took to me. Watching that man with Talon and Sophie? I'd have sold my soul before I'd have taken them away."

"Good man, huh?" Thea asked, matching stride beside Annika's stirrup as the trail widened.

"Tough, thoughtful, kind, and caring," Annika replied. "But anyone who'd lift a hand to hurt an animal, a kid, or a woman? Cal won't abide it. Makes him crazy. He doesn't talk much about it, but I think it has something to do with his father."

"What about this ranch?" Thea asked. "How big is it?"

"A little over three thousand acres, and then there's the Forest Service lease. We ran about three hundred head. Depending on what the packers were paying, times were always thin, or sometimes even thinner. We might not have had new clothes, but we always had food on the table. I've been thankful. Especially for Talon and Sophie. The only future they would have had in Casper would have been drugs and prison. Now, every day when I look at them, I'm proud. Talon's fifteen. And a man. Sophie's thirteen, and even if I die tomorrow, she's solid. Everything I wasn't back when my dad died."

Thea glanced up from under her hat brim, a wrist draped over the rifle balanced on her shoulder. "Sounds like you've done all right."

"The only thing that scares me? I'm terrified that Gaites is finally going to figure a way to get around us. They'll just kill the men outright. Me and Sophie?" She chuckled bitterly. "If we don't die right off, given the kind of scum-suckers Gaites has working for him? Yeah, you know what they'll use us for."

"Hard to think the country's come to this." Thea was squinting out across the valley. The haze was lowering like a muggy gray curtain. Lightning flickered in the distance.

Annika shifted her grip on the Sako. "Law of the jungle. Last we heard, they were fighting down around Cheyenne. Some rumor about people swarming north out of the cities along the Front Range in Colorado."

"No rumor. Governor Agar closed the Colorado border. Used the Wyoming National Guard and militia to enforce it."

"And then that business about Edgewater? The Homeland Security director? Heard he was taking people's ranches, confiscating merchandise from stores. Word was he wanted inventories of cattle, firearms, and stuff like that. Since Gaites was between us and Edgewater, his goons never made it to our door."

"Director Edgewater was the duly appointed federal authority for the state, and it was a national emergency. He had the law behind him."

Annika rode Jumper around the gray boles of the old cottonwoods that choked the canyon mouth and into the narrow valley, bounded as it was by the hogback on the west. The trail opened up on a hay meadow; a wheel-line sprinkler system had been rolled to one side of the alfalfa field.

Thea pointed at a man's body—face-down off to the right—almost obscured by blooming alfalfa. Two ravens had been ripping at the corpse and leaving white streaks of droppings on the blood-blackened denim; they took to flight, squawking as they winged into the sullen air.

"Who's that?"

"One of the twelve. Sophie shot him a little over a week ago. Just haven't had time to dig a hole and drop him in. Maybe we'll live long enough to get around to it."

Thea gave the corpse a distasteful scowl.

Annika said, "We heard Edgewater's goons were taking women. That he raided the wrong ranch over by Hot Springs, and some of their people took him and his thugs down. Blew up that mansion he confiscated up the South Fork."

"Yeah. Bad shit that day," Thea said softly as her gaze shifted from the corpse to the rich field, the alfalfa rife with blue blossoms that perfumed the air. Sounded like she was changing the subject when she asked, "Shouldn't you be cutting and baling this?"

"Can't." Annika pointed Jumper toward the ranch house, barn, and corrals where they were visible down the valley. "Like I said, there's just the four of us...and the people trying to kill us are only eight miles over to the west. Talon, Sophie, Cal, and me, we take turns on watch. Got to have eyes on the approaches to the ranch twenty-four hours a day. All it would take would be one mistake."

Thea pursed her lips, her long legs keeping pace. "You sure it's worth it? If they're killers like you say, you could just saddle up, ride out through the forest. Wouldn't that be safer for your kids? You'd get out alive."

Annika slapped a hand to her thigh. "It's like this: Calvin is fourth generation on this land. Doesn't matter that there's no law anymore. We're in the right. Gaites figured he could run us off. When that didn't work, he started shooting."

"Maybe that makes pulling out all the more reasonable."

"This is our land. We're not leaving."

Thea kept glancing back at the corpse. "What makes you think you can win?"

Annika took a deep breath. "If we can kill a couple more of them, maybe the others will wonder if it's worth it. Or, best yet, if we can tag Gaites, the others will quit. Figure they've got sixty thousand acres, what the hell do they need ours for?"

"Kind of long odds, don't you think?" Thea had an amused twist on her lips.

"It's what we've been dealt."

———

Looking out the ranch house's north window, Calvin caught sight of Annika as she rode in on Jumper. That she was accompanied by a...yes, given the way she walked, that was a woman. But where in hell had Annika found her? And more to the point, who was she?

He climbed to his feet and clenched his jaws against

the pain as he hitched his wounded leg over to the table. Now that he knew Annika was safe, he could tend his dressing. Untying the binding that held the compress to the back of his upper thigh, he dropped the bloody cloth into the wash pan. Once it was soaked, he wrung out the blood into another pan. Sniffing, he thought maybe he smelled pus. That would be bad.

Standing made the wound throb. Annika had cut off the left pant leg just below his crotch to allow access to the bandage. Made him look like a fool with that one white leg ending in a fancy-stitched Lucchese riding boot with high dogger heels. And the bloody bandage could have been mistaken for a frickin' woman's garter!

He heard Jumper's whinny, answered by the horses in the corral out behind the barn. Then the sound of boots on the wooden porch. Reaching for the vodka bottle, Calvin wet the compress, positioned it over the bullet hole, and tried the strangle the gasp as he pulled the binding tight and tied it.

Damnation and hell, that hurt!

The door opened as he turned, Annika giving him a worried look. He was panting, arms braced on the table as a wave of nausea rolled through his gut.

"You all right?" Annika asked, pausing only long enough to lay her .25-06 on the table with a clunk. The woman followed, glancing back at the yard before closing the door.

"Yeah…just chipper," he said through a weary exhale.

The woman had stopped long enough to lean a long-barreled bolt-action rifle against the wall. Thing had a huge scope on it. Then she pulled her battered hat from her head and walked over with her long slicker swinging. Dang, she was taller than he, maybe by a couple of inches. But, where…?

"This is Thea Salva," Annika told him, taking his left

arm. "Lightning killed her horse up in the forest. I think she's all right. Now, let me help you back to the chair before you fall over."

Calvin swallowed his grunt of agony as he braced himself on Annika and hobbled back to the chair. Each step made in brain-numbing pain.

"Looks like you caught a slug," Thea noted as she squinted down at Calvin's leg.

He puffed his relief as Annika helped him settle into the chair. His leg went from white-searing agony to a throbbing ache. "Yeah. Gaites's guys...a couple of them carry AR-15s. The rest have these stubby little semi-automatic machine gun-looking things. Like, I don't know. Uzis maybe? Nine millimeter...with big magazines. Might be good for up close security work, but worthless as tits on a boar long range. Or so I thought. Yesterday one caught me in the back of the leg." He grimaced. "Wasn't bad at first. Felt like a bee sting."

"What can I get you?" Annika asked. "Something to drink? You hungry?"

"I'm fine, darling love," he told her with a smile. To Thea, "Ms. Salva? Did Annika tell you about..."

"Yeah," Annika muttered, fretting over the binding on his leg. "All she needs is a horse. I thought she could take Smoke. He's got wind, surefooted. And what the hell? If Gaites ever gets the drop on us, it's one horse he won't end up with."

"I can pay," Thea said reasonably.

Annika sighed, pulled off her old Bailey hat and set it crown down on the table next to the bloody washbasin. "No, you take the horse. With the exception of more trouble than we can handle and the chance for a real short future, we got everything we need here. But Smoke might save your life. He's packed elk, won't balk at the blood. And he's surefooted."

Calvin added, "Ms. Salva, you got tack?"

Annika picked up the wash pan, heading to the sink where she dumped the bloody water. "Her saddle's trapped under her dead horse, and lightning-charred to boot. I thought maybe your mother's saddle?"

Calvin caught the surprised rise of Thea Salva's eyebrow as he said, "Might as well. It's the Newberry. Fifteen inch. Looks like it will fit you. Haven't waxed it lately, but it's better being used than collecting dust and going all hard in the tack room."

"Your mother's? You sure?" Thea asked hesitantly.

"She's dead, you're not. And I'd a heap rather you were riding it than leaving it for Gaites and his scum."

Thea gestured at his leg. "Bullet still in there?"

He jerked a nod.

She dropped down to a crouch, staring him in the eyes. "I can take that bullet out, debride the wound, and suture it. Call it a trade for the horse and saddle. I don't have anesthetic. You'll just have to scream. If you caught that slug yesterday, you're running out of time. You up for that?"

"How do you know how to do that?" Annika asked as she filled the wash pan at the kitchen sink.

"Guess I've spent too much time in bad places, Ms. Clint." Thea stood, looking around. "Can we put him on the table? Back of the leg? Into the quadriceps? As long as it didn't trend medial toward the femoral artery, should be a piece of cake."

That measuring stare Thea was giving Calvin unsettled him. Not that having a bare white leg in a cowboy boot wasn't humiliating enough. The damn ache was almost bad enough he didn't care. But not quite.

Calvin told her, "I don't want to cause you any—"

"You don't get that tended to, you'll end up with gangrene," Thea said. "Or dead."

"What about Gaites?" he asked. "He could hit us again at any time. Doesn't matter that it hurts, I can still shoot."

Thea shook her head. "I've seen what happens when untreated bullet wounds go bad."

Annika had crossed her arms, brow pinched with worry. "You sure you can do this?"

Something about the way Thea Salva nodded, left no doubt. "Won't be like I had a surgical kit, but I can make do. Now, there are some things I need..."

———

The pain lurked—filled the disjointed dreams that slowly faded from Calvin's head. The creak from the chair brought him fully awake. He lay on his stomach. In bed. Thea Salva dozed in his mother's old rocker. The tall woman's head was back, her brown hair in a ponytail. In the glow of the bedside light, he could make out faint scars on her right cheekbone and jaw.

He shifted, grunted at the sudden stab in the back of his left leg as the muscle contracted.

It might have been an electrical shock given the way Thea jumped. Instinctively, she'd reached for the pistol at her hip, fingers wrapping around the grip—a short-barreled .44 magnum given the holster and cartridges in the belt loops.

"Sorry, to wake you," he rasped. "What time is it?"

"Little after midnight." She stretched, stood, and bent over the bed to inspect his wound. Gently lifted the bandage and said, "Good. No bleeding. Don't see inflammation around the sutures."

"Where'd you learn to use a Phillips screwdriver for a bullet probe?" Calvin asked.

"Same place I learned to use a twist of number twelve

fencing wire for a hemostat." A pause. "On YouTube, of course."

"Of course," he said through an exhale. "Leg still hurts. Maybe a five on a one-to-ten scale."

"Better?"

"Yep. Not as bad as times I've been bucked off in the rocks. Or when I broke my ribs. Or the time a bull trampled the crap out of me. Or when I got kicked by the old red mule. Or when I fell off the haystack. Or—"

"You're a tough man, Calvin. You didn't so much as whimper when I was fishing for that bullet."

"Ranch kid, Ms. Salva."

"Call me Thea. Need to pee?"

"No."

"Then you're not drinking enough." From beside the bed, she produced what he recognized as a CamelBak water bag and offered him the tube. "More," she ordered when he would have quit.

Satisfied she placed it back on the floor.

"Where's Annika?"

"Up on the ridge in the lookout." Thea lowered herself into the rocker. "Sophie and Talon are both in bed. They checked in on you at sunset. Sophie kissed you on the forehead, but you were still out. Talon? He just patted your hand." She glanced absently at her rifle where it was propped beside the bedroom door. "You could have done a lot worse than those kids."

"Yep." He tried to shift, thought better of it when pain stabbed through his leg. "Breaks my damned heart that they're in this fix. The only thing they should be worrying about are grades and if their 4-H projects are going to place at state fair. Instead, they're in a shooting war."

"I've seen kids in worse," she said absently.

"Where?"

"Afghanistan. I was there at the pullout. My team was on one of the last flights out of Bagram. Remember the pictures of people falling off the airplanes? It was a hell of a lot worse on the ground."

"Military?"

She nodded. "You'd call it Special Forces work. In some missions, women can provide access, gain confidence, mislead, interrogate, get into places men can't."

"How'd you get here?"

She chuckled to herself, gaze going distant. "A long string of bad choices. After Afghanistan, I didn't re-up. Went to work for...well, we'll just call them military contractors. Volunteered for an op in Syria. We were working with some pretty rough characters and doing things the US didn't want to be associated with. It paid well, was exciting as hell." She paused. "Until an op went sideways, and a lot of people died who weren't supposed to."

For a time she sat, rocking, staring into the past.

"I guess you could say I was out of sorts for a while after that. Kind of crazy. Made some really bad decisions. The kind that carved out my guts and left my soul bleeding and numb."

Her expression pinched, and she went silent.

Calvin finally said, "You don't look like a lady with no guts. Not to me."

A wistful smile died on her lips, the gaze still empty. "Putin invaded Ukraine. Like a rope to a drowning woman, I grabbed it. Killing Russians? Now there, finally, was a chance for redemption."

"Killing Russians?" he asked softly.

"I had skills. A résumé. It was chaos at first. Stopping the Russians outside Kyiv. Then I met Tvorchi. He was a sniper. I'd had some training. He needed a spotter. Call it a match made in heaven. We both had our demons. Mine in Afghanistan and Syria, his in Bucha, Melitopol, and Kherson where his wife died and his children were sent to Russia as"—she crooked her fingers in quotation—"'orphans.' I ran on hate; he was powered by rage."

The smile that bent her lips was scary.

"I'll go out on a limb and say you were more than partners," Calvin said softly.

"Yeah." Her smile widened. "Sex in the middle of a shelling? Energizing as hell."

"What happened?"

"Bakhmut." Her gaze went vacant again. "Sam and I...I started calling Tvorchi Sam. We didn't use real names for security reasons, and when he'd spot an Orc—that's what we called Russians—he'd say, 'Play it.' Like in *Casablanca*, you know?" A pause. "Then the shot. And we'd scan for another target. They just kept throwing those poor bastards at us. Sometimes our biggest worry was keeping the guns fed. The body count. Shit, we lost track somewhere past two hundred.

"We had this tradition. We'd polish our cartridge cases until they were bright. After each kill, we'd leave the empty case standing. One time, we had this hide in the ruins of the Palace of Culture on Artema Street. We lined up the cases on a board. When we pulled out, there were seventy-eight. All shining and standing in a row." Her voice had trailed off.

"And Sam?"

"My fault. Russian lines were collapsing. One night we'd wormed close to gather intel. Sam heard the Russians talking about the general. He was coming to take charge. Stop the rout." She took a deep breath. "I made the call to infiltrate their lines. Wasn't hard. Those poor bastards were just cowering in the rubble. We slithered in like snakes, found a hide in a blasted building.

Could see their forward command post. Four hundred and thirty meters. Clear shot."

Her brow pinched, tension in the set of her mouth. "Next day, about noon, the Orcs really started to stir. And here he came. Colonel General Sergei Rizhmatov."

Sam said, "'Got movement. Patrol sixty meters to our left in the old bakery.' But I ignored him. I had Rizhmatov in the crosshairs, scope dialed. And I took the shot." A pause. "Gave away our position."

"They caught you?"

Thea shook her head, eyes fixed on the past. "I was in the lead, headed back toward our lines. All hell was breaking loose behind us. Shouts, gunshots. I ducked into a half-collapsed garage, scooted to the far side. When I looked back for Sam, I could see him. Atop a pile of rubble. He yells, 'I got this! Run!' Standing there, he opened up with his Kalashnikov, screaming, firing."

She swallowed hard. "And they shot him to pieces."

"But you got away?"

"Should have stayed. Fought it out. But I've never made good choices. So I exfiltrated. Never could make myself claim the kill on Rizhmatov. Couple of months after that, I quit. Couldn't take it."

"How'd you get here?"

Thea stretched her long legs, yawned again. "The only time in my life that I was happy was horse packing. Thought maybe if I could be a wilderness guide again, I could forget. So I applied for a job with the Shingle. They were full up, but the Rusty Spur Guest Ranch hired me on as a packer for the season. Then, bam. The Collapse hits. No guests are coming."

"So you hung out in the forest?" Calvin nerved himself, gritted his teeth, and shifted to ease a cramp in his good leg.

"That would have been smart, and I don't do smart. No, I signed up with Edgewater. Thought, like Ukraine, that I'd fight on the side of law and order in the face of societal meltdown." Her laughter sounded bitter. "Guess we all know where that ended up. And you know what, Calvin? In the end, I didn't care. I'd lost so much of myself, I was just another hired gun. Like some fucking robot. Following orders. Living the good life in my off hours."

"What about that fight up at Clark Ranch? You in on that?"

"I was down on the road. That's what spotters do. Put us out front to observe. No, the fighting, the explosion, all that was up canyon. But it sure as hell put me out of a job. Then Governor Agar tries and executes Edgewater? Kind of left me high and dry with a need to be far away from Cody." She paused. "But I've always had a skill... and that's what took me to the forest above your ranch. I've always been a hunter."

He glanced at the rifle. "Looks way too long and awkward to be an elk rifle."

"It's a Gunwerks long-distance rig chambered in 7mm PRC mounting a chunk of 5x35 Nightforce glass on top." Thea lifted a hand. "I know. It's not the optimum elk-hunting rig for sneaking around in the black timber. It's about as graceful as a shovel when it comes to tight places. But, like using a screwdriver for a bullet probe and wire for a hemostat, sometimes you've got to use what you've got."

"Yeah, I guess you do."

They sat in amiable silence for a time, Calvin hating the throbbing ache in his leg. Damn it, if he could just roll over.

"What's next?" he asked.

"Riding out in the morning," she told him, that absent

look in her eyes again. "You sure I can't pay you for the horse and saddle?"

"Nope. You're a good person, Thea Salva. Not enough of those around these days, so it's a pleasure to be of help when you're in need...and you need to be as far from here as you can get. After all you've been through, there's no sense in getting yourself shot on our account."

"Yeah," she said wistfully. "A good person." And then she shook her head, closed her eyes, and would talk no more.

Something was terribly wrong. As morning lightened from dark to a gray overcast haze, Annika rode warily down the hogback trail, cut across the hayfield. The smoke smell and stink seemed stronger this morning.

Depressing.

She let Jumper drink before crossing Taylor Creek. Where the hell were the kids? Talon should have been up to relieve her right at dawn. Each passing second they were overdue, her fear built. As it was, she'd forced herself to wait until full sunup to give the flats leading down to the Big Horn River bottoms a final scan with her field glasses.

Had Calvin taken a turn? Was that it? Damn! He couldn't have died in the middle of the night, could he?

Heart in her throat, she glassed the ranch. Saw nothing out of the ordinary except for Smoke. The big gray horse was saddled, tied off at the corral gate. But no sign of Thea or the kids.

Pulling her .25-06, Annika let Jumper trot back to the barn. Usually she held him back. Wasn't good to let a horse head for home like that. Today—that feeling of dread like lead in her heart—she didn't care.

Riding into the ranch yard, she pulled Jumper up, looking carefully around. Nothing seemed out of order. The only oddity was the Polaris side-by-side with its dump box that they used for fixing fence. Someone had pulled it out of the shop and left it beside the barn door. Why? The thing only had a couple of gallons of gas left in it.

"Talon? Sophie?"

"They're in here, Annika!" Thea's voice came from the barn. "You'd better come see. Something tells me this will be the end of all your problems."

Annika frowned, dropped the reins, and stepped off Jumper. Her thumb on the safety, she carefully walked up to the barn door, peered in. Could see Zigzag, Sophie's horse, saddled, while Soap, Talon's gelding, was only haltered.

"Where are you?"

With a weary exhale, Thea's voice called, "Oh, for the love of mud, Annika, stop being so suspicious. Everything's fine."

Annika took a step inside, peering around. That's when she saw Sophie and Talon, both securely tied, tape over their mouths, bandanas tied like blindfolds around their heads.

"Now," Thea said reasonably, "lay that rifle down and raise your hands. If you don't, you, or the kids, are going to end badly."

Heart hammering, Annika lowered her Sako and stared in disbelief as Thea Salva stepped out from behind the tack room door, a large-caliber short-barreled revolver in her right hand.

"Sorry, Annika," Thea said, walking up and pulling the pistol out of Annika's belt. "Now, down on your knees, and cross your legs. That's it. Now, hands behind your back."

"Why are you doing this?"

Thea, voice deadpan, said, "Just doing a job."

"We trusted you."

"Yeah. Another in your string of bad choices, huh?"

Thea Salva and Smoke got along great. He wasn't going to be the fastest horse she'd ever ridden. She wouldn't call him lazy, just curious to see what he could get away with. But once moving, Smoke had that feel like he could go for miles, strong, and definitely sure-footed as he climbed the hogback trail. Topping the rim, Thea pulled him up, stared back at the Clint Ranch. The buildings, corrals, and green hayfields looked somehow pristine despite the forever-brooding skies. Lightning flashed off to the south where a storm built over Worland.

From her slicker pocket, Thea extracted a walkie-talkie and thumbed the send. "Gaites? You there?"

It took three tries before her radio, with a background of static, announced, *"Thea? That you?"*

"Roger that. Job's done. Everything's tied up. If I were you, I'd load up my guys and beat feet. The place is yours."

"How'd you do it?"

"Damn fools trusted me. Bought my story about being left on foot up in the Big Horns. Made me feel right at home."

"And the kids?"

"Why would they have been a problem? World's full of kids."

"Edgewater always said you were cold and calculating when it came to getting the job done."

"Giving a damn just leads to a broken heart. Now, you got my money?"

"Ten thousand in cash. Just like I promised."

"Bring it with you."

"We're on the way. See you in fifteen!"

———————

Leon Thomas Gaites had been many things in his life, and more than once, he'd stumbled into uncommonly good luck. Not that he'd always recognized that fact in the beginning. When JaXX-EE-JaZZ had selected Gaites as detail leader for his ranch security, Gaites—born and raised in Newark—had thought the rapper had exiled him to hell.

Until the Collapse.

Rumor was that everyone on the East Coast was dead. All the cities burned to ash.

And Gaites was not only alive but building an empire.

He reclined in the passenger seat as Marko drove the big black Suburban into the Clint Ranch yard. Today, it felt really good to be Leon Gaites. Life at the end of the world had a lot going for it. Edgewater might have been taken out by the local yokels over in Cody, but if Gaites played his game smart, who knew? He might be able to step into the role as the Big Horn Basin's kingpin.

Marko stopped in front of the house, shifted the Suburban into park and killed the ignition.

Gaites chuckled to himself, opened the door, and stepped out. The only thing that would have made the day better would be if the sun had been shining. But, word was, that might take months, even years, for the smoke to clear. Slamming the door behind him, he watched as Jenkin's fancy Tahoe pulled in behind the Suburban, the rest of the team piling out. HK MP5s in hand, his six guys began to clear the property.

The walkie-talkie crackled, and Gaites pulled it from his jacket pocket. "Yeah?"

"Got my money?"

"As soon as the team secures the place."

It didn't take more than five minutes. Marko stepped out of the house, calling, "House is clear, boss."

"Clear!" Sven called as his team finished their sweep of the barn, shop, and sheds.

"Where's my money?" came from the walkie-talkie.

Gaites reached for the rear door. Under his breath, he muttered, "Yeah, you heartless bitch. I hear you." But hiring her had been a good choice. And there was a ton more cash in the safe back at the mansion.

He reached out the small toiletry bag, a glitzy Armani piece. But then JaXX-EE-JaZZ always bought the most expensive thing he could find.

Gaites pulled out the walkie-talkie. Thumbed the button. "Got it right here. Pleasure doing business with you." He held it up, turning, curious about where she'd step out from.

The bullet hit him full in the sternum. Punched through him like a battering ram.

He never heard the shots that followed as his team was picked off, one by one. Was stone dead when the big gray horse was ridden into the yard, and the tall woman stepped off only long enough to pick up the fancy Armani bag.

———

"Up here!" Talon called. He stood atop the hogback, Sophie at his side where she stared pensively down at the ground, wind flipping her ash-blond hair. They waited up on the rimrock, not more than twenty yards up from where Calvin and Annika hitched their way, step by step, up the steep trail.

They didn't look like kids, Calvin thought. But then—with Calvin's leg out of order—Talon had run the backhoe. Dug the grave where they'd dumped the bodies—including the one Sophie had shot dead in the alfalfa field. No one could be called a kid after what they had been through.

"Take a breather," Annika told him, keeping a tight grip on Calvin's arm lest he stumble.

He pointed. "It's like you can see it all unfold. There's the aspen grove where Thea left us hidden in the side-by-side. From here, she could keep an eye on us. And that's where the Orcs drove into the ranch yard."

"Orcs?"

He gave her a wink. "Thea's term. And I guess she knew we'd figure a way out of those zip ties eventually."

"You up for the last little bit?" Annika asked.

Calvin turned his attention to the trail. One step at a time. Right foot first, then bring his left up. Took him nigh on ten minutes to make it, his breath puffing like a steam engine.

He thankfully stopped at the top, gasping for air. Hating the ache in his healing leg. But damn it, last thing he'd do was laze about the ranch house. And he'd really wanted to see this.

Sophie pointed. "Right here, Dad. They're just like I found 'em."

Calvin nodded, all the pieces falling in place.

He didn't need to pick one up to know what the head stamp read: 7mm PRC. Seven of them, polished to a mirror-like gleam, standing upright on the weathered sandstone.

THE HAMMER

KATHLEEN O'NEAL GEAR

There is a danger inherent in writing about historical figures, especially those who've become legends. Some such figures, like Bonnie, tempt us. So many questions. While her young life is filled with blanks, perhaps we can fill some of them in with what-ifs. And, in doing so, conjure images that will haunt us with nightmares. (WMG)

The uncomfortable thing about legends is that people think they know the story. In the case of Bonnie, no one will ever really know her story. The information is too scant. But there are clues. For example, we know she grew up hard in an impoverished and crime-ridden part of Texas. We know her family said she was sterile due to some "operation" in her teenage years. We know she was a very talented writer. What could have spurred a beautiful and gifted honor student to travel down such a tragic road? My guess is desperation.

As to "Hell's Belle..." She is also a historical figure.

The facts of her life that you will find here are historically accurate. She vanished after her house burned down, but people claimed to have seen her in Mississippi and California. Did she pass through Texas on her way? Well…who knows? (KOG)

Bonnie walks fast.

The first rays of dawn are filtering through the dust spewing from the cement factory and turning the sky an ugly shade of burnt orange. This is the poor part of town, the part of town that Mama says people take desperate measures to escape. There's a lot of stray animals and crime. Squatter's camps have sprouted up everywhere. Folks that can't afford tents are living under bridges and overpasses. Bonnie's scared but not scared enough to stop. Horse-drawn wagons and a few automobiles rattle by on the dirt road.

Shoving strawberry blond hair behind her ears, she hurries toward the huge cottonwood tree that shades the little house on Eagle Ford Road. Mama says Bonnie is runty, four-foot-eleven and ninety-two pounds soaking wet, but being small makes it easier to hide. The tree trunk is twice as wide as she is and the lowest branches break up her image, so when she peeks around the bark, she's sure the spring green leaves make her invisible. The fumes from the factory get stronger as day comes on, stinging her eyes.

As usual this time of morning, Hell's Belle—the old woman across the street—is bent over weeding her vegetable garden. She's a big woman and has her gray hair pinned in a bun on top of her head. The style makes her dark eyes look enormous. She wears an old-fashioned black dress with a white ruffled collar that blows in the cool breeze. Bonnie thinks she could have just stepped out of a historical novel, the kind Bonnie reads in school.

Bonnie pulls the yellowed *Chicago Tribune* article from

her pocket and unfolds it. The headline reads: "Fire Victim's head missing." It says the corpse was horribly mutilated, but there's a picture of the woman when she was alive. Bonnie examines every detail, then darts back to the old woman's face. Back and forth, comparing the shapes of the eyes, the nose, the mouth. It's *her*. Bonnie is sure of it. She's been following the old woman for over a month, watching her to see where she goes and what she does. Some of the clippings call her the "La Porte Ghoul."

When the woman rises and stretches her aching back muscles, Bonnie slips behind the tree trunk. She's breathing hard with excitement. She waits for another five minutes, then chances a glance back at the garden. Belle's back is turned to Bonnie. Bonnie leaps from behind the cottonwood and races down the street for school.

———

That night, Bonnie stands before the kitchen window, watching evening settle in a dusty, brown haze over Cement City. The western sky glows a lurid purple. She waits for darkness to come. The darkness here is alive. It spawns demons, disembodied voices, and people who can change into animals. Her teacher says she's very imaginative. But Bonnie knows demons are real. She has smelled their fetid breath and felt their claws on her skin.

She clenches her jaw. She's smart. Way smarter than the other girls at school. She's always on the honor role. She won the last spelling bee and got a brand-new Kodak camera and one roll of film for a prize. One of her teachers paid to have the roll developed. That's the only teacher Bonnie likes. She hates all of the others. They say Bonnie is hot-tempered and mean to the boys, but she never gives them anything they don't deserve. Fiends. Every one of 'em.

"Bonnie, I told you to get to bed. You're thirteen! I'm tired of you whining 'bout the dark all the goddamned time."

"But Mama, I—"

"Get in there!" Mama points down the dingy hall where peeling blue paint looks faintly green in the light of the coal oil lamp. Other folks have electric lights, and there's gas streetlights in places, but this house will likely never see such doings.

Bonnie bites her lip to hold back tears. The look on Burt's face scares her. Bonnie's daddy died when she was four, and Mama's new boyfriend is a giant. He works laying bricks. His arms are as big around as tree trunks.

Burt says, "You sure are a purty little thing, girl. Now go on, get yourself to bed like your Ma told you. And close your door good. Me and your Ma got things to do."

"Mama, can I go upstairs and sleep with Granny?"

"Hell, no," Burt answers. "Your brother and sister are watching her tonight. She don't need you. Now, get to bed."

Bonnie knows that Mama is struggling to pay the bills. What little she makes goes to take care of five people. Maybe Bonnie should quit school and get a job to help her? The idea is like a knife in her soul. Bonnie loves school, and she studies hard. She has to learn everything she can, because someday soon she's getting out of here, and she's going to be somebody. Maybe she'll be an actress, or a big-time magazine writer for *Harper's* or *Collier's Weekly*. She writes all the time. She doesn't really understand it, but there's a blinding light that appears in her head, and it breathes poetry. The words are born in aching, unbearable brilliance. Maybe she'll write a poem and call it, "The Ogress Down the Street."

"Go on!" Burt shouts.

Bonnie runs down the hall, opens the door to the small room that was once a tool shed, and tiptoes through the darkness to crawl under her blankets. They smell musty, like they've been laying in a cave for ages being pissed on by mice. Mama works as a helper at the printing company, and sometimes as a seamstress. She sews beautiful blankets, but she has to sell those. Bonnie only gets the stained old castoffs.

Don'tsleepdon'tsleepdon'tsleep. The demon comes when she's asleep.

She starts crying again and smothers her face in her blankets to muffle the sound.

When a sob escapes, she goes rigid. God almighty, what if it's Burt who comes to shut her up? Bonnie shoves the whimpers behind the door at the back of her throat and holds her breath until they die—holds it so long she doesn't know where she is. This might be Cement City or Rowena, or another place far away, but dark. So dark in here.

Dim moonlight seeps through her tiny window and crawls across the floor to Bonnie's face where it sets and rests a bit. Bonnie pulls the old, yellowed newspaper clippings from the shoebox beneath her bed. Mama's friend in La Porte, Indiana, sent them in a card a few years back. When Mama threw them in the trash, Bonnie fished them out and kept them to read over and over again. By now, she's memorized every word. Bonnie loves to read. In school, she gets to read romance novels. She'd give anything to have a book of her own, but Ma says such foolishness will just get Bonnie stirred up and make her start dreaming of things that will never be. Says the wanting will get Bonnie into trouble. But Bonnie's already in trouble, and she knows it.

When the moonlight meanders across the room and

flares on the doorknob, Bonnie tucks the clippings back in the box and shoves it under her bed again.

It takes another hour or so before she works up the courage to close her eyes, then she starts praying with every ounce of strength in her body. "Dear Jesus, please let me grow hooves so I can gallop far, far away. Or just take me home to heaven? I'll be a good girl. I won't make any trouble."

Deep inside her, she's underwater, looking up at a glitter like dove wings fluttering in sunlight. Coming down to fetch her and carry her off where there'll never be darkness again, and pearly gates, and streets paved with gold. Bonnie hears laughter coming from Mama's bedroom, and whimpers sneak into Bonnie's mouth. They taste foul, like dirty underwear stuffed down her throat.

Finally, her breathing goes deep, and she drifts into the shining footlights. She's on a stage in Boston, singing and dancing. Below her, the audience claps...

Sometime in the night, her door creaks open and footsteps whisper too close. A man's gravelly voice and stinking breath, and a calloused hand across her mouth. "You tell your family, and I'll blow their brains out. Where'll you be then, purty little Bonnie? All alone on the street starving to death. That's where."

———

The next morning, Bonnie slips on her frayed wool coat and tucks one precious newspaper clipping in her pocket. Mama's already gone off to work, but Burt's still asleep. Tiptoeing to the door, Bonnie slowly pulls it open, then eases it closed, and runs off as fast as she can. Heading straight to the old woman's cottonwood-shaded house down the street.

She flies through the open gate, past the mailbox with the name "Esther Carlson" painted on it in careful black letters, and dashes up to the door. The tiny bungalow sits a ways back off the street. It's white with black shutters and gray trim. A hedge of flowers encircles the yard. Bonnie has taken pictures of the old lady out here clipping plants. Everything looks so perfect it reminds her of pictures in magazines. Even if Mama won't buy her any more film, Bonnie takes pictures with her eyes. *Snap. Snap.*

There's a copy of the *Dallas Morning News* laying on the step. Bonnie reaches down, rolls it up, and tucks it under her arm. Takes a while to nerve herself to go through with it.

Then, brushing hair away from her blue eyes, Bonnie lifts her hand and knocks on the black door. Her heart's racing while she waits. It's past six o'clock. The old woman is always up by five. Bonnie knows, because she watches.

When no one comes, Bonnie puts her ear against the door and listens for footsteps. It's quiet in there. Maybe the old woman is gone. Bonnie's insides wither at the thought. She knocks again, hard, and calls, "Good morning! Hello!"

Somewhere far off in the house, she hears a cane tapping the floor.

Bonnie knocks again, then kicks the door for good measure. "Hello!"

"Hold yer horses!" a woman's deep voice yells. "I'm coming quick as ay can."

A thrill of fear goes through Bonnie. Belle has a faint accent. Norwegian, Bonnie suspects. Bonnie knows she was born on a small farm in Norway. Her father was a stonemason. While she listens to the tapping, Bonnie reflects on corpses that refuse to stay buried. Like vampires that claw out of graves and go hunting for fresh blood.

The knob rattles, then the door slits open, and those odd eyes look out at Bonnie. They're as cold and alert as a cougar's. "What do you want?"

"Ma'am, I was wondering if you needed someone to help you work in your yard. I reckon at your age, it's getting harder for you, if you don't mind me saying so. I'd work for dirt cheap."

The monster studies Bonnie's face. "How cheap?"

"Two pennies a day. I'd come whenever you need me." Bonnie turned and pointed up the street. "I live just right up there. Won't take me long to get here."

Belle's eyes are watchful, then she leans farther out her door and scans the street in both directions. While she does, Bonnie's gaze goes over every detail of her wrinkled face, comparing it to the pictures in the newspapers. She has gray hair now, and she's heavier. But she's tall, as tall as the papers said, five-foot-nine or thereabouts. She towers over Bonnie. Her black dress is old and faded, but clean and pressed.

"Go away, child. Ay don't need any help."

The door starts to close, and Bonnie rushes to shove her foot in to block it open. "Ma'am, I picked up your paper for you." Bonnie hands it through the gap in the door.

With a worried expression, the old woman snatches the paper, kicks Bonnie's foot away, then slams the door in Bonnie's face.

Bonnie's a little breathless. The "Ogress" isn't nearly as terrifying as she'd imagined. She's just an arthritic old woman with a strange accent and an eerie light in her eyes.

Determined, Bonnie leans closer to the door and shouts, "You were born on November 11, 1859. When you were a girl, you went to a dance and a man kicked you in the belly, causing you to lose your baby. He was a rich man. Never even got arrested. After that, folks said you changed. You came to America in 1881."

There's a long silence.

The knob turns, the door opens a slit, and one blazing eye looks out at Bonnie. "Get away from my door!"

Bonnie smiles. "Ma'am, I don't mean no harm. I just want to come in and talk to you for a spell."

"No." The door closes again.

Bonnie leans her forehead against the cool wood. "You married Albert Sorenson in Chicago, and you had four children. Two of them died as infants from cramping in their guts. You collected the life insurance and built a house."

"Nonsense, child!" The voice thunders from right behind the door. "Where'd you get such notions?"

"Newspapers. The articles said your husband died the day two of his insurance policies overlapped. The doctor said it was strychnine poisoning. Couldn't be proved, though, and you collected the insurance and bought a farm in Indiana."

It takes a full minute before the door creaks open.

The old woman's face has gone florid. Her arthritic fingers tighten on the edge of the door and pull it open wider. "My name is Carlson. You have mistaken me for someone else, child. Go away."

"Your next husband died from a tragic accident and one of your kid's told a classmate that her mama had killed her papa, hit him with a meat cleaver and he died. Coroner said he'd been murdered. You sweet-talked your way out of it and got three thousand dollars for that one."

The old woman stares at Bonnie through eyes that are too wide and shiny. "You get bit by a rabid dog, girl? Ay told you to get away from my door."

Bonnie rushes to continue before her courage fades. "I don't know what happened after that, not exactly. The papers just say that your next fiancé woke one night and found you standing over him with a candle and the look on your face was so sinister he let out a yell, threw on his clothes, and caught the first train for Missouri. Guess he's the only man ever left that farm alive. And there were aplenty. Cops called it 'the murder farm.'"

The old woman balls a knobby fist and shakes it in Bonnie's face. "If you do not leave, ay'll call the police!"

"All righty, ma'am. Maybe I'll hang about and ask 'em if they truly did find another forty hacked-up bodies buried on your land."

The door slams again, but not before Bonnie sees straight-up fear in the old woman's eyes. Hell's Belle is getting the idea now.

Bonnie shouts, "Your house burned down with you in it, along with all your children. Four bodies were found. The headless corpse of a woman and three children. But the woman was only five-foot-three. Coroner said it couldn't be you." Bonnie took a breath. "They never did find that woman's head. You died. 'Cept, of course, you didn't."

Bonnie puts her ear against the door and hears heavy breathing.

"I'm not planning on tellin' anyone, ma'am. I could have done that last month when I knew for sure it was you, but I didn't. I just want to ask you some questions. Can I come in for a little bit?"

Bonnie listens to the sounds of the cement plant chugging away, and her insides curl up like a dying dog's. Burt must be at work by now, but he'll come home for lunch. He'll expect Bonnie to be there waiting for him.

"Please, ma'am? I need your help."

Bonnie puts her cold hands in her coat pockets and

fingers the newspaper clipping. The photos she's taken of Hell's Belle, the Indiana Ogress, look identical to the pictures in the newspaper. It's got to be her. No one could mistake those insane eyes. When you look at ole Belle, you know it's death looking back.

There's a tap-tap-tap from behind the door. Then another tap-tap-tap. What's she doing? Pacing back and forth?

Finally, the door opens wide, and Belle gives Bonnie a bizarre smile, the kind of smile a wolf gives an unsuspecting rabbit. "Forgive my rudeness. Please, do come in. It will give me a chance to set you straight, child."

Belle turns, props her cane, and walks away, leaving the door ajar.

Bonnie enters and closes the door behind her, assuring they have privacy. Wouldn't do to have Mama or Burt know she's been here.

Large pink roses twine across the pale green wallpaper. Vases of flowers sit everywhere. The mix of fragrances is so overpowering it makes Bonnie slightly ill, or maybe that's the knot twisting up in her empty stomach. She watches Belle slump down hard on the old brown couch. The Ogress pats the place beside her. "Come and sit, child. Let me get a good look at you."

Bonnie figures Belle is likely picturing where to land the first strokes of the meat cleaver. But Bonnie is desperate. Stiffening her spine, she walks over and sits on the far side of the couch from Belle. "You're different than I imagined."

"How's that?"

Bonnie lifts her shoulders. "I guess I thought you'd have, you know, claws for hands or cloven hooves hidden in your shoes." Bonnie glances down at Belle's polished black shoes, wondering.

A small grimace comes to Belle's face. "What makes you think Ay am this woman you speak of?"

"Oh, I have lots of newspaper clippings from Indiana. Mama's friend lives on a farm near La Porte, and she sent a big bunch of clippings after it happened. I bet I've read 'em a thousand times."

Belle cocks her head in a curiously birdlike manner. "Why would you do that?"

"Don't know, I guess I like 'em. The skeletons they dug up in the mass graves, all hacked apart? I just can't stop looking at them. It's like my eyes can't close for a second. I want to know every detail of how they were murdered."

Belle studies Bonnie. Then, very quietly, she repeats, "Why?"

"Well, ma'am…it—it makes me feel good to see those hacked-up men."

Belle blinks. After a few moments, she lets out a breath. "Ah. Ay see."

Bonnie tucks her hands deep into her pockets and strains against the threadbare gray fabric. "How did you do it and get away with it?"

Belle leans back against the couch and folds her hands in her lap. Bonnie notes that the nails are neatly clipped.

"What is his name, child?"

"Who?"

"This man you wish to kill."

Bonnie goes rigid. "I'm not sure I want to kill him, maybe just hurt him enough to make him—"

"Every woman wants to murder a man, child. Don't be ashamed of it. Usually, it's her husband. But just as likely her father."

"That's not true," Bonnie says. "My mama loved my daddy. He died in 1916. And she loved her own daddy, too. He died in 1919."

Belle looks bored. "How did your daddy die?"

"Folks say he was working construction and fell off a scaffold. Broke his neck, but Mama never talks about it."

"Lost his balance, did he? What about your grandfather?"

"Stomach cancer."

A tiny smile tugs at the edges of Belle's mouth. "Yes, my husbands died from accidents and stomach cancer, too."

Barely above a whisper, Bonnie asks, "Did they have life insurance?"

Under her breath, Belle says, "A girl. A *little* girl. Of all the—"

"Yes, ma'am." Bonnie pulls the newspaper clipping out of her pocket. "I thought you looked familiar, but I couldn't place you, so I took a whole lot of photographs of you when you weren't looking."

"You did what?" Belle explodes.

"Oh, sure, when you were walking back and forth to your house, or out weeding your garden, I'd hide behind a tree and snap a picture. One night, I was puzzling over your face—it seemed so familiar—when it occurred to me where I'd seen it. In the clippings. I spent hours studying your nose and mouth, but it was your eyes that gave you away. The eyes in my pictures and the ones in the papers were the same. You got unique eyes, ma'am."

"Do Ay?"

Bonnie nods vigorously as she unfolds the clipping. "I like 'em. They're powerful."

"Hmm," says Belle.

"Do you want to look at this clipping here?" Bonnie asks as she spreads the clipping out on the coffee table. The photo shows Belle sitting upright, her eyes staring into the camera with that evil look. "See the shape of your nose? And that long earlobe you got? They're the same." She hesitantly points to Belle's face.

The Ogress does not look. There's nothing in her eyes now. They're just blank, like those old people in crazy houses, staring at nothing for all their lives.

Bonnie focuses on the precious clipping. Mama tried to take the clippings away from Bonnie once and learned pretty quick that Bonnie was capable of a roar like a wounded lion. She'd leaped upon her mother and beaten her with her small fists until Mama had tossed them on the floor and stamped out of Bonnie's room. Mama said it wasn't natural for a little girl to like staring at dead bodies.

Bonnie starts to feel a little awkward and rushes to say, "You know…at first, I thought I'd kill myself. I'm blue all the time. I mean *all the time.* Truly, I—I just can't stand it any longer, but then I thought—"

"What has he done to you?" Belle asks and her teeth set so her jaw sticks out on one side.

Bonnie stares at the clipping on the table. If Burt ever found out…

"Hmm," Belle says again and fiddles with her cane, wiggling it against the couch. "How old are you, girl?"

"Thirteen."

"Thirteen." Belle's gaze takes on that far-off gleam of unpleasant memories passing by, and Bonnie wonders if she's hacking somebody apart in her mind, or maybe thinking on the fella that kicked her in the belly. "So…"

The word hangs in the air for so long Bonnie feels like she might throw up.

"Your father and grandfather are both dead and Ay suppose your mother is worthless—"

"Oh, no, ma'am. She's a good woman, but I can't tell her because he says he'll kill my whole family if I do."

"You got any brothers?"

"Buster."

"How old is he?"

"Fourteen. Almost fifteen."

Belle grabs her cane, props it on the hardwood floor, and grunts to her feet. Step by step, she makes her way over to the rocking chair and sits down. As she rocks, she squints at Bonnie. "Your grandmother lives with you, doesn't she? Ay see an old woman sitting on the step of your house."

"Granny? Yes, ma'am. But she's sixty-eight and frail as a sick cat. She sleeps most of the time."

There is a long pause. "Tell the truth. Have you told anyone about me?"

"No! No, ma'am. I swear to God, I wouldn't do that. I need your help."

Belle looks suspicious and maybe a little dazed, not sure what to do about Bonnie. "You're a funny little bird, child."

"Yes'm, I know it." Bonnie's gaze subtly examines the living room, looking for the telltale glint of metal. Meat cleavers aren't all that easy to hide. "Ma'am, I'm here because I was hoping you would tell me how to do it."

Belle clutches the knob of her cane, and her lips press into a thin pale line. "You're skinny as a blade of grass, child. Are you hungry? Ay got good cheese and fresh-baked crackers in the kitchen."

"I could eat. I was afraid to have breakfast. 'Fraid I'd wake him and he'd come looking for me. He does that on occasion, after Mama goes off to work."

"Run in the kitchen and fetch the plate on the counter."

Bonnie leaps to her feet and hurries into the kitchen. Everything is perfect. The glasses sparkle on the shelf, all arranged by height. A clean dish towel lies neatly folded beside the flowered plate, where slices of cheese and a handful of crackers rest. The old woman must have been about to eat when Bonnie knocked.

Bonnie carries it back to the living room, and offers the plate to the Ogress, who shoves it away, and says, "You eat it."

"Thank you, ma'am. I'm obliged to you." She carries the plate back to the coffee table and gobbles three pieces of cheese, then stuffs two crackers in her mouth. Her belly button is rubbing her backbone. "Thank you again, ma'am. I really do appreciate it."

Belle frowns as she watches Bonnie. Bonnie has to hold herself back from eating the entire plate. Instead, she stops at four slices of cheese and four crackers, pushes the plate aside, then plucks up every cracker crumb that has fallen on her skirt and puts it in her mouth.

"Better?" Belle asks.

"Yes, ma'am. I can breathe easier now."

"Good. Carry the plate back to the kitchen."

"You don't want any? Wasn't this your breakfast?"

Belle waves a hand at the plate. "Ay'm not hungry now."

"All right, ma'am." Bonnie carefully carries the plate to the kitchen and sets it on the counter, exactly where she found it. The whole place smells like fresh-cut flowers, but it doesn't make Bonnie ill now.

When she returns and sits down on the couch, Belle starts rocking faster. Her black hem hisses across the floor. Belle seems to be considering something. Her gray brows have pulled together. "Here is your first lesson. When it gets bad enough that you want to kill yourself, it's because you're a coward, and you know it. Stop being a coward."

Bonnie swallows hard. She dreams of murdering Burt all the time, but if it came right down to it...

Belle seems to read her face perfectly. "You ever killed anything, girl?"

"I squash mosquitos and miller moths with some regularity."

"Umm."

Bonnie waits. In the great quietness, there is one clock. Bonnie's blood in her ears. It's a strange painful sound, like a beast licking its own wounds. *Shish. Shish. Shish.* If there was ever real hope in her heart, she doesn't remember it. Her hopes always die before they can stand up. *Dead babies on distant shores, bloating in the sun, finally chewed to bones and left on the sand like maggots turned to stone.* Bonnie smiles for an instant. Poetry. She loves rhymes. Then her smile fades, and she wonders what it would be like not to grow up having to put your soul in the wall every night. So it can't see.

"That's a strange look, child. What were you thinking?" Belle asks.

"I was trying to figure where to hide my soul next time."

Belle stops rocking. "Hide your soul?"

Bonnie crushes her skirt in her fists. "Yes, ma'am. Mostly, I hide it in the wall. Sometimes, I can will it to fly outside onto the porch to watch the stars 'til it's over."

Belle's mouth opens as though to speak, then she closes it, and grinds her teeth for a long time. "Do you have a sister?"

"Billie Jean? She's two years younger than me. Eleven."

"Ay see," the Ogress says so low Bonnie almost doesn't hear it.

"Yes'm. I figured that out myself. You understand now, don't you? I don't have much time. I have to get this done before he gets tired of me and—"

"Do you have rats in your house?"

Bonnie pauses, wondering at the abrupt change of subjects. "'Course, we do. Big ones. I know the state has been waging war on them since the Bubonic plague in Galveston a few years back, but they still seem to be everywhere."

"What poison does your mama use?"

"It's called *Rough on Rats*. She won't even let me touch it. Says it'll kill me just as dead as a rat."

"Cancer or coma first, though, in the right doses."

"Like…stomach cancer?"

It doesn't take a genius to understand what Belle is saying. And Bonnie suddenly wonders if her grandpa's death was natural after all. Then again…maybe her daddy's fall off the scaffold was a coma setting in. Maybe Mama had problems with men, too.

Bonnie scratches her throat. It has a strange itch. You don't think…? No, Belle didn't know Bonnie was coming this morning. Still, it would pay to be more careful in the future. No more cheese and crackers at Belle's abode.

Bonnie monitors the old woman, who has her eyes narrowed and is staring wolfishly at the door. She isn't thinking of bolting, is she?

"Ma'am? You don't have to tell me all the details, but I'm hoping you'll teach me how to mix poisons and maybe the way to swing an axe hard enough to chop a man apart. So I can hide my handiwork."

Bonnie is especially interested in hearing about the human bones wrapped in loose flesh that dripped like jelly. That's how the police described the contents of the burlap sacks they dug up at the murder farm. Bonnie dreams of that, of using an axe on Burt and watching him turn to jelly.

"Why would Ay do that?"

"Well, I don't want to, ma'am, but my other clippings and my photos of you are in a shoebox under my bed. If you don't, I'll trundle off down to the police station and hand it over. You don't want that, do you?"

Belle gives Bonnie the strangest smile. "You're a brave child."

"You're the brave one. Chopped up forty men and poisoned five or six of your own children, too. What kind of poisons did you use?"

Belle's eyes have a euphoric glow, as though remembering how her victims writhed as they died. Or, jeez, maybe wondering how Bonnie will writhe after Belle poisons her. "Ay never poisoned anyone."

"Sure you didn't." Bonnie smiles broadly. "Which poison was the worst? The one that caused the most pain?"

Something changes. It's as though the old woman suddenly understands Bonnie better than any other human being on earth. Her evil expression slackens, she blinks, and looks away. While Belle's gaze drifts around the house, landing here and there on a vase of flowers or a table leg, Bonnie thinks, *Arsenic is easiest. Good ole Rough on Rats will do the trick. How much is the question. Can't use so much that folks will know or I'll be warming a bed in Hell right beside him.*

"Are you speaking to me or yourself?"

Bonnie sits up straighter. She hadn't realized she was talking out loud. That was a bad sign. She didn't do that at home, did she? Good Lord, what if she accidentally told Burt what she was planning? "What did I say?"

"You're afraid of going to Hell."

"Well," Bonnie says with a shrug. "Aren't you afraid of that?"

"This is Hell, child. Right here. Right now."

"That's not what the preacher says, and Mama says if I don't mend my ways I'm going to fry for eternity."

"Then get used to the idea and stop fretting about it."

"Well. That's hard to do."

Belle glances at the clock on the wall. "What time do you go to school?"

"I have to start walking about seven to get there on time."

Belle leans forward in her rocking chair, stares hard into Bonnie's eyes, and says, "So. Ay do need help in my garden, after all. Ay will hire you, but at a rate of one nickel per week."

"Oh, yes, ma'am. That's fine with me!"

Belle props her cane and stands up. She's giving Bonnie a curious look when she says, "Come back at six tomorrow morning."

———

Bonnie tiptoes across the floor at dawn, eases the door open, then slowly pulls it closed and runs off like a frightened jackrabbit. There's no wind this morning, and the thick cement dust that's settled on the road puffs up with her every step. When she looks back over her shoulder, the puffs resemble smoke signals hanging in the sickly yellow gleam. Down under the bridge, the campfires blink as squatters move back and forth in front of them. The whole town is coming awake.

A horn blares as Bonnie sprints across the dirt road in front of an automobile—just before it can run her over—and opens Belle's gate. She briskly walks toward the old woman who is twining bean vines through her chicken wire trellises. The patterns are so green and frilly they resemble Granny's crocheted shawls.

Belle is already watching her with hard unblinking eyes. Bonnie wonders how it's possible to stare without blinking for that long? Like a hunting cat evaluating prey. Bonnie feels the bottom of her throat shrinking up.

She croaks, "Here I am."

"Ay see that."

Bonnie has to lean her head far back to look up into Belle's face. The "Black Widow of the Midwest" has eyes too big and far away, and the rising sun behind her gray head hurts Bonnie's eyes. She squints against it. "Want me to help you arrange the bean vines?"

Belle shakes her head, and her arm extends to point at a hammer leaning against wall of the house. "Go fetch that."

"Yes'm." Bonnie runs over, grabs the hammer, and suddenly feels sick to her stomach. She props a hand on the wall and vomits silently into the dirt. Then she trots back with the hammer clutched in her hand. "What do you want me put the hammer to?"

Belle studies her for a second, as though wondering about something. "Walk the garden. Every time you find a grasshopper, kill it."

"With a hammer? Can't I just stomp it?"

Belle stares at her. "Use the hammer."

Bonnie searches beneath tomato bushes and around corn stalks, until she spies a grasshopper, then she smashes it with the hammer and watches the guts shoot out across the dirt. Belle's right. This is way more gratifying than stomping the pesky leaf-chewing insect.

For an hour, Bonnie kills bugs in the garden. When it's almost time to run to school, a rat darts from beneath the broad leaves and Bonnie lets out a yip and dances away with her heart pounding. "Good Lord, that scared the—"

"Don't let it get away." Belle orders, "Kill it."

Bonnie charges after the rat, leaping through okra

plants and radishes while the rat skitters beneath leaves. Finally, the rodent leaps out and, with Bonnie in hot pursuit, races for the house where Bonnie corners it and starts whacking it with the hammer. At first, the rat's screams startle her, but she keeps pounding that small furred body until she's crushed the skull and the screams stop.

When Bonnie rises to her feet, the hammer head is covered with blood and bits of brown fur. She leans the tool against the wall again and wipes her runny nose on her sleeve.

Belle calls, "Dead?"

"Dead as it gets."

Belle examines Bonnie's face, as though searching for some sign of emotion. "Do you regret killing it?"

In truth, Bonnie feels a bit dazed. "Maybe a little."

"Why?"

"Well, he looked up at me with scared eyes."

Belle's brows pull together into a solid gray line over her nose. "They always look at you with scared eyes, child. Here's lesson number two: They deserve it. Remember that. Now, come over here."

Bonnie jumps two rows to get to Belle and stands obediently awaiting instructions. Belle's voice is deep and matter of fact: "It's you or them. You understand?"

Bonnie nods. "Oh, yes, ma'am. I do."

"Very well. Get to school. Stop on your way home. Ay have one more task for you."

"Yes, ma'am. Thank you, I'll be back!"

Bonnie races through the garden and out the gate, trying to get to school before she's late. ...*through the gate before she's late, thinking on bait and getting ate...*

———

As she walks home that afternoon, the dust from the cement plant is thick enough to choke her. She has to cover her mouth with her sleeve and breathe through the faded green fabric to get air. A man and a woman whiz by on bicycles with their white sleeves flapping and wearing scarves pulled over their noses. Bonnie watches them until they swoop around a corner and disappear. She got in another fight at school today. Roy Thornton pulled her hair hard enough to jerk out a hank, so she hit him in the back of the head with a rock. Roy is sweet on Bonnie, that's why he torments her. Strangely, hitting him with a rock only seemed to inflame his passions—as romance novels put it. After she'd bloodied his head, he'd smiled at her every time he saw her. Tough to figure that one out.

Bonnie breaks into a trot while she thinks about Roy.

If she married Roy, it would get her out of the house, and Roy is a fighter. He beats up every boy in school. Maybe he'd protect Bonnie if Burt ever came around. That makes her wrinkle her nose. She doesn't need any man to protect her. She needs to know how to do the deed herself. It's a skill that can't be overrated. No telling when she might need it again in the future.

When Bonnie trots up Belle's path, she notices that the old woman has set a bowl of milk on the porch. Does she feed the strays that roam the streets? Mama says that some of the squatters eat stray cats, and dogs, too.

Bonnie starts to knock, but Belle calls, "Come in, child. Leave the door ajar. The house is hot. Ay want some air in here."

Bonnie leaves the door open about the width of her body, then walks into the dim living room where she finds Belle sitting on the couch with a cup of tea in her hands. The porcelain is blue and painted with tiny golden flowers. Bonnie has never seen such a beautiful cup. Is it

Norwegian? Did Belle bring it with her when she came to America in 1881?

Bonnie sits down on the opposite end of the couch. "What's my next job? You said you had one more task for me."

"Yes, but not so soon. You vomited this morning. Are you feeling better?"

Bonnie pales a little. "Yes. Thank you for asking."

"Did you eat something that made you sick?"

Bonnie licks her lips and looks away. "Must have."

Belle takes a sip of her tea and swallows. "Do you wish to be put straight?"

"Put straight?" Bonnie has to think about what that means.

Belle reaches into her pocket and pulls out a small bag and hands it to Bonnie.

Bonnie takes the bag and sniffs it. "Smells like bitter herbs. What's in it?"

"Pennyroyal, black cohosh, ergot of rye, cotton root, and other things."

Bonnie shakes the bag, listening to it rustle. Might contain a good dash of arsenic, as well. But what if it is just the thing she needs to get 'put straight'? A sense of almost overwhelming relief surges through Bonnie. "Did you ever use it?"

Belle blinks in a lazy, almost bored way. "Make yourself a strong tea and drink it all down. Strap on a diaper under your skirt. Your Ma will think it's your flux."

"Is it going to hurt?"

"Does that matter?"

Bonnie rises to her feet. When she looks down, Belle's eyes are fixed on some far point of memory. Her expression is cold but touched with a strange wistfulness. "Put the bag in your pocket. Time for your last task."

Bonnie stuffs it in her pocket. "What is it?"

Belle jerks her chin to the door. Outside, Bonnie sees a skinny yellow cat lapping milk from the bowl as fast as it can. "Go catch that kitty. Then find the hammer."

Bonnie feels her face go fishbelly white. "You want me to kill a stray cat? Are you going to toss it in a stew pot?"

Belle doesn't reply. Just watches Bonnie as though evaluating her strength of character, or maybe lack of.

Bonnie turns and sneaks across the room, trying not to scare the starving little animal. In one quick leap, Bonnie grabs the cat and holds it out by the scruff of its neck. "Where's the hammer?" she calls.

"Where you left it this morning."

Yowling and hissing, the cat squirms in Bonnie's hand. By the time Bonnie walks around the house to where the hammer leans against the wall, the cat is wild to escape and twisting so hard it's difficult to keep hold of it.

Bonnie sees movement from the corner of her eye as Belle walks around the corner of the house and stands watching.

"Ma'am? Don't you have any rat poison? If you want to be rid of it, can't we just put some in a bowl of milk?"

Belle doesn't seem to have heard the question. She glares unblinking at Bonnie, waiting as though the fate of the world rests on the next few moments.

Bonnie reaches for the hammer but can't make herself grab hold of it. The cat is screaming and scratching, staring up at her with pleading green eyes. Bonnie can't stand it. She drops the cat, which streaks off across the garden as though scalded. Bonnie turns to face Belle, but the old woman is gone.

She runs around the house and tries the doorknob; it's locked.

"I'm sorry!" Bonnie calls. "I just couldn't do it."

There's no answer, and Belle's words ring in her memory: *Stop being a coward.*

———

Sometime after midnight, Bonnie awakes struggling with her blanket. She's running sweat, and her belly is cramping up bad. Must be the pennyroyal mix taking hold. She followed Belle's instructions exactly. The tea had tasted awful, like she was drinking poison, which made Bonnie recall that two of Belle's children had died from cramping in their guts.

Doesn't take long to feel the first gush of warm blood soaking into the folded towel Bonnie placed in her underwear. She sits up in bed and holds her belly. When the cramps get so bad she's sure her insides are going to squeeze out, she squats on the floor and holds her hands over her mouth. After about an hour, the towel is soaked and Bonnie pulls it out of her underwear. When she stands up to fetch the clean towel she hid under her bed, a clot the size of a lemon splats on the floor. Breathing hard, Bonnie studies it.

The demon's spawn looks dark in the starlight streaming through the window.

Evil, evil, evil.

Bonnie pulls out the clean towel and tucks it in her underwear, then she uses the soiled towel to pick up the biggest clot. She'll clean the rest up when she gets back.

Dressing in a warm coat, she runs down the street to Belle's house with the towel cradled in her arms like a precious baby. The hammer still leans against the wall. Bonnie's hands are sticky with blood when she picks it up. Kneeling on the ground, she places the towel before her and pounds the clot to bits. *Burt. Burt. Burt.* Every strike of the hammer makes her feel better.

At last, she rises on shaking legs. Starlight coats the leaves of the cottonwoods with a shine like liquid silver. The cool air feels good in Bonnie lungs. For a time, she just breathes. Dear Jesus, the relief surging through her is so great she feels dizzy.

Bonnie bends over, gathers up the towel and the hammer, and carries them to Belle's front door.

Apart from the stray dog trotting down the street, Bonnie and the devil's spawn are quite alone. She's light-headed, floating like a feather on a soft spring breeze. When she kneels and gently places the bloody towel on the step, it feels like a church ritual—a bundled baby being left on the doorstep of a convent for the nuns to find and raise in the light of the Holy Spirit. Bonnie neatly places the hammer on top.

Afterward, she feels tired and weakly slumps down on the step to cry. Part of her wants that baby to live so badly her pain becomes poetry. In her mind she's dressing that little girl in pink gingham and combing her blond hair and dusting her pretty face with kisses.

The other part of Bonnie wants it to live just so she can kill it again.

Pain like a rhyme, pounding in time,
to a hammer.
Pound, pound, chop.
Watch Bonnie rot.

She can already feel it starting deep down. Her belly is swelling with rot. Soon it will rise up into her chest and poison her heart. Then who will purty little Bonnie be?

Fifteen minutes later, she feels strong enough to slowly walk home. She has her hands tucked in her pockets. As the blood dries, her fingers stick together and she has to repeatedly pry them apart. She can't help wondering what that little girl would be like at the age of five or fifteen. She can see an older version of herself sitting on a bench beside a boy. Maybe the girl would be a little shy, breathing quickly because she feels uncomfortable beneath the boy's gaze. Or maybe she's more like Bonnie and whacks him in the head to make him stop looking at her like that. Bonnie wishes, she wishes so hard, that the little girl had been born to a different mother, a mother who could have protected her.

When another bad cramp twists her insides, she stops and bends over. How long will this go on? She forces her feet to walk again. The houses on the street are varnished with moonlight and every agonized breath tastes like cement. There are a few men lurking about in the shadows. She hurries past them. When one man calls to her, Bonnie breaks into a run, flying down the dirt road for home.

She leaps up the front steps breathing hard, eases the door open and closes it softly behind her, then she tiptoes down the hall to her room. The door is ajar. She must have left it open.

When she slips inside, there's a square of moonlight resting on the bloody spot on the floor. It's mostly dried up now. First thing after Mama leaves tomorrow morning, she'll mop it up before anyone sees the evidence.

Pulling off her coat, she tosses it on the floor and silently walks toward her dark bed. God almighty, she hurts, and not just in her body. The black ruins of her heart are haunted by a baby's whimpers that she will never hear in this world, but they will always be there inside her—a small ghost begging to be held in loving arms.

Just before Bonnie reaches her bed, a big shadow moves, then sits up.

She gasps and backpedals so fast she stumbles and has to grab for the wall to stay on her feet.

"Where you been, girl?"

The disembodied voice of the demon is deep and gruff.

"Just out walking."

"What's all that blood on the floor? I skidded in it when I walked in. You kill something?"

Bonnie's heart flutters like a dying bird's. Dear God, does he suspect? She has to think fast.

"No, I got my flux. It's bad this month. That's why I was out walking. Helps to ease the cramps."

Burt rises and walks into the moonlight to loom over Bonnie. The demon is huge and has its fists balled at its sides. It could squash her like a bug if it wanted to. It grabs a lock of her blond hair and twists it around a finger. "How long are you going to bleed?"

"Three or four days, at least."

Bonnie can tell it's thinking of doing the deed anyway.

Then the demon drops her hair and pounds a fist on top of her head hard enough to jar Bonnie's spine. "I'll be back at the end of the week. Make yourself purty for me."

———

When Bonnie walks into Belle's fragrant garden the next morning at six, the old woman is standing with her back ramrod straight, staring at Bonnie with those huge glittering eyes.

"Here I am, again," Bonnie says as she trots up to stand in front of Belle.

Belle doesn't say a word. She extends an arm to point.

Bonnie follows her hand to the bloody towel which rests beside a shovel next to the okra plants.

"Yes, ma'am." Bonnie hurries to the shovel and starts digging a hole in the soft garden soil. When it's deep enough, she uses the shovel to scrap the towel into the hole.

"Not deep enough," Belle calls.

It occurs to Bonnie that she's right. Any hungry dog could dig this up in a few scratches. Bonnie lifts the towel out of the hole and puts her back into making the hole deeper and deeper.

"Now?" she says when she's breathing hard from the effort.

Belle nods. "Now."

Bonnie quickly covers it with dirt, then tromps the dirt down. *Down, down, down. Bonnie drowns, drowns, drowns.* It looks like a small fresh grave, maybe a dog's grave. As she lays the shovel aside, a sob catches in Bonnie's throat.

"Why are you crying?" Belle asks.

Bonnie wipes her face on her sleeve. "I don't know. I guess...I guess I feel guilty."

"For what?"

"For doing it."

Belle crooks a finger and motions for Bonnie to come over.

Dutifully, Bonnie marches forward and stares up at the old woman like a supplicant pleading for forgiveness. Belle's face is still as death, but her eyes blaze. "You didn't do it. He did."

"Well, I know that, but I feel guilty. I just want to die and have it over with." Bonnie adjusts the scarf around her throat. "I tried to hang myself last night, but I guess the rope was too long. If I had a car, I'd try to wreck it. Drive headlong into a tree, maybe."

Belle reaches over and pulls the scarf down to examine the rope burns around her throat, then she grabs hold of Bonnie's chin and wrenches it upward.

"Look at me." The words are ice splinters. Cold and

hurtful. "Lesson number three: You never deserve to die. He does. Understand?"

Bonnie's vision is blurry and makes Belle's wrinkled face appear vaguely unreal. "Yes, ma'am, but I've had the blues so bad that I could lie right down and die. I don't know what to do. This is over, but there'll be more. Won't there?"

Belle gazes at Bonnie without blinking for so long that Bonnie feels like a bughouse rat about to have its guts stomped out. In a voice as dark and soft as black velvet, Belle asks, "Are you a coward or not?"

Bonnie sits alone in the kitchen staring out the window. Billie Jean and Buster are both at school, and Mama is at work. She got to stay home today because she told Mama she was sick, which she is, but it's mostly sick at heart. There's a shadow crawling around inside Bonnie. Sometimes that shadow grows into a brilliant light that becomes a poem or a story, but today it's a small human-shaped darkness that breathes behind her eyes. It is alive.

In school she learned that ancient people used to measure time by the length of a shadow on a sundial. It was invisible at high noon and shaped like a long sharp dagger at nightfall. Without a shadow there was no way to tell time. Time stopped. Will darkness ever swallow the small shadow moving around inside her? Bonnie hasn't slept in months. She longs for the deepest darkness where all shadows die.

Coward.

Hands pressed close over her ears, Bonnie sings a little song, trying to drown out the echo of Belle's voice that keeps bouncing around like an iron wrecking ball smashing her brain to dust.

Coward, coward.

When she can't stand it any longer, she drags herself out of the chair.

The doorknob feels cold. She turns it. The hinges squeal when she pulls it open and looks down the steps into the dark basement below. A musty smell rises.

Bonnie leaves the door wide open to let the light in and takes the steps down one at a time.

At the bottom of the steps, a faint whimper startles her. The sound seems to be coming from the darkness to her right, but when she walks toward it, she knows she's wrong. It's coming from the top of the steps. No, from behind her. Now, it's circling her head.

Bonnie cranes her sore neck, trying to follow its course. It flies close, then soars far away in one long barely audible infant's cry, as if trying to draw her into the blackest corner of the basement.

She doesn't want to go back there.

The rope still dangles from the rafters. She can't see it, but the chair that rests beneath the rope is dimly visible. Bonnie turns her head aside and veers wide around it.

This is the way death always works, she supposes. The living do everything in their power to shut their eyes and avoid it. Nobody really wants to see the head-on coming. But someday Bonnie is going to, and she knows it.

Her eyes are starting to adjust. She carefully places her feet as she walks toward the shelves that line the wall in the rear of the basement. The old coffee can rests on the highest shelf to the far right. Even on tiptoes, she won't be able to reach it.

Sucking in a deep breath, she clenches her fists and forces herself to walk back to fetch the chair. Before she lifts it, she gently pets the rope.

"Wasn't your fault," she whispers. "It was mine. I'll do better next time."

Bonnie carries the chair back and sets it on the floor beneath the coffee can. She can just barely reach inside it.

She pulls out the smaller can.

Rough on Rats.

Rat-a-tat-tat

Heartless and mean

I am keen

To watch him scream

They'll find my body

Bloody and gaudy

Death is the wages of sin

Bonnie clutches the can to her chest and jumps down off the chair.

Burt will be home for lunch. She'll bake him some biscuits.

No more turning back for purty little Bonnie.

———

1930

There are no other mourners. Just Bonnie and Bud standing in the rain at the cemetery, watching the gravediggers shoveling as fast as they can in the cold downpour that started at dawn. The cottonwoods fling rain in their faces every time the storm gusts across the graveyard.

Bud rolls his cap in his hands and lightly shakes his blond head. "She was an odd one, wudn't she? Folks said she was peculiar. Kept to herself."

In a tight voice, Bonnie answers, "She was my friend."

Bud gives her a long speculative look. "Well, I reckon

242

that's enough. Hope somebody will say the same about me at the end."

Bonnie doesn't know exactly how long she's been standing here, perhaps longer than it seems. Even in the best of circumstances, she has trouble reckoning time and has since she was thirteen—the worst year of her life. That's when the nights got longer and longer, until all she saw was darkness, even in the daylight. But on this gray day with the cold wind whipping her strawberry blonde hair into her eyes, she's certain she's been standing her since the first moments of creation. *Let there be light, Lord?*

"How long did you know her?"

Bonnie thinks back. "About six years. I tracked her with my vest pocket camera when I was a kid. Snapped pictures of her going down to the mercantile and working in her garden."

"Why'd you do that?"

Bonnie ponders for a time. "It was...her eyes," she says softly. "Something in her eyes. Drew me like a cat to milk."

God Almighty, that little camera had been her savior. At night, she'd pull her photos out of the shoebox, line 'em up on the floor, and arrange and rearrange them to create new stories. She could be a glamorous Hollywood star or a world-famous poet.

Bud flips his cap back on his wet hair and exhales a breath. To the gravediggers, he calls, "Y'all 'bout done here?"

"Hell, yes, we are. Cain't take much more of this damned storm."

"Awright, then." Bud turns to Bonnie. "You must be freezin'. Let me walk you down to the café and get you a hot cup of coffee."

She looks up at him. Bonnie doesn't know him well. Just met him in the kitchen at a friend's house a few days ago, but there's something about him that draws her as powerfully as Belle's eyes did the first time she saw them in the newspaper clippings. Bud Barrow is seven inches taller, which makes her tilt her head back. "I'd like that. Thank you."

Before she can convince herself to leave, Bonnie has to take one last long look at the fresh pile of dirt. With tears in her voice, she whispers, "So long, Belle."

Bud frowns. "Who's Belle? Headstone says Esther Carlson."

Bonnie barely hears him. She's still staring at the grave with tears in her eyes. "Thanks for everything you taught me. Without you, I'd have been keeping company with Suicide Sal long ago."

As Bud slips his warm arm over her shoulders and starts guiding her toward the café, he says, "Who's Suicide Sal?"

"Oh, it's nothing. Poem I just started. It's not finished." She wipes her cheeks with her hands. "Belle would have hated it. Told me killing myself was the stupidest thing in the world. At the time, I needed to hear somebody say that."

Bud's pale brows pull together. "Well, I been there a time or two my own self. Don't reckon it'll be the last time neither."

He smiles down at her. "While we sip coffee, you can tell me how you met Belle. Was Esther her nickname? Like Bud is mine? Most folks call me Clyde. Clyde Barrow."

Bonnie shakes her head. "Esther Carlson was her alias. She had many. We wrote letters back and forth for years, 'til she died of tuberculosis last week. She taught me things no one else could have."

"Like what?" Bud asks as they charge across the street for the café.

When they dash beneath the red awning outside, thunder rumbles through the sky and lightning splits the gray morning into blazing, crackling zigzags.

Bud removes his cap and bats off the rain on his pant leg, then he stares at her, awaiting her answer.

Bonnie hesitates.

Let there be light…please, God?

Deep emotion constricts her throat when she replies, "She taught me how to save myself."

A LOOK AT: PEOPLE OF THE LONGHOUSE
THE PEACEMAKER'S TALE BOOK ONE

New York Times **bestselling authors W. Michael Gear and Kathleen O'Neal Gear weave another vivid narrative thread into their stunning tapestry of Native Americans.**

Born in a time of violent upheaval, young Odion and his little sister, Tutelo, live in fear that one day Yellowtail Village will be attacked. When that day comes and Odion and Tutelo are marched away as slaves, their only hope is that their parents will rescue them.

Their mother, War Chief Koracoo, and their father, Deputy Gonda, think they are tracking an ordinary war party herding captive children to an enemy village. What they don't know is that Odion and Tutelo have fallen into the hands of a legendary evil: Gannajero the Trader. Known as the Crow, she is a figure out of a nightmare, a witch who captures children for her own nefarious purposes. No one can stand against her powers—except perhaps the mysterious Forest Spirit whose tracks have crisscrossed their own throughout their journey.

Odion and the other children struggle to survive their brutal captivity. They, too, have seen the Forest Spirit. But like their parents, they can't be sure if the Spirit is a friend—or a foe.

AVAILABLE NOW

ABOUT W. MICHAEL GEAR

W. Michael Gear is a *New York Times, USA Today*, and international bestselling author of sixty novels. With close to eighteen million copies of his books in print world-wide, his work has been translated into twenty-nine languages.

Gear has been inducted into the Western Writers Hall of Fame and the Colorado Authors' Hall of Fame—as well as won the Owen Wister Award, the Golden Spur Award, and the International Book Award for both Science Fiction and Action Suspense Fiction. He is also the recipient of the Frank Waters Award for lifetime contributions to Western writing.

Gear's work, inspired by anthropology and archaeology, is multilayered and has been called compelling, insidiously realistic, and masterful. Currently, he lives in northwestern Wyoming with his award-winning wife and co-author, Kathleen O'Neal Gear, and a charming sheltie named, Jake.

ABOUT KATHLEEN O'NEAL GEAR

Kathleen O'Neal Gear is a *New York Times* bestselling author of fifty-seven books and a national award-winning archaeologist. The U.S. Department of the Interior has awarded her two Special Achievement awards for outstanding management of America's cultural resources.

In 2015 the United States Congress honored her with a Certificate of Special Congressional Recognition, and the California State Legislature passed Joint Member Resolution #117 saying, "The contributions of Kathleen O'Neal Gear to the fields of history, archaeology, and writing have been invaluable…"

In 2021 she received the Owen Wister Award for lifetime contributions to western literature, and in 2023 received the Frank Waters Award for "a body of work representing excellence in writing and storytelling that embodies the spirit of the American West."

www.ingramcontent.com/pod-product-compliance
Lightning Source LLC
La Vergne TN
LVHW041036290125
802441LV00025BA/338